Swift as was the attack, Conan was swifter. He grabbed the easterner's wrist, stopping the fingers an inch from his eyes. With a mighty wrench, he twisted the arm around and down, and Tsongkha grimaced as bones snapped and tendons tore. His other hand shot up, the heel of the palm aimed to smash Conan's nose, but the Cimmerian batted the hand aside and smashed an elbow in the man's temple.

Tsongkha collapsed upon the ground, and servants came to drag his inert form from the tent. Conan stood relaxed.

CONAN
THE
MARAUDER

Look for all these Conan books from Tor

CONAN THE CHAMPION
CONAN THE DEFENDER
CONAN THE DESTROYER
CONAN THE FEARLESS
CONAN THE INVINCIBLE
CONAN THE MAGNIFICENT
CONAN THE MARAUDER
CONAN THE RAIDER
CONAN THE RENEGADE
CONAN THE TRIUMPHANT
CONAN THE UNCONQUERED
CONAN THE VALOROUS
CONAN THE VICTORIOUS

CONAN
THE MARAUDER

BY
JOHN
MADDOX
ROBERTS

A TOM DOHERTY ASSOCIATES BOOK

CONAN THE MARAUDER

Copyright © 1987 by Conan Properties, Inc.

First printing: January 1988

A TOR Book

Published by Tom Doherty Associates, Inc.
49 West 24 Street
New York, N.Y. 10010

Cover art by Ken Kelly

ISBN: 0-812-54266-5
CAN. ED.: 0-812-54267-3

Printed in the United States of America

0 9 8 7 6 5 4 3 2 1

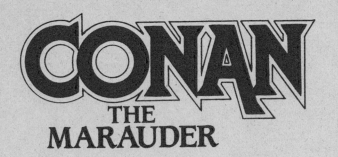

CONAN
THE
MARAUDER

One

Behind him were the hills, hills that would have been mountains in comparison to the puny elevations of the west. Beyond them towered the true mountains, climbing level upon level, growing white with snow as they rose. The mountains ascended seemingly without end until they reached the roof of the world, Mount Pajaram, Pillar of the Gods.

Before him lay the steppe, a sea of grass stretching from the Vilayet to distant Khitai, from the northern border of Vendhya to the pine forests of the far north. It was a land of few rivers, much of it semi-desert during the long dry season, when its parched grasses could become a terrifying ocean of flame, ignited by lightning or the actions of men. Few but steppe nomads roamed the vastnesses of the plain, but its southern periphery was crisscrossed by the ancient caravan routes that linked the lands of east and west, and at intervals along these routes, wherever there was an abundance of water, there were the legendary cities of the caravans: Lakmashi of the Silver Gates, where precious metals were worked before transshipment to east and west; Malikta, where the jewels, stones, pearls and jade of the east were traded by the hundredweight; Bukhrosha, city of incense and spices; and lordly Sogaria, where the silks of Khitai were dyed with pigments from Vendhya and the far isles of the eastern sea, and then woven into wondrous fabrics by the artisans of the city.

Conan thought of these far places as he made his leisurely way westward. For years he had heard tales of the caravan cities, told around the campfires of the *Kozaki*, in the cave lairs of the Himelian hillmen, and on the starlit decks of the sharklike galleys of the Red Brotherhood. Predictably, all of these men had spun dreams of sacking those rich, soft cities. But the steppe was vast, and only a well-organized expedition of experienced caravaneers could hope even to cross the enormous distances between those cities, much less conduct a siege at the end of the journey.

The Cimmerian adventurer hoped to visit those places someday, when his ever-restless spirit led his steps in that direction. Just now, though, he was of a mind to go back to the western kingdoms. He had been living among primitive raiders in the high hills, until the great cosmopolitan cities of the Hyborean lands had beckoned him. He would find which of them had a war in the offing, and there he would surely find an army in need of an experienced officer.

As was his usual practice, the Cimmerian was traveling light. A broad-bladed Zhaibar knife, sword-long and razor-sharp, hung from his wide, silver-nailed belt in a cunningly worked scabbard of carved leather. Its bone hilt showed the wear of much handling. A short, curved dagger and sheath were thrust through the belt in front. Over his tunic he wore a shirt of the lightest Turanian mail, silver-washed to prevent rust. A fluted helmet of steel with a neck guard of similar mail covered his thick black hair. The season was warm, and besides the tunic, he wore only a loincloth and sandals. A case slung from his saddle bore a short bow of layered horn and wood, and its arrows fletched with eagle feathers.

As he rode, Conan pondered his course. A few days' ride would bring him to the southern shore of the Vilayet, in a region often fought over by Turan and Iranistan. There he would meet his old friends, the *Kozaki*, and would share their fires and tents. He would have to cross Turanian territory, and he did not wish to fall afoul of King Yezdigerd's patrols. Little fear of that. A man who had led Afghuli tribesmen would have no difficulty in avoiding the overmanned, lumbering horse-squadrons of a civilized army.

Such were the thoughts with which Conan passed his hours upon his journey westward. Rolled behind his saddle in a spare cloak were his sparse camping gear, his means of making fire and a few days' supply of emergency rations. He would depend upon wild game for most of his food. The only lack that bothered him was that of a remount. He had lost his spare mount to the bite of a deadly serpent not long after entering the steppe. This would be an unforgiving land for a man afoot, but there was no sense in worrying about it now. He would do all he could to spare the horse until he could trade for another, and should something happen in the meantime, he would walk and make the best of it.

On the dawn of his sixth day upon the steppe, he rose with the first gray light, rolled up his few possessions and kicked out the embers of his small fire. He saddled his horse and prepared to mount when a tiny movement far to the east drew his eagle gaze. Eyes less keen than the Cimmerian's would never have seen the

distant figures. Against the bloody shield of the rising
sun, he descried five riders, and behind them were more
horses, at least four or five beasts for each horseman.

Before he mounted, Conan strung his bow and replaced it in its case. Perhaps the newcomers were of
peaceful intent, but he had not reached his present age
by making such assumptions. Once in his saddle, he
urged his mount westward. There was no sense in
running just yet. They had seen him by now. If they
wished to pursue him, he had little chance of avoiding
them. As his horse tired, they could switch to fresh
mounts.

As the sun climbed across the blue cloak of the sky,
Conan paused occasionally to rest his horse and to scan
to his rear to see whether he were being pursued. By
midday the riders had closed the distance by half, but
when next he looked, they were nowhere to be seen.
Conan shrugged, thinking that perhaps they had no
interest in him and had gone on their way. Still, he did
not unstring his bow.

As the sun was beginning its long descent to the
west, Conan saw a movement to his left and bit off a
curse as two riders began closing upon him. They were
no more than a half-mile away and shortening the distance by the minute. He began to wheel his mount to
the right when he saw three more horsemen bearing
down upon him from that direction. It had to be straight
ahead, and he spurred his mount into a rapid trot as he
sought to leave his pursuers behind.

How had they flanked him so neatly? The question
burned in his mind as he looked for an easy route.
Obviously they were familiar with this stretch of steppe.
Nowhere is the steppeland truly flat, but always gently
rolling. They had taken advantage of that and had ridden in natural declivities while catching up with him.

Now they had him herded onto a long slope that would tire his mount quickly. What manner of men was he dealing with? As they rode closer, he saw that three of them wore leather armor; the two others were naked except for loincloths and knee-high boots of felted leather. Across their backs were curved sabers, and at their saddles were bows larger than Conan's.

Hyrkanians! From their headgear—tall pointed caps with dangling earflaps—he judged them to be of one of the southwestern tribes. As he watched, he saw one of the armored men leap with insolent ease from a tiring horse to a remount, taking his cased bow and arrows with him. Hyrkanians were said to be the finest horsemen in the world, and Conan was beginning to believe it.

Now he knew whom he fled, but why? Surely they were not wasting a whole day just to take his horse. They could see that he had little worth stealing. Perhaps this was their idea of sport. He vowed that should they run him down, he would teach them how high was the price for their amusement.

As his mount's sides began to work like a bellows and foam from its jaws lashed back over him, Conan was forced to admit that there was no use in further flight. There was no sense in riding the brave beast to death and then having to fight on foot. He scanned the ground near him and saw that there was nothing resembling an elevation to yield him any advantage. He slowed his horse to a canter and pulled his bow from its case. Fitting arrow to string, he turned in his saddle and let fly at the nearest pursuer.

The man had a small shield of Vendhyan steel, barbarically ornamented with fur around its edge. As Conan's arrow streaked between them, he raised the shield almost lazily and deflected the missile. The Cimmerian tried again, this time shooting at one of the unarmored riders. This one deflected his arrow as well, with the same contemptuous ease. The glancing arrow flew straight for one of the other riders, but that one merely leaned aside and let it pass.

"Crom!" Conan swore. Compared to these men, his old companions, the *Kozaki*, were children when it came to mounted fighting. But why were they not using their bows? Little question about that: They could have only one use for a live prisoner. He smiled grimly. Before they hauled him to some slave market, they would have a fight on their hands. He slowed his horse to a halt and drew steel. Matchless horsemen they might be, and legendary archers, but the Hyrkanians had no reputation as swordsmen.

"Come and let us discuss this matter man-to-man," Conan called out. He thumbed the edge of his Zhaibar knife. "I have here an argument that will let some light into your skulls."

The riders began to trot around him in a wide circle. They twirled something in their hands, but so swiftly did these objects move that he could not make out their nature. He did not waste time seeking to keep all of the men in view at once. His ears would tell him should one of those behind ride too close. He had a single advantage: He knew that they wished to keep him alive. He had no such benevolent intentions toward them.

One of the riders called out, and Conan saw something long and thin pass before his eyes before jerking tightly around his arms and chest. Instantly he knew it was a rope. He flexed his arms from his sides, expecting the rope to break. It merely bit into the flesh of his arms below the short sleeves of his mail shirt. Awkwardly he sought to twist around and cut the rope with his knife, but one of the riders streaked in and lashed out with a long whip. It wrapped around his sword wrist just as two more nooses descended over him.

With a mighty heave Conan managed to jerk the whip-wielder from his saddle, but then another loop circled his neck and drew tight, cutting off his wind. A redness descended before his eyes as he fought the ropes. They were no thicker than his little finger, but they were stronger than any cords he had ever known. A concerted pull from three horses brought him crashing to the ground, and his last sight before he lost consciousness was the grinning face of one of the Hyrkanians, framed by a drooping brown mustache.

When he awoke, it was dusk and the last lurid rays of the sun stained the western horizon. Conan found that he was lying on his left side and that his left arm had gone numb. His head throbbed like a Vendhyan war gong, and his throat was swollen and sore, making his breathing raspy. He tried to swallow, but between the swelling of his throat and its excessive dryness, he could not. He tested his arms and legs and found that his arms were firmly pinioned to his sides. His wrists were lashed together as well. The bonds were tight, though not so tight as to cut off circulation completely. These men were experienced and knew that no one bought a limbless slave.

Awkwardly Conan lurched to a sitting position. He found that his feet were unbound, for obvious reasons. Where could he flee on this steppe that a horseman could not run him down? He wore only his loincloth and sandals. That came as no surprise either. He heard voices behind him, and he twisted around to face them.

Four of the Hyrkanians were seated around a low fire, grilling quartered sections of a small animal. Each had a single horse picketed within a few paces, and Conan surmised that the fifth man was away with the other mounts, probably taking them to water. The men were conversing among themselves, sometimes laughing quietly, and paying him not the slightest attention. The smell of cooking meat reached Conan and his stomach rumbled.

"You!" Conan called, his voice a rusty croak. He recognized their language as a distant relation of Iranistani, and he assumed that they would speak the trade tongue of the borders. "Yes, you, oh long-mustached father of children who resemble the village shaman. Are you going to feed me or do you expect to obtain a good price for a skeleton?"

All four faces turned toward him. He saw that their complexions were fair but darkened by sun and wind, and two of them had blue eyes. A brown-haired man who had set aside his armor stood and walked over to the Cimmerian. His bandy-legged waddle bespoke a life spent in the saddle. He wore a thin tunic of felt and the inevitable cap, which exposed only the thin braids that fell nearly to his waist in back.

"It is not fitting that the hulking ape of the Vendhyan jungles should address the lordly riders of Hyrkania. Be still, oh pursuer of hairy, tree-dwelling females, and perhaps tomorrow or the next day we shall toss you a well-gnawed bone." He kicked Conan in the jaw and the Cimmerian fell onto his back.

The Hyrkanian was too busy laughing to notice that Conan had drawn his legs in toward his chest as he rolled back. Then, as the Cimmerian rolled forward, he lashed out with both feet, catching the Hyrkanian squarely in the stomach. The wind went out of the man with a loud whoosh and he flew backward, tumbling end-over-end to roll over the fire as his friends snatched their skewers of meat out of harm's way. The three seated men laughed uproariously at their companion's discomfiture.

The Hyrkanian forced himself to his hands and knees, gasping hoarsely and clutching at his belly. He glared at Conan with feral rage. When he had breath, he staggered to his feet. As he made his painful way back to Conan, he drew a wickedly curved knife.

"Perhaps you are not good slave material, ape," he said, grinning. "Perhaps I will skin you instead. I need a new bridle and saddle cover."

Conan stared into the man's eyes. "Cut me loose and we'll see. I've seen toads under a rock show more spirit than you."

"Cut you loose?" echoed the man, honestly puzzled. "What manner of fool gives an advantage to one he intends to kill?"

"Of what use is it," Conan barked back, "to speak of courage or honor to a Hyrkanian?" He prepared himself for a last effort. If nothing else, he would bury his teeth in this one's throat before the others knifed him.

"Put up thy blade, Torgut!" someone called. The man addressed stepped back and sheathed the knife instantly. Conan squinted toward the fire to see who had spoken. The command had not been phrased as conversational speech. It was an imperative form of the language, meant to be obeyed. A man with a black mustache and wispy chin beard rose from his place and walked toward the Cimmerian. He looked little different from the others, but Conan caught the glint of gold earrings and bracelets. His felt tunic was embroidered with animal designs. This man might be a subchief, commander of this little band. He squatted before Conan fearlessly. The trick would not work twice.

"Of what land are you, slave?"

Ostentatiously, Conan looked to right and to left, as if searching for someone. "I see no slaves here. Do you refer to those baboons by the fire, or perhaps this lout with the sore belly who stands beside you?"

Dispassionately, the subchief slapped him. "You need not convince us that you have spirit, man. We know that. Do not try my patience. What is your homeland?"

"Cimmeria," Conan grumbled. He had made his point. They might kill him, but they would not seek to degrade him further.

"I have never heard of this land," the man said. "Your arms and armor are from Vendhya and Turan and the border hills."

Conan looked at the pile of gear by the fire, near where this man had been sitting. "Yours are from Khitai and Iranistan. What of it?"

"Listen closely." The man's blue eyes stared into Conan's own. "We are Hyrkanians. We are of the Arpad people, of the noble horde of the Ashkuz. We go to join the great chief, Bartatua, who is gathering all the clans and minor hordes for a campaign such as has not been seen in many generations. Bartatua has sent out orders that all who come are to bring in prisoners from among the inferior peoples. I know not what his purpose is. It is possible that you might survive what he has in store for his prisoners. You will not survive my displeasure should you keep upon your present course."

Conan shrugged and spoke as though he were making some great concession. "Very well, I'll go with you. I am a warrior by trade. Perhaps this Bartatua will have better employment for my skills than that of slave labor."

To his chagrin, the Hyrkanians broke out in shrill laughter. "You!" said the man he had kicked. "You ride like a ten-year-old child. You shoot less expertly than such a child.''

Conan's face burned with humiliation when he remembered how easily these men had ridden him down and captured him. "I could carve the lot of you to dog meat with my sword," he said. "There are other ways of fighting besides shooting from a distance off the back of a horse."

"We have no use for such ridiculous styles of fighting," the chief said. "We have encountered such things before. The armies of the cities come out against us. They stand in lines or ride in formations and seek to tempt us into coming within reach of their spears and swords. We laugh as we shoot and then go to gather up our arrows from the corpses."

"If you are so mighty and invincible," Conan mocked, "why have you not taken the world?"

The man shrugged. "Why do we need the world? We have the limitless steppe and the Everlasting Sky." He and the others made a gesture of reverence, and Conan understood that the man had named their deity.

"Cities?" he went on. "They are good for sacking. What other use have we for them? We are the only free men beneath the sky. Should we become tax collectors, or spend our days watching farmers trudge behind their bullocks so we can make sure they are not cheating us?" He spat in disgust. "Never! When one is free to hunt and hawk upon the steppe, one would be a fool to covet such a life. We overawe and terrify the princes of the world with our invincible hordes, and we take their tribute as our rightful due. Thus we gain the gold and silks and perfumes that it is our pleasure to use. It is fitting that the contemptible dwellers in cities should toil to produce these things for us, for we are the true princes of the earth.'' The other Hyrkanians shouted their approval of these words.

"Give me a horse," Conan said, "and in the turning of a moon I will be a horseman better than any of you. Give me one of those bows to practice with, and in the same time I will be a better archer than any Hyrkanian. I have never taken up a fighting skill without excelling at it.''

The chief rose and looked down coolly at Conan. "We have a few days' ride to join Bartatua. You shall have ample time to prove your worth. What is your name, foreigner?''

"Conan.''

"Know that I am Boria, of the Blue Stag clan of the Arpad tribe. I am a fifty-leader, and I will test you along the way. If there is anything to you besides talk, I will know of it by the time we join the great chief. It may be my pleasure to say to him a few words in your favor. It may be his pleasure to act upon those words.''

"This is foolishness!" said the one called Torgut. "What use can the great Bartatua have for this city-dwelling, swine-eating ape?" He spat, but was careful to stay out of range of Conan's feet.

"That is not for you to say, Torgut," said Boria. "The ways of a great *kagan* are not the concern of a common saddle pounder. Do you wish to dispute my judgment?''

Torgut raised the back of his hand to his forehead. "I meant no disrespect, commander." He shot Conan a look of close-reined hatred.

"See that it is so." Boria turned to the men by the fire. "Give the prisoner some of the dried food from his saddlebag." He turned back to Conan. "At dawn we ride. Your journey shall not be easy. You may not

survive it. This means little to me. I shall know more
when we reach the great camp.''

The officer left and one of the others, a man tattooed
from shoulders to knees in animal designs, tossed a few
strips of dried meat near Conan. The Cimmerian had
to inch over on his side and pick up the strips with his
teeth. Boria had called him ''prisoner'' instead of
''slave,'' and that might mean something. He choked
down one of the tough, leathery pieces of meat.

''Water,'' Conan called. The tribesmen ignored him.
Boria finished cleaning the bone he had been gnawing
on, then spoke to the man who sported the elaborate
tattoos. That one rummaged in his saddlebags and brought
out a shallow bowl. He filled this with liquid from a
skin and set it near Conan, who wrinkled his nose at
the smell but knew better than to be finicky about what
he ate and drank. There was an ordeal ahead, and he
would need all his strength in order to meet it.

The bowl was not filled with water but with fermented milk, whether that of sheep, cow, goat, yak or
mare, Conan neither knew nor cared. The steppe peoples lived largely off their flocks and milked the females of all their animals. He noticed that the bowl had
been cut from the top of a human skull. Awkwardly he
emptied the vessel. Bound as he was, there was no
possibility of finding comfort, but with the coming of
night, he did his best to sleep. His fitful rest was
tormented by stinging insects, and dawn came all too
soon.

''There is no need to tire our horses with your bulk,''
said Boria as he fastened a halter around Conan's thick-
muscled neck. ''You who dwell in cities and villages
are accustomed to using your feet. Keep up with us, or
you will be dragged.''

When the men were mounted, they set out at an easy

trot, their path taking them eastward. Conan ran with the remounts, carefully judging the gait of the slowest horse and pacing himself with it. If these arrogant riders hoped to see him dragged gasping upon the ground, they were in for a surprise. Conan was a matchless runner, and he kept up easily.

As the morning progressed, the Hyrkanians would occasionally glance back at him and each time they did, their eyes went a bit wider to see him trotting with the horses, his tether swinging loose, his breathing light. To these men who never walked more than a score of paces save in dire emergencies, it was inconceivable that a man could keep pace with a horse. At this easy pace, Conan knew that he could run all day. To a Cimmerian hillman, running came as naturally as breathing or fighting.

But Conan knew, too, that he had trouble when Torgut took his tether from the man who had been holding it. "Our prisoner looks bored and low in spirits. Perhaps some exercise will improve his humor." With that, the Hyrkanian kicked his horse's flanks and the beast began a steady lope.

As the tether drew taut, Conan lengthened his stride. He had expected that something like this might happen. He could trot as long as any horse. At this speed, he could run longer than any other man, but not as long as a good horse. If the Hyrkanian put the animal to a rapid gallop, Conan would have to take desperate measures or be dragged. Sweat began to run into his eyes and his breathing grew deep and hard. He was far from exhausted, but he would reach that state eventually.

The other riders drew level, laughing and shouting at this rare sport. Conan caught Boria's cool, evaluating gaze as the tall, dry grasses flashed by him. He considered catching the rope in his teeth and trying to bite through it. Success would be unlikely; he had never encountered rope so thin and yet so strong. And they would only drop another noose around his neck anyway.

Torgut looked back and saw that Conan was keeping up. Fury knotted his features and he lashed his horse's rump with a short quirt. The mount sprang forward at a full gallop. Conan took a deep breath and began to run at top speed before the rope could grow taut and jerk him off balance. With his hands bound, he lacked his customary superb equilibrium. The ground was rough and should he fall, the long dragging that would ensue would result in severe lacerations at the very least. More likely it would be a race between strangulation and a broken neck. Boria might be displeased, but Torgut hated the Cimmerian. To a barbarian, what was a mere dressing-down by a superior compared to the sweetness of revenge?

Conan ran with a purpose now. He sought a stone, a stump, any protrusion that might give him purchase. If he was to die here, he wanted the pleasure of taking Torgut with him. Then he saw what he was looking for. A few hundred paces ahead was one of the rare trees of the steppe. Low, stunted, gnarled and twisted by the wind, it was little more than a shrub. But Conan knew that it had a tortured, scrawny trunk of amazing strength. He knew also that his luck was with him, for one might encounter no more than four or five of these tiny trees in a day of travel on the steppe.

As they neared the tree, Conan saw that Torgut was going to pass close by it on the right. The Cimmerian inclined his steps slightly to the left so as to pass the tree on the other side, with the rope between. Boria, riding somewhat behind Conan, saw his plan and called out, "Torgut!" But he was too late. Conan darted to the tree, ran completely around it and leaned back, snubbing the rope effectively around the trunk.

Torgut had time only to look back. Then he was jerked violently from his saddle by the rope that was wrapped around his wrist. He struck the earth with a bone-jarring shock that drove the air from his lungs. Grinning, Conan ran back around the tree and made for the man.

The others were slowing and turning their mounts, but they could not reach Torgut before Conan. The Cimmerian, still a few paces from the inert Hyrkanian, leaped as nimbly as an antelope. He came down with both feet in Torgut's midriff, causing what little breath the man had left to explode from his lungs in a pain-filled bellow. Conan then dropped to his knees and was rewarded with a gratifying snap of ribs.

He sprang to his feet and prepared to jump onto Torgut's face when Boria rode up behind him. In one hand the leader held his unstrung bow, and he swung it with all of his considerable strength. The heavy, whiplike construction of wood and horn cracked into the base of Conan's skull with the force of a spear butt swung with intent to kill. A red sunburst blazed before the Cimmerian's eyes, and he collapsed across his unconscious enemy.

Two

A lurid crimson glare outlined the spires of the city as the sun settled beyond the steppeland to the west. Two riders sat their mounts atop the escarpment overlooking the small but fertile valley in which beautiful Sogaria nestled like a great jewel on a cushion of green silk. All around was the arid plain, but within this tiny valley, water worked its ancient magic and caused the land to blossom. Many caravan trails converged upon this land of well-kept fields and orchards, where the very field hands wore silk, which was bartered in Sogaria as cheaply as was cotton in Vendhya or linen in the western kingdoms.

"The gongs will sound soon, my lady," said the man, whose flat features and tilted eyes identified him as a member of one of the eastern Hyrkanian tribes, those renowned for their terrible periodic raids into Khitai. "They will shut the great gates for the night." He spat upon the ground. "That is the way of the dwellers in cities, so fearful that they must lock themselves within their walls at night, then go to their homes and bolt the doors and shutters against the clean air. You will not be able to enter until morning."

"I know what cities are like, Bajazet," said the woman impatiently, "and I will find a way in. We waste time here."

The two coaxed their horses gently down the escarpment. The animals were eager to descend once they smelled the water below, and had to be restrained from taking dangerous steps in the uncertain, treacherous footing.

The man wore the typical dress of the steppe nomad, although in the heat of summer he had stripped off all but his loose trousers and his high, soft boots. He was heavily armed, but only his dagger was belted directly upon him. Lance, bow and sword hung about his saddle. To a Hyrkanian, weapons borne on a mount were the same as those borne on the person.

The woman wore an all-enveloping garment that covered her from scalp to ankles, the black cloth pierced only by a pair of holes for the hands and a narrow slit for vision. The vision-slit was itself covered by a band of fine netting, so that nothing of the woman's face could be seen. Boots and gloves covered what little of her the cloak left exposed.

As they neared the city, they came into an area of pens and common pasture where the camels, horses and oxen of the visiting caravans were kept. Nearer the gates were the campgrounds occupied by those caravaneers who had arrived after the closing of the gates or by those who chose to sleep without the walls. Around the smoky fires were spoken a score of languages as men told tales in the cool of the evening, continuously switching their fly whisks against the night-flying insects.

The woman dismounted and handed her reins to Bajazet. "I will be back before the sun is up. Take the horses where they can find grass and water and be back here with them at first light. And stay sober." The weakness of the steppe men for strong drink was legendary.

"As you command, my lady."

Bajazet led the beasts away and the woman began to make her way among the campfires. The caravaneers paid her not the slightest attention. She might as well have been invisible. A veiled woman was another man's property and not to be acknowledged.

There were other women moving among the campfires, though, as well as boys and men who were plainly not from the caravans. The women were for the most part unveiled and engaged in selling a multitude of wares: food, wine, trinkets or, occasionally, themselves. There were fortune-tellers and letter-writers, musicians and mountebanks, all of them eager to provide weary caravaneers with goods and entertainment, as well as with a few items and services forbidden within the walls of the city.

The woman traced this colorful stream back to its source: a small, door-sized gate set into one of the great wooden gates of the city. Beneath a small lantern, a single guard leaned on a spear and passed through any who could show him a lead seal stamped with the mark of some magistrate's office. The veiled woman walked up to the guard as soon as there was no one else near him.

The man regarded her curiously. "May I help you, lady?" Surely only the woman of an important man would be veiled so heavily.

"I wish to enter the city," she said.

"Have you a license?"

The universal passport appeared in her gloved hand: a glint of gold in the light of the lantern. The guard looked about swiftly, assured himself that no one stood near. The gold disappeared into his belt and he jerked his head toward the city. The woman stepped through the gate and disappeared.

Khondemir stood upon his high balcony, studying the stars. On one of the marble rails rested a delicate, intricate device of brass and crystal. The mage peered silently through the artifact, his long, thin fingers making minute adjustments. Finally he straightened and crossed to a table where he dipped a quill in ink and noted upon fine parchment the exact day and hour when the carmine planet would enter the House of the Serpent.

Then a sound from below drew his attention and he looked over the railing and down into the street. He lived in an area of the most sumptuous homes, and it was rare that any walked abroad at night. In the light of the lanterns that hung from poles every twenty paces, he saw a black-swathed figure approaching the gate of his courtyard. He knew who it was by the confident stride and he returned to his study. At the tug of a bellpull, a servant appeared.

"There is a lady without the garden gate. Admit her and bring her hither immediately. Then fetch wine and refreshments." The servant bowed profoundly and left. A few minutes later there was a scratching at the door. "Enter."

The servant bowed the woman into the room and departed. The instant the door was closed, she grasped the hem of her cloak and pulled off the garment, shaking a wealth of rich black hair over her bare shoulders.

"I thought I would suffocate in this thing!" she said. "Greeting, Khondemir."

"Greeting, Lakhme," said the mage.

The woman thus addressed bore the features of the upper castes of northern Vendhya. Though small, her form had the voluptuousness of the temple sculptures of that land, and beneath the cloak she wore naught but a narrow silken loincloth and knee-length boots. Her beauty was dazzling, but most striking of all was the perfect ivory whiteness of her skin, protected from sun and wind every day of her life and kept soft with scented oils.

"I have little time," she said, stripping off her gloves. "The great horde of Bartatua shall set forth this season, before the turning of another moon."

"So I have already detected," said Khondemir portentously. "The stars have foretold it, as have certain spirits with whom I commune."

Her beautiful eyes cast him a look of weary cynicism. "You wizards always try to pretend that your powers give you knowledge of the future and of events far away. I would wager that your human spies are of far greater value to you. Else what use would you have for me?"

His thin lips turned up at their corners in the faintest of smiles. "Truly, my human agents are of a certain value, to confirm that which I already know, you understand. As for having another use for you . . ." He stepped forward and placed his arms around her.

She put a hand against his chest and looked up at him mockingly. "Did your wizardly mentors not tell you that indulging your carnal nature would seriously sap your magical powers?"

"They did," he said. "It was one of several matters in which they spoke foolishly." He released her as a discreet noise at the door announced the arrival of the servant. Lakhme stood behind the door as the man entered, set the tray on a low table and backed out.

The Vendhyan woman took the goblet of wine proffered by Khondemir and paced slowly about the room, admiring its furnishings. She was as unselfconscious in her near nudity as an infant. "It is good," she said, "to be among civilized things again. The Hyrkanians have no appreciation of the sensual pleasures of life save for a joy in good horses and bestial drunkenness." She ran her fingers across a casket of fragrant sandalwood inlaid with mammoth ivory.

"Some of them," Khondemir observed, "have a taste for beautiful women."

She shrugged her smooth shoulders, causing her alabaster breasts to quiver. "As mere battle trophies. Bartatua values me highly because he took me from Kuchlug, the greatest of his enemies. When his followers see me, they are reminded that the great Bartatua slew Kuchlug with his own hands and took his woman." She grasped a handful of embroidered drapery and drew it to her face, inhaling the scent of incense that clung to it. She began to rub the cloth languorously over her body. "You have no idea of what it is like to live in the squalid tents of those savages, to have to do without the simplest pleasures of life." She dropped the hanging and went to the tray, selecting a skewer of grilled meat rolled in herbs and wrapped in vine leaves.

Lakhme read the wizard's eyes and breathing far more accurately than he could read the stars. "Bartatua's first prize is to be Sogaria. It has wealth and a strategic position between east and west. There are no cities nearby to offer assistance, and the city is soft and fat. It has not known war in a generation."

With an effort of will, Khondemir dragged his thoughts away from her soft white body. "It has walls, and granaries full of grain. Even if he can unite the tribes, how will men who know only how to shoot from horseback lay siege to such a city?"

"He is a savage," she said, dropping the bare skewer and picking up a sugared date, "but he is not stupid. He has plans for that eventuality. And a siege of Sogaria will be good practice for other conquests. He has a mind to be a conqueror of nations.''

"Turan?" Khondemir asked.

"He wants to take Khitai first, before turning west." Her kohl-rimmed eyes studied his every expression.

"That army," Khondemir half-whispered, "will take Turan ere I am done with it."

She stepped close to him and traced with a fingernail the outline of a dragon embroidered on the breast of his robe. "But that is not Bartatua's plan," she said.

"You and I shall take care of Bartatua," said the wizard. Once more he sought to enfold her. This time she pushed him away forcefully.

"Not so soon, wizard! Bartatua killed my former master to possess me, and you must do the same. I'll be a conqueror's woman, but I yield to no lesser man. If you would have me, slay Bartatua and take control of his army."

Khondemir took a deep, shuddering breath. "You place a high value on yourself, woman. Be glad that you are of use to my plans." He was dizzy with a combination of rage and lust.

"I must be away," she said, gathering up her cloak and gloves. "Bartatua believes that I need these ten days to myself every six moons for certain religious rites. I must be back in his tent within five days or face questions I would rather not have to answer. Swiftly now, tell me what you would have me do."

As the lovely body disappeared beneath the cloak, the wizard found himself in better control of his thoughts. "To advance our aims, I must first gain mastery of Bartatua's mind and soul. For that, there is no aid more powerful than substances recently taken from his person. These things give my spirit servants a kind of . . . focus, or route, by which they may invade his being and bend him to my will.''

"What sort of substances?" she asked.

"Hair, nail parings, bits of flesh, and," he paused, "those things that a concubine is in the best position to gather."

"You shall have them," she said, as simply as if he had asked her to bring him produce from the market. "Now I must go. When we meet again, it shall be in the City of Mounds. Farewell." She swept out in a whisper of rustling cloth.

Khondemir poured himself another goblet of wine. He reflected upon what a dangerous woman this one would be should he keep her near him after his plans came to fruition. That could wait. Soon he would have her. More important, he would have control of Bartatua's horde and would lead it against King Yezdigerd of Turan. The thought of that sweet vengeance made all the risk worthwhile.

As she walked back through the quiet streets, Lakhme had far different thoughts than those entertained by the wizard. Always she marveled at how easy men were to control and manipulate. If a woman had beauty, intelligence and ruthlessness, she could bend the most powerful man in the world to her will. How simple it was to convince a strong man that by winning her, he became a hero beyond compare! Even children were not so foolish.

From the day her starving parents had sold her to an itinerant trader, Lakhme had learned the arts of transforming her helplessness into power. As she had ripened from a skinny child into a beautiful woman, she had learned what the basis of her strength was to be. The trader had pampered her, providing her with the most expensive of beauty treatments and sending her to retired courtesans for lessons in the arts of pleasing men. She had been far more interested in the tales the courtesans told of the loose-tongued folly of wealthy and powerful men when they relaxed with skilled, compliant women.

The trader had dreamed of making his fortune from Lakhme. He would take her to one of the great cities and sell her into the harem of a fine lord, perhaps even that of a king. When he had decided that the time was right and that she had reached the peak of her beauty and desirability, he bundled her into a curtained, camel-borne palanquin and set out on a caravan to the king's summer court in the beautiful northern vale of Kangra.

Still scarcely more than a girl, Lakhme had quickly grown bored with sitting in the airless conveyance, subject to the camel's ever-swaying gait. One afternoon, hearing an untoward noise from outside, she had parted the curtain to see what was happening. She found herself staring into the face of the captain of the caravan's guard: a fierce Hyrkanian warrior. The man's narrow eyes had widened at the vision of loveliness within the palanquin.

That evening she had heard the sound of voices raised in argument. One of the voices was that of the trader, and it rose to an angry screech before it was cut off by the sound of a sickening blow. A moment later she was terrified when the curtain was jerked aside and the Hyrkanian stood framed in the opening. He was mounted, and a powerful arm around her waist hauled her from the palanquin and threw her over his saddle. As he galloped away, she saw the trader staring sightlessly at the sky, lying in a pool of his own blood.

She felt no sorrow at the death of the trader. She had been nothing to him except prime livestock, no better than a blooded horse. But through him she had learned a valuable lesson: Men would kill to possess her. The brute power of the Hyrkanian warrior did not impress her. What she wanted was a man who commanded thousands of such warriors.

Within the turning of a moon, the leader of a band of twenty nomads had slain her abductor and taken her for himself. She learned the language quickly and soon convinced him and her subsequent masters of how important it was that she preserve her beauty from the ravages of the sun and wind of the steppes. Wives and older concubines found themselves evicted to provide her with the finest of tents. In this way she earned hatred, but never for long. Among the arts she had learned from the courtesans was the brewing of potions to induce passion, sleep and death. When priests or learned men visited the camps, she conversed with them through a sheer curtain. Thus she learned how the powers of the world were distributed and the manner in which wars and royal marriages shifted borders and redistributed the influence of nations. But when the holy men and philosophers spoke of such things as compassion, pity or conscience, she dismissed all such irrelevancies from her mind.

Any time a higher chief visited her current master, Lakhme contrived to display herself to him. No Hyrkanian would surrender his woman to another, no matter what his rank, so inevitably there was a fight and Lakhme would follow her new master, always looking for the next.

By the end of her third year on the steppe, Lakhme was in the tent of Kuchlug, the chieftain of a great horde. This was a bitter time for her because there was no greater chief around than Kuchlug, and he was a brainless brute who would never amount to more than the savage leader of other savages. Then, one day, Bartatua called on Kuchlug.

Bartatua was the chief of a minor horde, the Ashkuz. She knew his story, knew of how as a boy he had become chief upon the death of his father and had gathered all the scattered families and clans of the Ashkuz into a unified army. By diplomacy, persuasion and force, he had caused several other small hordes to join his host. The moment she saw the still-young, auburn-haired lord of the Ashkuz, she knew that this was a man of power and destiny.

He would be her most brazen conquest of all. Through a long evening she listened as Bartatua tried to persuade Kuchlug to join his alliance and form a super-horde against which nothing could stand. Arrogantly Kuchlug laughed and cursed the younger man as an upstart. Condescendingly he said that he himself would assume leadership of such a horde and that Bartatua could take the position of subcommander, after Kuchlug had given the best commands to his sons and nephews. In a rage, Bartatua stormed from the tent.

Lakhme found out where Bartatua would take his horses to water in the morning and was there when he arrived. The Hyrkanians bathed only in sweat lodges and had a taboo against polluting running water. Vendhyans had no such rule, and when Bartatua reached the stream, he was thunderstruck to see Lakhme knee-deep in the water, dressed only in her streaming black hair. Feigning surprise and embarrassment, she managed to gasp out her name and to whom she belonged.

That night the dispute between Kuchlug and Bartatua broke into violence. As a gesture of goodwill, Bartatua had arrived unarmed. In the midst of a roaring tirade, Kuchlug seized a sword from the tent wall and pursued the younger man outside, where Bartatua turned at bay.

The men of Bartatua were greatly outnumbered by Kuchlug's, but no Hyrkanian would interfere in a mortal combat between chiefs. After letting Kuchlug slash at him long enough to convince all witnesses that the older man was in no way incapacitated, Bartatua wrested the sword from him and broke his neck bare-handed.

All could see that the fight had been fair, and a council of Kuchlug's subchiefs agreed to the overlordship of Bartatua. Kuchlug's closest kinsmen fled while they still had their lives. Most important, Lakhme had the man she had dreamed of. He was ruthless and boundlessly ambitious. Best of all, he was intelligent enough to listen to good advice, even from his concubine. Within a year she was guiding him in nearly every aspect of his plan of conquest. And she had lied to Khondemir about Bartatua's feelings toward her. The chieftain of the Ashkuz loved her beyond all reason.

Three

The little band led by Boria rode into the huge camp on the afternoon of the fifth day following Conan's capture. The Cimmerian was tightly bound, but at least he was riding instead of running. His arms were bound close to his sides and his ankles were tied together beneath his horse's belly. Torgut wanted him slain, but Boria refused to kill a valuable slave and Torgut was still in too much pain to wreak any harm by himself.

With his arm in a sling and his sides lashed with sticks and thongs to keep his broken ribs in place, Torgut looked poisonously at Conan. "This is where your soft treatment stops, ape," he hissed, wincing at the pain the words drew from his flanks.

Conan surveyed the camp. It stretched along a small stream for many leagues and was roughly divided into upstream and downstream halves. Upstream were the odd, humped tents of the Hyrkanians. Downstream were huge pens of horses and other livestock. He noted that the sheep and cattle were few, only enough to feed the camp. The real herds would be in summer pasture, tended by the women and boys. This was a war camp.

As they rode in, they passed men shooting at incredibly distant targets. Some shot dismounted, but most shot from horseback. The most skillful shot at a full gallop, and some actually shot backward over the horse's rump while riding away from the target. Conan began to have second thoughts about his boast that he could master Hyrkanian archery within a month.

The Cimmerian knew little about the dress and accoutrements of the Hyrkanian tribes, but he could see that many diverse peoples were gathered within the camp. Tribesmen whose clothing was predominantly Khitan, Vendhyan, Turanian or Iranistani obviously rode the borders of those nations. These nomads could make little for themselves, and only the thickly padded clothing of leather, felt and furs thay they wore in winter was of native make. Woven cloth, most of the metalwork, even the bows and saddles, were made in the cities and villages bordering the steppes.

The western peoples tended to lighter complexions, fairer hair and blue eyes, and they favored heavy and elaborate tattooing of their skin. The eastern tribes were more squat of build, with flat features, tilted eyes and thin beards. All had the bandy legs formed by a lifetime in the saddle. The Hyrkanians admired strength, but unlike other peoples, they did not prize height. They held that a man on horseback was as a giant to any man on foot, however tall he might be.

Boria halted to ask questions of several warriors, and they pointed upstream. Riding on, they eventually came to a pit that had been excavated near the center of the camp of tents. The enclosure was perhaps twenty feet deep, with sheer sides and only a narrow ramp for access. Guards with strung bows paced their horses along its rim and conversed in bored tones. The floor of the pit was filled with men.

Boria turned Conan over to a scarred warrior who stood next to a Khitan scribe. The Khitan sat behind a folding desk, with brushes, blocks of dry ink, and paper rolls before him.

"Be careful of this one," Boria warned. "He is a fire-eater, for a village man."

The warrior looked Conan over contemptuously. "This place takes the fire out of the toughest prisoner." He glanced at the elaborate bindings that held the Cimmerian. "He must be tough. You've used three slaves' worth of rope on him."

Carefully Boria and his men retrieved their ropes from the Cimmerian's body. The cords had bitten deep, and Conan stretched his limbs to revive his circulation. He looked at the miserable mass of humanity in the pit below, then turned to the warrior in charge.

"It's a waste of time putting me in there. Take me to Bartatua."

The warrior stared at him in amazement, then turned to Boria. "You should have told me that he is mad as well as vicious."

"You are the slavemaster," Boria said, grinning. "Do with him what you will. But I advise you not to turn your back on him." Except for Torgut, they all laughed as they wheeled their horses and rode in search of their fellow tribesmen.

The slavemaster shook his head, frowning. "Those westerners are all crazy." He turned to Conan. "Tell the scribe your name and nation, slave."

"I am Conan of Cimmeria."

The shaven-headed Khitan picked up a brush, wet it and swirled it on a block of red ink. "Your name is a mere sound that I have no way in which to write, and I have never heard of your nation." With a few quick, deft strokes, the Khitan sketched two complicated characters.

"What do they mean?" Conan asked.

"They say 'big, black-haired foreigner' in my language. Slaves who have so little time to live have no need of names in any case."

"Into the pit with you, slave," ordered the slavemaster, rapping Conan on the arm with a coiled whip. The Cimmerian turned and glared, and the slavemaster backed off a step, his hand going to his sword hilt. Conan considered killing him. Horses abounded everywhere, and it would be but the work of a moment to seize the man's sword, cut him down, leap on a horse and ride away.

Had he been dealing with any other nation, he would have done exactly that. Here it would be futile. Such archers as these would riddle him with arrows before he reached the edge of the camp. And probably without damaging the horse, he thought as he turned and walked to the ramp.

Conan had been in slave pens before, and he knew what he would find when he reached the bottom. As he stepped off the ramp, few faces even turned his way. They were so defeated, so fatalistic or apathetic, that they neither knew nor cared what went on around them. Most of them sat motionless or lay staring at the ground vacantly. Conan was filled with contempt. Had this slave pen, like many others he had seen, been filled with helpless women and children, he might have been moved to pity. But these slaves were healthy, able-bodied men. Hardy specimens who were not rebellious, or even angry, were beneath his notice.

There would be others, though. There always were wherever slaves or prisoners were herded in large numbers. Somewhere, in some corner, would be congregated those who still had a spark of spirit and were not more dead than alive. He scanned the huge pit until he saw the place where a number of men were standing, some of them pacing, many waving their arms in animated discussion or argument. Men who would argue yet retained some life in them.

There were perhaps a hundred men gathered in the shade of one of the walls. Heads swiveled to scan the newcomer as he approached, and Conan discerned the features of a dozen or more races. Some he recognized, most he did not.

"I am Conan, a Cimmerian by birth and a warrior by trade. Who among you knows why these dogs want so many prisoners?"

A huge, burly man came forward. His expression was truculent and contemptuous. Conan was familiar with this situation as well. Men in such degraded conditions became pack animals, like dogs. And as with dogs, a newcomer had to learn immediately who was top dog.

"What gives you the rigt to ask, foreigner?" the brute challenged. He wore rags of brown homespun, and Conan read him for an Iranistani serf who had run to the hills and turned bandit.

The Cimmerian placed his fists on his hips, leaned back and laughed for the first time in days. "Foreigner? I don't see a dozen men here of any one nation. Who here is not a foreigner?"

Like any other petty bully whose dominance is based on instilling awe and fear in those weaker than himself, the Iranistani could not bear to be laughed at. With an inarticulate howl, he reached for the Cimmerian with huge furry hands.

Conan stepped straight in between the reaching hands.

His left fist sank to the wrist in the other's capacious belly as his right looped over and down, smashing into the brute's jaw and dropping him like a steer under the slaughterer's hammer.

He stepped over the motionless body and spoke as if nothing had happened. "Now, some of you good fellows tell me why these half-horse Hyrkanians want so many slaves all of a sudden."

"We are not sure," said a Vendhyan, whose ears still bled where rings of gold and silver had been torn from their piercings. "There is talk that the dogs want to besiege a city and we are to do the digging and carry the ladders."

"Aye, that would make sense," Conan said. "Else why would they want only able-bodied men?"

Surely these nomads could have little use for huge slave gangs unless it were for purposes of war. Conan had been present at a number of sieges and he knew that there was much digging and carrying to be done, tasks that the lordly horse-archers would never deign to perform. There was also a great deal of dying. He had known only a few of the most-civilized armies to have regular sappers, those who worked beneath enemy defenses and were protected by armor, shields and mantlets. Most often the work was performed by huge drafts of slaves or peasants, who were slain in droves as they toiled to undermine walls, push siege towers or carry scaling-ladders.

"There is little future in such work," Conan said. "Not one in a hundred of us would survive, and once they had no more use for us, the Hyrkanians would kill such as were left, to be spared having to feed them." Nods and growls of assent told him that he was not the first to have such thoughts.

"You have the truth of it," said a man who wore a

kozak scalplock. "The Hyrkanians have little use for slaves, and none for prisoners. Such slaves as they want, they take as children so that they can raise them properly. Comely women they will sometimes take for concubines. Grown men, especially if they are warriors, are simply slain. They do not want to rule over conquered peoples, but over great pastures."

Conan stroked his bristly chin. He had not been able to shave in many days. "This man Bartatua must be different. He wants to take a city, and it must be a great city if he needs so many slaves for the siege works. If he wanted only tribute, he would ride around the walls with his army and make his demands. But these are serious preparations. I suspect that he plans to move soon, within half a moon."

"Why do you say that?" asked the Vendhyan.

"I observed the land as I was brought here. They are running short of pasture. This is a great horde assembled, and there are at least five horses for every warrior. I will wager that the wealthy ones have twenty or more. The grass will not last and it has been a dry summer. They must march soon or the beasts will begin to deteriorate."

"You did not lie about being a warrior," said the *kozak*. He straightened from where he had been squatting, drawing designs in the dirt. "I am Rustuf, of the Dniri *Kozaki*." He held forth a gnarled, filthy hand and Conan took it. The man grinned, exposing a gap an inch wide between his front teeth. He retained a wide, nail-studded leather belt and the rags of a pair of baggy trousers, but his feet were bare.

"I have ridden with the Zaparoska," Conan said, "and have been a *hetman* among them."

"The Zaparoska are worthless dogs," Rustuf said,

"but any *kozak* is a hundred times better than the lesser breeds of men."

The *Kozaki* were not a true people, but a polyglot collection of horseback bands comprised of runaway serfs, outlaws, former pirates and other dregs of the surrounding nations, united only by their courage, love of adventure, and fierce independence. The different bands were called after the rivers, rapids and river islands where they made their camps. They were by turns bandits, raiders and irregular cavalry for the civilized armies.

"Tell me," Conan said, "have any of you planned an escape?"

Rustuf laughed sourly. "Where would you have us escape to? Truly, they do not even need this pit to confine us. We could force our way up the ramp, but then we would simply be out on the steppe, where they would ride us down for their sport. Even if we could seize some of their horses and bows, look at this lot!" He waved a massive arm disdainfully at the huge mass of apathetic slaves. "They've no spirit. If they had the guts of real men, I would still chance it. Among five thousand fleeing horsemen, a few of us might hope to make our escape. But most of these cannot ride and are too fearful to run."

"It is as I thought," Conan said. "And yet there must be some way out of here. Perhaps alone, and at night."

At that moment a drum thundered and the slaves rose lazily to their feet. Men appeared at the rim of the pit, dragging great skin bags that they proceeded to dump over the edge. The slaves swarmed toward the piles of food, showing their first signs of spirit as they fought and argued over the bounty.

Conan and Rustuf strode to the nearest pile and shoved

aside a knot of scrambling men. Conan picked up a flat, round loaf. It was not much, but it might keep him alive. It was made of coarse, dark meal, gritty and bristling with chaff, slave fare of the roughest sort. He bit into it and choked down a mouthful.

"Is there water here?" he asked.

"When the sun is lower, they will march us out in small groups, under guard, to the stream," Rustuf told him. "There we may flop on our bellies and lap up water with our tongues, like curs."

"Then we had better hope that Bartatua moves out soon," Conan said, "for before long we will weaken and die on such fare."

The kozak led him to a relatively uncrowded spot, and the two men sat on the ground and ate, a laborious process since they had nothing with which to wash down the dry bread.

"There may be a way," said Rustuf in a low voice.

"Speak on," Conan urged.

"Bartatua likes to have sport at his banquets. He sets slaves and captive warriors to fighting one another as entertainment for his guests."

Conan saw the possibilities. "Wrestling? Fist strokes? Or with weapons?"

"All manner of combat," replied the kozak. "He likes to see how other peoples fight. He thinks it is good for his officers to see these things as well."

"Is it to the death?"

"They fight until one is finished. Bartatua does not care greatly whether the defeated man dies or not." Rustuf picked a small pebble out of his bread and tossed it away. "I have for some time considered getting myself chosen for these fights. It may be that should a man fight mightily enough, Bartatua might enroll him in his army. Better a soldier than a slave, and I would not be ashamed to follow such a man. A conqueror is a conqueror, even if he is a dog of a Hyrkanian.''

''Why have you hesitated to take this path?'' Conan asked.

''It has a certain drawback,'' the *kozak* replied, ''that causes even a warrior like me to question the wisdom of such a course.''

''And what might that be?''

''I have spoken with some of the slaves who have been called up to serve at these banquets. Bartatua usually has a banquet whenever some allied chief joins him here. Often when a man triumphs skillfully in such a fight at one of these entertainments, the onlookers enjoy it so much that they wish to see him fight again.''

''And so they pit him against another opponent immediately,'' Conan said.

''That is true. Sometimes there will be five or six bouts in succession. Eventually even the greatest fighter tires and is defeated by a man perhaps no more skillful than he, but less weary.''

''It is also,'' Conan said, ''a good way to eliminate the most-likely troublemakers among his prisoners and slaves.''

Rustuf grinned, nodding. ''That, too, has occurred to me. And yet, a small number of men have impressed him enough to earn a place in his army.''

''The chances may be slender,'' Conan observed. ''But anything is better than being a slave. How do we get chosen for these fights?''

The *kozak* laughed. ''I could tell that you are a man of spirit and quick decision. Wait until they take us for water this evening. At that time we will make ourselves known.''

''What if they pit us against one another?'' Conan asked.

"Then," said Rustuf, clapping him on the shoulder, "we will find out which of us is the greater fighter."

Conan lay on his belly, easing his parching thirst for the first time that day. The water had already flowed through the camp, but it did little good to worry about that for it was the only water for many leagues. When he had drunk his fill, he rejoined the crowd of slaves waiting to be led back to the pit. He stood next to Rustuf, but the two men ignored one another.

"Back to your kennel, dogs!" shouted a slavemaster with a snap of his whip. "Move smartly now. Your brethren of the lash want to drink as well."

The slaves began to shuffle back toward the pit. Conan and Rustuf stood on the edge of the group. As a slavemaster passed, Rustuf stumbled, knocking Conan directly into the man, who snarled and struck at Conan with his lash. "Keep your distance from your betters, dog!"

"No man lays a lash on me!" shouted the Cimmerian. Before the startled Hyrkanian could defend himself, Conan leaped in and grabbed him by the throat. Snatching the whip from the man's grasp, he reversed it and struck a tremendous blow with its weighted butt. He was careful, though, to strike at the lower edge of the man's helmet. His captors would not take a killing lightly. The slavemaster dropped unconscious, and several more guards came rushing up, drawing swords.

As the first came in slashing, Rustuf stuck out a booted foot and the man fell sprawling. The *kozak* twisted the blade from his hand and gave him a rap with its pommel. As another charged in, his blade descending to split Conan's skull, the Cimmerian grabbed him by the wrist and belt, lifted him and slammed him to the ground. Appropriating the weapon from the stunned man, he was now armed and ready to take on the rest of the guards.

Two came slashing in from his left and he leaped joyously to meet them. Although they were matchless archers, he found that the Hyrkanians were indifferent swordsmen, especially when on foot. He parried their clumsy strokes without difficulty and dropped one of them with a blow of the flat of the blade to the side of his head. The other cursed and cut, but Conan batted his sword aside and kicked him in the belly. As the man doubled forward, Conan smote him on the back of the neck with the base of his fist.

He turned to see Rustuf lustily engaging another two Hyrkanians and rushed to join him. Conan took charge of one, and the ring of steel on steel continued for a few moments longer before a band of horsemen surrounded them.

"Hold!" shouted the head slavemaster. The combatants stepped back and lowered their arms. Conan saw that a dozen arrows were trained on them, the bows at full draw.

"Drop your weapons!" the slavemaster ordered. Sullenly, they complied. The slavemaster came closer. "So, you two are fond of fighting? Then we must find something better for you than mere slave work." He turned to the bowmen. "Take them to the Great Enclosure."

They were herded toward the center of the camp. There a large area had been enclosed by a huge curtain that kept out the cutting, dust-laden winds of the plains. The curtain was fifteen feet high and covered with barbaric decorations. Towering above it were the equally barbaric standards of the Hyrkanian chieftains: poles topped with horns, horses' tails and the skulls of beasts.

The slavemaster arrived on his mount and led them

within the windbreak. There were perhaps twenty large tents inside, each with a standard before its entrance. Beside the largest of the tents stood the highest pole. From the spreading yak horns topping it there dangled nine white horses' tails. This, Conan thought, must be the tent of Bartatua.

Well away from the tents, near the windbreak, was a small area enclosed by a folding lattice-fence. Within were a number of thick stakes buried deep in the ground. From a ring at the top of each stake hung a six-foot chain ending in an iron neck ring. Conan counted twenty-five men already chained to these stakes, and there were several neck rings still awaiting an occupant.

"It is good that you have so fine an urge to fight," the slavemaster said. "Our chief holds a great banquet this night, and he also enjoys close combat. Get in there."

The two did as they were told, having little choice. The bowmen still followed, and their strings were still taut. Only when Conan and Rustuf were firmly locked in the neck rings did the guards relax their weapons and leave.

"We have been successful thus far," Rustuf said. "Although a chain and a neck ring are no more comfortable than the slave pit."

Conan stood and gripped the chain. He tugged on it, but the stake would not budge. He stood directly over the stake and tried with all his might to pull it up. It did not move. He knew then that not only was the stake buried many feet deep, but that its base was fastened to a crosspiece. Even his strength would not be sufficient to uproot it.

"The company seems to be no better here, either," said Rustuf.

Conan studied their neighbors. They were a hard-bitten lot, scarred and burly, with the look common to soldiers, bandits and pirates: an air of truculence that expressed belief in their own strength and very little else.

Nearest him was a huge man whose features were eastern but who belonged to no people that Conan knew. "Who are you?" Conan asked in the tongue of the nomads.

"I am the one who will kill you at this evening's fights, dog."

The man was grim but he did not bluster. He meant every word, and Conan did not seek to draw him out further. Instead, sat down and leaned against the stake, conserving his strength against the evening's work.

Four

Khondemir gazed into his scrying glass and saw there visions that only a wizard could interpret. Vague, inhuman faces appeared and spoke to him, although no sound was heard. At last he waved a hand over the glass in a gesture of dismissal. The glass cleared and he replaced it in its chest.

From a tower nearby came the call of the watchkeeper, giving the citizenry notice that the gates would close in one hour. The wizard had an important appointment upon that hour, and he began to prepare himself. He donned his finest robe and his best collar of gold and jewels. He combed out his forked beard and wrapped his tall skullcap in a turban of jeweled silk. He was a man of considerable height, lean and well formed. His features were those of the Turanian aristocracy, and he could move with confidence in any civilized court.

The servant appeared at his ring. "Have my sedan chair waiting at the garden gate in one half hour," he commanded. The servant bowed and left to do his bidding. Khondemir would take with him none of his sorcerous paraphernalia. The fathers of the city knew well his powers, and he had no need to impress them.

As his chair was carried through the bustling streets, the mage admired the surrounding beauty. Sogaria was indeed a splendid city. Its public buildings were towers of white marble, and the homes of the wealthy were only slightly less magnificent. Few were truly poor in the city, which was founded on the rich caravan trade rather than upon the estates of the nobles.

From the balconies and the flat rooftops a profusion of hanging plants swayed in the wind, for like all dwellers in arid regions, the Sogarians loved gardens. Flowers grew in profusion everywhere, and rich hangings were aired in the sunlight daily, adding to the brilliant colors of the city. The streets were paved with cut stone, and fountains played at most of the street corners.

The palace of the prince, Amyr Jelair, stood upon a low hill surrounded by gardens raucous with the cries of exotic birds brought from far lands. The brilliance of their plumage outshone even the spectacular, ever-blooming flowers. Khondemir took deep pleasure in the splendor of the place, and in the knowledge that one day soon he would possess many such palaces.

The bearers set the sedan chair down in a courtyard in which fountains of colored and perfumed water splashed. An officer of the palace bowed deeply and conducted the wizard into a great audience chamber, where a number of distinguished men of the city sat on cushions around the periphery. Tall windows freely admitted air and light, and the floor was a splendid mosaic that formed a map upon which the caravan cities were depicted in precious stones and the features of the surrounding lands were identified in lettering of obsidian.

Khondemir seated himself upon a cushion and held

his silence while the others conversed in low tones. Some of them he knew to be magistrates and officials, others were soldiers. There were several present whom he did not recognize, but that did not surprise him. He had been in the city for but a short time and his circle of acquaintance was not wide.

All bowed to the floor when Amyr Jelair entered. He was a portly man of middle years who wore a harried look. He acknowledged their salutes and seated himself on a low couch.

"I have summoned you here," Jelair said without preamble, "because the emergency we have long anticipated may soon be upon us. I wish all of you to hear the words of the great mage, Khondemir, who has come from Turan to aid us in this time of peril."

At Jelair's nod, Khondemir stood. "My prince, distinguished nobles, most of you know me. Since I was cast out of my native land by the usurper, King Yezdigerd, you have taken me in and made me one of you. I have come to regard Sogaria as my home, and this danger to my adoptive city strikes me as deeply as it does you." A courtier by training as well as a necromancer, Khondemir knew well the value of honeyed words.

"When first your prince suspected that the Hyrkanian barbarians had designs against Sogaria, he summoned me hither that I might put my sorcerous powers at your disposal, and I have wielded them unstintingly in his service." The audience applauded politely, tapping their fly whisks upon the floor. "My supernatural agents have confirmed your worst fears. The savage Bartatua has gathered the greatest host the nomads have seen in a generation, and he shall lead it against the city within thirty days."

At this there was much agitation. One of the men in

military dress rose to speak. "Can we be sure of this? We have had nothing but the reports of traveling merchants thus far. They have said only that the hordes gather. The target could as well be Malikta or Bukhrosha." There were those who agreed with him.

"Honored sir," Khondemir said in mock humility, "I must insist that my sources of information are infinitely more reliable than those of these travelers."

"What boots it in any case?" asked a magistrate whose turban sported a pearl the size of a child's fist. "If the savage means to take one of the caravan cities, he will want to take them all. Whether we are first or last, he will come to Sogaria in time."

The Turanian inclined his head toward the magistrate. "Exactly, sagacious sir. With the Hyrkanian nation on horseback, it is no good to wait until their raids begin. They campaign at a gallop, and they will be before the gates of your city before you know that they have crossed your borders."

Amyr Jelair turned to a somewhat younger man whose features resembled his own. "My brother, as governor of the city, you must see to it that the granaries are full and that all appropriate livestock are brought within our walls." To another man: "Master of the armories, see to it that all weapons are in order and ready to be issued to the citizens at need."

Khondemir suppressed a grim smile at the thought of these merchants and artisans taking up arms against the wild warriors of Bartatua. "These preparations are noble and proper, my prince," he said, "but I have weapons at my disposal that will be of far more use to you. Your pardon for my saying so," he bowed toward those in military dress, "but your warriors, though they be brave as lions, have spent their lives on routine patrols and in chasing bandits across the plain. Sogaria has not seen real war since your father's day.''

"I have the utmost confidence,'' Amyr Jelair said, "in your great powers. Tell us of your plans.''

"What need have we of sorcery?'' asked a tall captain in a gold-chased breastplate. "Are the walls of Sogaria not strong? Have these unwashed subhumans not come here before? Arrows cannot take a great citadel. We can stand atop our walls and jeer at them while they rage, sicken and die. In the end, they will look for easier prey: unwalled villages and helpless caravans.''

"This chieftain, Bartatua,'' Khondemir continued, "knows more of war than did his predecessors. He has gathered a great host of slaves for his siege works. Your walls will be undermined, your ramparts assaulted by siege towers. Even if the siege were not successful, your land would be ravaged, the outlying villages destroyed, the profits of many caravans lost. Sogaria would be many years in recovering from such devastation.''

"These are words of wisdom,'' Amyr Jelair said. "And your proposal?''

"I know of a way to draw this horde away from the city. Then, once it is in the place where I shall lead it, I shall call upon the most powerful of my demon servants to smite it.''

"Can you truly do this?'' Amyr Jelair asked in awed tones.

"I have not wasted such of my time here as I have not devoted to the wizardly arts,'' said the Turanian. "I have spent many hours in the city archives poring over ancient writings that tell of the steppe tribes. In one of them I discovered a fascinating tale.''

He had their total attention now, and the room sat quiet as they followed his story like children in the marketplace listening to the fables of a master storyteller.

"Some five centuries ago, when Sogaria was a part of the short-lived kingdom of Katchkaz, that kingdom suffered the raids of one of these hordes. The king at that time, one Karun, was a warlike sovereign, so he gathered his army and gave chase. For many days they pursued the will-o'-the-wisp horsemen, who always fled mockingly before them. Sometimes the raiders would turn, ride within bowshot and loose a brief hail of arrows. Then they would flee once more, before King Karun could catch them.

"Finally, in exasperation, Karun sent an envoy under a flag of truce. The envoy bore the king's words to the chief of the raiders: 'Why, oh warriors, do you flee before me? Come and fight us, for we fear you not. Come and give us battle, lest the world mock you for cowards.'

"The chief of the raiders answered thus: 'Wherefore should we do battle with you at your pleasure when it is not ours? We have already invaded your land and seized your treasure and your women. What profit for us lies in battle at this time? Yet if you would feel the full weight of our wrath, you may find the tombs of our forefathers near here. Molest those tombs and see whether we will come to fight you.'

"But," Khondemir went on, "the king and his host were already short of water and food. Instead of seeking out these tombs, they prudently turned their steps homeward."

As if at random, the wizard stepped across the mosaic floor, crossing the line of caravan cities and moving onto the steppe to the north. "I found this story to be fascinating, for it means that there is one solid, rooted place in the lives of these restless people. They have burial grounds that are sacred to them, and they

will stop whatever they are doing to defend those ne-
cropolises. I summoned spirits of the steppe, and I sent
them forth to find the burial ground sacred to Bartatua.
This day they brought me word of their success. They
found it . . . here." He pointed to the mosaic beside his
slippered foot; it was a featureless yellow field of topaz.

Amyr Jelair leaned forward to look. "The Steppe of
Famine! Surely there is nothing in that desert place save
the bones of dead men bleaching in the sun."

"There is no mistake. This is where the ancestors of
Bartatua's people rest, in a place they call the City of
Mounds. Give me a strong wing of cavalry, and certain
other items, and I shall lead the horde there, and there I
shall summon such a creature as shall wipe the barbarians from the face of the earth as though they had never
been."

"A wing of cavalry," mused the soldier who had
spoken earlier. "It is foolishness to send away so many
men when the city most needs them."

"But if Khondemir is correct," said the prince, "the
city may need no protecting."

"You said that this place is sacred to Bartatua," said
the prince's brother. "Will the others of his horde seek
to protect the tombs?"

"It matters little," said Khondemir with a wave of
his hand. "Bartatua and his Ashkuz will come. Without
him and his people, the others will fall out and break
up. They would never attempt anything as ambitious as
a major siege without his leadership."

"I can spare you perhaps a thousand men," said
Amyr Jelair. "Even so, they would be little protection
against such a host."

"They will be more than adequate, sire," Khondemir
assured him. "For I have learned other things about

these people. By the time they reach us, we will be well within the City of Mounds. These tribesmen have many superstitions and taboos. Among them, none may ride a horse within sight of the mounds. Better yet, none may shoot an arrow into the necropolis. Dismounted, with only their swords and lances, these barbarians will be no more formidable than any other undisciplined rabble. Give me good swordsmen under the command of capable officers and we need have no fear of any number of mere tribesmen.''

"That sounds quite reasonable, does it not, my advisors?'' Some agreed heartily, some less so. Then another thought struck the prince. "Good Khondemir, you mentioned that besides the cavalry, you would need 'other items.' What sort of items?''

"Oh, minor things having to do with my needs upon the trip. A pavilion, wherein I may work my craft during the halts, certain pieces of furniture for the same purposes . . . and one other thing.''

"And what might that be?'' Amyr Jelair asked.

"You must understand, sire, that summoning one of the great powers of another world is not like simply hiring a soldier or a workman. The rituals involved are quite complicated. Since this rite is being performed in your behalf, ideally you should be there in person.'' At the prince's look of alarm, the wizard put forth a forestalling hand. "I know, of course, that it is unthinkable to take you from the city in the midst of its preparations for siege. Someone of your blood will do nicely. Best of all would be a child of yours.''

Amyr Jelair paled. "One of my sons? How could I bear to part with one of my sons?''

"I did not say a son, sire. A daughter will do quite as well.''

The prince sat back in relief. "A daughter? That is different. I have several daughters. Ishkala is the eldest. She is difficult, and I despair of ever making a good match for her. You may take Ishkala."

"Very well, sire. Barring accident, she will return to you unharmed. Now, sire, if I am to conform to the schedule I have drawn up for this plan, I must have the soldiers and your daughter ready to depart at dawn on the tenth day from today."

"It shall be done," the prince said. "Now that business has been taken care of, let us repair to dinner."

That evening as Khondemir was conveyed back to his mansion, he congratulated himself on having carried out his plan so well. The prince was credulous and unused to situations of such urgency. Even had he been a sharper and more suspicious man, though, the result would have been the same. The plan was a good one, and everything the wizard had said was true . . . except for what he really planned to do when he reached the City of Mounds.

While Khondemir was being carried from one banquet, another celebration was still rollicking along in the city of Sogaria. A crowd of young men made merry in one of the many taverns bordering the city's bazaar. These taverns catered to the caravan trade, but this one was frequented by the better-educated classes: the students, the higher artisans, and the more disreputable sons of the nobility.

One table was especially noisy this night. The men who sat around it were very young, and they had been there since early evening. The wine flask had made many rounds in that time, and had been refilled frequently. One young man in particular was holding forth, and his words were forceful, although he stumbled over them upon occasion.

"We live in decadent times, my friends," he proclaimed. "The men of this age care for nothing but amassing money, buying palaces and objects of art, and overindulging themselves with food and wine."

"What is wrong with money, Manzur?" asked a companion. "What is wrong with palaces and objects of beautiful art?"

"And what is wrong with food and wine?" asked another. "You have done more than justice by such as has come your way this night." The table roared with laughter.

"There are greater things!" said the one called Manzur. He was young even in this company, and the suns of scarce eighteen summers had shone upon him. His garments were a bit threadbare and not nearly so fine as those worn by some of his friends, but his features were aristocratic, straight, narrow and cleanly formed. The soft new beard that framed his jaw was chestnut in color, and many a serving maid let her gaze linger upon him. The lad seemed to have no interest in them, though.

"What greater things, oh Manzur?" cried one, and his tone made it clear that this raillery was a common thing among these young roisterers.

"Glory! And adventure! And love eternal! Where in this soft age is the clash of steel, the whir of arrows, the shouts of brave men in battle?"

"Not far from here, if the rumors be true," said an older friend. But Manzur paid no attention.

"How may a man prove himself to his fellows and to his lady-love save by great deeds?" he demanded.

"Tell us!" chorused his friends.

"It just so happens," said the young man, "that I

have with me some verses I have composed upon this very subject.'' He rummaged within the breast of his robe and undertunic. ''Let me see, I know they are here somewhere.'' He fumbled at his sash and opened a case in which he kept his writing instruments.

''By the gods, we are doomed!'' shouted one in mock despair. ''Manzur wants to read us his poetry!'' There were groans and curses.

''I must fortify myself for this ordeal,'' said another, hastily pouring himself a fresh goblet of wine.

''There are some things a man simply cannot endure,'' said a youth who wore the sleeveless robe of an architect's apprentice. From his sash he drew a short, curved dagger, placed its tip against his breast and pretended to attempt suicide.

Manzur paid them no attention, at length locating his errant verses tucked into the top of his boot. ''Ah, here they are! Attend me closely, my friends. In years to come you may tell your children that you were present at the first recital of these verses.''

Hand spread over his heart, papers held at arm's length, Manzur began to recite:

> *Where, O Gods, are those warriors,*
> *Lion-brave, who in our fathers' time*
> *Did hold their battle lines*
> *'Gainst nomad fierce and Turanian proud,*
> *Not to mention the scurvy Bukhroshans.* . . .

As many of those at the table leaned over, feigning the symptoms of severe illness, the would-be suicide tugged at the poet's striped robe. ''Manzur, as highly as we all esteem your poetic works, it is about your lady-love that we wish to hear.''

''Ah,'' sighed the youth, ''my beautiful—but I may

not let her divine name pass my lips where others may hear." He folded his verses and put them away. Those seated about the table made gestures of gratitude to the gods.

"Why is there such mystery about this lady, Manzur?" asked a youth in a student's turban. "For a fortnight you have sighed and moped about her, and yet we have naught but your word that she is worthy of such suffering." He refilled Manzur's goblet in hope of loosening his tongue, an operation the poet scarcely required.

"I swore an oath to her," Manzur said, "that I would never reveal her identity. The consequences would be terrible for us both."

"Hah!" said the suicide. "Did I not tell you? She is married! The wife of some fat-bellied merchant, she entertains Manzur amid opulent surroundings while her husband is away on business. Admit it, Manzur."

"Beware!" cried Manzur, fumbling for his sword. "You sully the *name* of a great lady!"

"How can we do anything to her name?" asked another. "You will not reveal it to us."

Manzur resumed his seat. "Alas, her identity must remain a secret within my heart. She is too highborn for such as me to raise eyes to, and yet I have dared. We have pledged our love, but it is doomed because of the difference in our stations."

His friends were rapt. At last he was speaking of the woman of mystery. "Describe her, Manzur," said one craftily. "Surely a poet must be able to delineate such a beauty in such wise that we may see her without knowing her name."

"Her hair, my companions, is as black as the midnight sky."

"There is scarcely another color of hair in all Sogaria," said the crafty one, disappointed.

"Her skin is as pale as the rising moon."

"Be more specific, Manzur," said the suicide.

A thought seemed to strike the poet. "But wait! There is a way I may yet tell you of her incomparable qualities." He reached into his other boot and withdrew a sheaf of papers. "This very day I have composed a poem to her. It is a trifling thing, still in rough form, of some two hundred ninety-seven lines, and I—"

He looked up from his verses to see the last of his friends storming out of the tavern by doors and windows. Perplexed, he surveyed the deserted table, then drained the last cup of wine.

"As courage and honor have fled our age," he proclaimed, "so has the appreciation of fine poetry." He looked about for agreement, in time to see the proprietor approaching with the look of a man who expects to be paid. Manzur decided it was time to take to his own heels.

Outside, he wended his way toward the prince's palace and brooded upon the many tragedies of his life. As a poet and philosopher, he knew himself doomed to a life of neglect, forever misunderstood by his fellow men. As a lover, he was likewise doomed, for only the greatest and fairest of women could stir his heart. While, much to his surprise, he had found just such a lady right in his native city, it was inevitable that she should be of the very highest birth and therefore unsuitable for the reprobate son of an impoverished minor noble.

Like many another such youth, Manzur was too proud to work and too poor to have connections at court. Such slight income as he had came from giving lessons in swordsmanship at the studio of Master Nakhshef. It called for little effort, merely the teaching of fundamentals to first-year students, but anything having to do with arms was honorable.

At least he could take pride in his swordsmanship. He had begged his way into the school as a young boy and had endured much scorn from the old master in his first years. Gradually the scorn became acceptance, then approval. Finally the old man took Manzur on as an assistant, and even hinted that someday the youth might replace him as master.

Manzur drew his blade and went through a complicated drill that would have been demanding of a sober man, but his performance was flawless. His sword was a variant of the Turanian talwar: single-edged, razorsharp, with the slightest of curves. Light and slender, in the hands of a skilled man it was exceedingly deadly. Master Nakhshef had insisted that he attain proficiency in all weapons, but the light sword was his favorite.

His steps had led him to the rear wall of the prince's palace, and he sheathed his blade in a single, flowing motion. There was an ancient vine growing up the wall, thick and gnarled. He looked along the lane he had come by and saw that it was deserted. The garden facing the wall was likewise deserted. No sentries showed themselves atop the wall. Satisfied that he was unobserved, he began to climb.

It was a sign of the decadence of the times, he thought as he ascended, that a veritable scaling-ladder had been allowed to grow up a wall of the palace. Likewise, that the sentries rarely walked their rounds. The fact that these derelictions allowed him to visit his love did nothing to dim his indignation.

Once atop the wall, he dropped lightly into the small courtyard beyond. All was quiet. He skirted the central pool and entered a veranda where, during the days, certain ladies of the court took shelter from the fierce sun. Stepping cautiously to an intricate tracery of marble, he whispered urgently, "Ishkala!"

With his heart in his mouth, he waited. Each time he did this, he knew that instead of his lady, a guard might be waiting.

"Manzur?" A slight form in voluminous garments came through the doorway next to the marble lattice. He swept her into his embrace.

"My lady, my love, how I have longed for you since—"

She drew back from him sharply. "Manzur! You have been out carousing with your friends again! You smell as if you had slept in a wine cask."

"I must drink to forget, love, lest thoughts of you so dominate my soul that when called upon by honor to draw my sword, I—"

"Cease this prattle," she hissed. "Something terrible has happened!"

For a moment, he almost sobered. "You have not been betrothed?"

"Almost as bad. That fearsome Turanian wizard visited the court this evening. As usual, I hid behind the throne to hear what was being said. There is to be war!"

"War!" Visions of glory danced in his head.

"The wizard, Khondemir, says that he can prevent this war."

"What a pity," said Manzur, disappointed.

"He plans to take an expedition far into the desert steppe and there wreak some horrible magic to destroy the nomads."

"These wizards have taken all the honor out of warfare," he protested indignantly.

"Worse than that. He claims that he needs *me* for his spell!"

"You? Perhaps you had better explain from the beginning."

She told him all she had heard from her hiding place. "This night," she went on, "the mayor of the palace came to say that I must prepare for a long journey. We are to be escorted by the Red Eagles. The wizard says I shall not be harmed, but I am not so trusting as my father. I know that the Turanian plots evil against the city!"

"I'll not allow this," Manzur vowed. "I shall demand an audience with the prince."

"You would not get past the gatekeeper, my love," she said. "I must obey my father, even when he acts foolishly."

"I cannot let you do this," he said. "Ever since I felt your heart calling out to mine, forcing me to climb yonder wall and find you—" He went on in this vein for some time.

In truth, he had been passing this way some weeks earlier with a pack of friends after a drunken party, and they dared him to climb the wall of the prince's palace. He accepted the challenge, ascended to the battlement, turned to take a bow, and then lost his balance and fell into the courtyard, straight onto a fragrant bush. When the world stopped swimming about him, he found himself staring up into a vision of loveliness such as he had never dreamed possible. By now he had forgotten the more-embarrassing details of the event and believed the story he had made up for her.

"You must go," she said. "The eunuch guards will be making their rounds. You must forget about me. If I return from this journey, well and good. If not, then find another love." Sobs distorted her last words.

"I shall do something, my love," he said. "I know not what, but I shall find some way to be with you."

They broke apart at the sound of tramping feet and

jingling metal. The guard was coming. With a final kiss, Manzur ran to the wall and eschewed the tree he usually climbed, using the more-prosaic gardener's ladder.

In the park near the palace, he wandered despondently. How could he contrive a way to be by his lover's side in her hour of need? He considered going to the house of Khondemir and challenging the mage to a duel. He discarded the thought. Doubtless the man would make use of some dishonorable, wizardly advantage. He watched the beautiful crescent of the moon between two spice trees and considered composing a poem to Ishkala, comparing her beauty to that of the moon. It seemed to be an original idea.

He awoke in the morning with a shattering head and the distinct feeling that he was at the bottom of a great sea. He sat up and saw some men trimming hedges in the garden, paying him no heed. He sought to remember the events of the night before. First, someone had attempted to insult his poetry. Then— Ishkala! Her words came flooding back to him. There had to be something he could do. Shakily he rose on unsteady feet and walked from the garden.

As he descended into the city proper, he became aware of a great deal of untoward activity. People were running hither and yon, officials were proclaiming importantly, armed soldiers were marching up and down. The city was preparing for war. At any other time Manzur would have thrown himself into the thick of things. It was what he had been dreaming of for years. Now, though, he could only think of Ishkala and the terrible fate that might befall her.

A half-squadron of colorful cavalry cantered past, and a wonderful idea came to him. Without bothering to return home to refresh his appearance, he hurried to the southern gate of the city. Here, just without the walls, was a vast area of pens, barracks and stables where the soldiery of the city was kept in garrison.

A few questions addressed to several hurrying soldiers brought him to a wide parade field where several squadrons were going through their drill with the precision of seasoned professionals. Because they wore nodding red plumes in their helmets, he knew that these were the famed Red Eagles, the prince's elite cavalry force. He saw an officer observing the drill and he ran to the man's side.

"I am Manzur Alyasha, sir, and I wish to join the Red Eagles."

The officer's mouth bent into a tolerant smile within his beard. "Now that the city faces war, many young men will want to join. Is there some reason I should take you into the finest cavalry unit of Sogaria? By the state of your clothing, I can tell that no court nobleman is going to procure you a commission."

"I have no court influence," Manzur admitted, "but I am excellent with a sword." He whipped his weapon forth and executed a dazzling practice form.

"Very pretty," said the officer. "I can see that you have studied the blade long and well. But in the army we do not use those little weapons. Can you wield a man's sword?" He drew his own blade and handed it to Manzur. It was long and broad, with more curvature than that of Manzur's sword. It had the reach a cavalryman needed, and the weight to split armor.

Manzur thanked the gods that old Nakhshef had made him practice with weapons of war. He went through a heavy-saber form, its motions simpler and more forceful than those used for the light sword.

"That is nice," said the officer, "but can you ride?"

"I can," Manzur asserted confidently. He was an

adequate horseman, although he lacked the special skills of the cavalryman.

"Then go to yonder compound, where all the nags are being gathered. A new troop is forming, and if you get there soon enough, you might have a mount."

"No," Manzur insisted, "it must be the Red Eagles."

"Young man," said the officer, "you cannot simply ask to be admitted to the Red Eagles. Many apply for a lowly trooper's place and are turned back, though they be seasoned warriors. Only the most proven are admitted. Go join some other regiment. After you have a few years of experience within your armor, apply to me again."

Manzur turned away, his hopes dashed. Somehow he had to find a way to follow Ishkala into the Steppe of Famine.

Five

As the sun lowered, a meal was brought to the men who sat chained to the posts. A slave deposited a platter and a flask between Conan and Rustuf, and the two fell upon them with gusto. There was bread of good quality, and cheese, but best of all, there was plenty of smoking meat.

"At least the food here is better than that of the pit," said Rustuf. He seized a joint and tore at it with his teeth.

With more moderation, Conan did likewise. It was the first decent meal he had eaten in many days. "Like men about to be crucified," he said, "we are well fed. Go easy, though. No man fights his best on an overfull stomach." He took the flask and drank. It was a decent wine, diluted with water.

"Aye," said Rustuf through a mouthful of lamb. "Our companions are not so delicate." The others in the enclosure were seizing their food like feeding jackals, quarreling over the prize bits and throwing blows when they could reach one another. Conan snorted disgust at such lack of self-control.

As they were finishing their dinner, a visitor arrived in the compound. It was a woman, cloaked and scarved so that only her face showed. She was accompanied by the head slavemaster, and she began looking over the prisoners like a buyer at a cattle market. As she approached, each man stood for her inspection.

Conan ignored her as she reached him.

"You!" said the slavemaster. "Stand for my lady."

Conan brushed some crumbs from the corners of his mouth.

"Is he deaf?" asked the woman. "Or does he not understand the language?"

"This one understands," said the slavemaster. "He is arrogant, though. Bested a parcel of my guards this afternoon. The warrior who brought him in said that he is prouder in bonds than most men walking free." He rapped on Conan's shoulder with his coiled whip. "Stand, hero. You shall have plenty of opportunity to show off your courage this night."

Slowly Conan unwound to his full height. The woman looked him over, missing nothing: the long legs, the deep chest, the thick neck, the arms heavily cabled with muscle. She walked around him, cataloguing his scars, admiring his size and symmetry. She felt an arm, kneading the tough muscle. She punched his midsection with a small, gloved fist. Her hand bounced back as if it had hit a tree trunk. Last of all, she studied his face.

"Cleaned up and properly shaved," she said to the slavemaster, "it might be presentable." Then, to Conan: "How do you fight, foreigner?"

"I am a swordsman, but I can use all hand weapons: ax, lance, mace, dagger. I am a warrior."

"Perhaps you are, as your nation defines such things. Can you fight bare-handed?"

"I have yet to meet my better," he answered. He studied her frankly. He could see little of her except for her face, but that was as lovely as he had ever seen. Her graceful, confident stride told him that her body was as well made.

"You are amusing, slave," she said. "You shall be yet more amusing tonight." She turned to the slavemaster. "Give him means with which to wash and shave. My lord will see him fight first tonight." With that, she went on to examine the rest of the slaves.

Rustuf grinned at Conan. "Already you have attracted attention, although it may be of the wrong kind. You may have the longest night of us all, or the shortest."

In the great tent, Bartatua held revel for the new arrivals. Two allied chiefs had come into the camp that day, bringing their hordes as well as a gaggle of slaves for the pit. He feasted them upon unaccustomed delicacies: imported wines and spices, birds that were not native to the steppe, even fish raised in the ponds of Bukhrosha, brought in by courier, still living in skin bags of water. It was important to his future plans that the austere *kagans* of the steppe acquire a taste for the exotic delights of civilization.

"Your reputation for hospitality was not exaggerated, chief of the Ashkuz," said a leather-faced *kagan*. His narrow eyes drank in the sight of a dozen Vendhyan women, clad only in elaborate jewels and executing one of the lascivious dances for which their land was famed.

"It is my pleasure to share with my friends all that I have," said Bartatua. "If you see aught that pleases you here, ask it of me and it shall be yours. Do you desire one of these dancers for your stay? Take your pick. They have been selected and trained by my own concubine, whom I took when I slew Kuchlug." It did no harm to remind them that he had slain the great chief bare-handed in the midst of his people. It was the kind of feat that made the reputation of an ambitious man.

"Your generosity is far-famed," said another, younger chieftain. "We are much intrigued by your scheme to take Sogaria. But we are puzzled by your plans for this great crowd of slaves. Would you explain this?"

"Aye," said leather-face, who sat upon Bartatua's other side. "We have always defeated the city folk easily because we ride like the wind across the plain. While they lumber about in their armored formations, we strike behind them and are gone. It is our swiftness and our incomparable bows that give us mastery. If we must take along these slaves, we shall be slowed to a walking pace and much of our advantage shall be lost."

"Attend me, then, and I shall explain."

The *kagan* of the Ashkuz was taller than most of his race, with the long arms and tremendous shoulders of a great bowman. He was of the western Hyrkanians, with green eyes, and auburn hair worked into a number of small plaits. His handsome features had a slightly eastern cast, but his skin was fair beneath its weathering. Tattooed swirls decorated his cheeks, adding to the powerful ferocity of his countenance. Although Bartatua had no more than thirty years and was quite young to be so great a *kagan*, his personal force and aura of power were those of a great leader of men. He sipped at his wine as he prepared his explanation.

"Within a few days, we shall begin our campaign. The slaves will not be needed until we commence siege operations, so they shall not move with the regular army. Instead, they shall be sent forth *first*, under a small herding force. A few days later, the cavalry squadrons under their leaders shall move out. They shall pass the slaves before the borders of Sogarian territory are reached.''

The others nodded, understanding the thrust of his tactics.

''The first stage of operations,'' Bartatua went on, ''shall be much like our accustomed raiding into the territory of the city people. A large number of detached forces shall hit several targets at once. These shall be outlying forts, villages and the like. Our purpose shall be to harry and terrify. It is important at this stage that we do little killing, no more than necessary.''

''Why is that?'' asked the older chief. It was ancient Hyrkanian custom to massacre all the defeated who were deemed of no value once their goods had been taken.

''Because the people are more useful to us alive at this stage. Once they realize that their homes and garrisons are no longer safe, they will flee, and they will all go in a single direction.''

''Straight into Sogaria!'' said the younger chief.

''Exactly, my friend,'' Bartatua said with hearty approval. ''We shall herd them like sheep. They will pour into Sogaria until the city bulges like a wineskin, eating up its stores, fighting for space to live, stirring up hatred among the regular inhabitants. Each batch of fleeing peasants shall make our task easier for us.''

''Soon even the city folk must see the foolishness of taking in so many useless mouths,'' said the older chief. ''They will close the gates against them.''

Bartatua waved his hand in an airy gesture. ''Such as

huddle without the walls we can dispose of handily. Some we may press into siege works. By the time we have herded the whole countryside into the city, our entire horde will be reunited and we shall have the place surrounded. By then, the marching slaves shall have arrived and we may commence siege operations.''

"This is a most sagacious plan,'' said the older *kagan*, ''and you may count on my horde for this campaign.'' The younger man vigorously assented as well.

Bartatua was deeply satisfied. His plans went much further than the taking of a single city, but he did not wish to burden these simple warrior-chiefs with anything too complex. In any case, he needed a season as sole leader of the united tribes so as to cement his position as overchief of all the hordes, *Ushi-Kagan*. Let the tribesmen get a taste of the loot to be had and they would demand that he lead them to further conquests. In the meantime, he would accomplish much more with deeds than he would with talk.

His ambitions spanned a far greater compass than these chiefs, and the others who sat in the tent, could ever comprehend. As a boy, he had listened to the tales of travelers describing distant lands and their great cities. He had gone on raids that probed the borders of those lands, and he had seen how soft, slow and poorly organized the civilized powers were. He wanted nothing less than to conquer them all, and to take all they had as his personal property. He would take great Khitai first, then voluptuous Vendhya, and after that, perhaps Turan and the gleaming kingdoms of the west, then sorcerous Stygia, and the lands south of Stygia, of which he had heard that the people were black and that there were elephants greater than those of Vendhya.

He was confident that nothing could stop his hordes

of horse-archers once they were united under a single rule. He had accomplished much by force of personality and native intelligence. Now he had as well the aid and advice of his beautiful, utterly ruthless concubine, Lakhme. A great deal of his tactical planning in the taking of Sogaria had been her idea, as had the concept of gaining a stranglehold on the caravan routes between east and west. He meant to have the world eventually, but he had grasped instantly the importance of controlling all the goods and virtually all the information passing between the great lands. Thus at will he could either terrify or lull into complacency the kingdoms at both ends of the routes.

He dragged his thoughts back to his tent. Dreams were for the future. For the present, he had yet to firmly cement his alliances with his fellow *kagans*.

"Tonight," Bartatua announced, "we have special entertainment. I have selected my most rebellious slaves and prisoners, but only those best skilled in arms. They shall be pitted against one another for our amusement, and so that you may see how your enemies are accustomed to fighting."

A great cheer greeted this announcement, and slaves came in bearing chests from which protruded a great variety of weapons. The Vendhyan dancers scampered off amid a shower of coins, and the rich carpets upon which they had been dancing were taken up, revealing the bare ground. Silent anticipation reigned.

"Bring in the first pair," Bartatua ordered.

Two men were led in on chains. One was the hulking brute with whom Conan had spoken when he entered the fighter pen. "This one I know," said Bartatua. "He was the victor in the last combat a few evenings ago. But you," he said to the other, "I know not. Who are you, slave?"

"I am Conan of Cimmeria, and I am a warrior, not a slave." He folded his arms across his massive chest and glowered from beneath lowering brows. He was clean-shaven once more, and he had contrived to bathe with a bucket of water and a rough cloth. His skin was now oiled and caught highlights from the torches.

"Say you so? Yet you wear my neck ring, and that makes you my slave."

"No," Conan said, "it makes me your prisoner. There is a great difference." There was nothing subservient in his pose nor in the volcanic glare of his blue eyes.

"This one has a sharp tongue," said a warrior as he drew a dagger. "Let me split it for you, *Kagan*."

Conan turned his baleful gaze upon the one who had spoken. "You had best dip your dagger in yon bowl of sauce, warrior," he said.

"And wherefore should I do such a thing, slave?" asked the man scornfully.

"Because," said Conan, "if you seek to use it on me, I shall make you eat it." The tent rocked with laughter, and the dagger-bearer would have leaped upon Conan but was checked by a gesture from Bartatua.

"Nay," said the *kagan*. "A free man may not fight with a slave as if with an equal. You amuse me, man of Cimmeria, but the time has come to see whether there is more to you than talk." He signed to a slavemaster and the neck rings of the two were unlocked. "The first fight," said Bartatua, "shall be without weapons. Begin."

No sooner had the command been given than the huge easterner burst into motion. With a speed incredible in a man so large, his foot whipped up and around, aimed for Conan's face. The Cimmerian was still facing Bartatua and had not even glanced toward his opponent beside him. Any other man would have died in that moment, his neck snapped by the terrible force of the easterner's kick.

Conan's muscles and nerves acted without hesitation and without need for thought. When the callused foot hissed through the space where his head had been, Conan was three paces away. The easterner's first assault flowed into his second as if it were a single motion. The instant his kicking foot touched the ground, his pivot foot lashed out at the Cimmerian's midsection. Conan slapped the foot aside with his open palm and the easterner spun away, out of range.

There was a ferocious cheer for the vicious assault and for Conan's superb recovery. The Cimmerian never let his eyes move from the man opposite him, who now stood with one leg slightly advanced, fists clenched before him at waist level. He could see that the easterner was using a highly sophisticated style of unarmed combat and that the man was accustomed to killing unskilled opponents with it.

Conan had no use for highly structured styles, with or without weapons. They taught a man to think in terms of set situations and left him vulnerable to the unexpected. He preferred to rely upon his own strength, speed and reflexes.

"Come, foreigner," taunted the easterner. "Meet your death at the hands of Tsongkha. I have slain hundreds with these hands and feet. Do not fear, I shall not make you suffer."

Conan grinned fiercely. The man had expected his first assault to kill, and now he had to boast to prop his shaken courage.

"I have no intention of suffering," Conan said. "Let us see more of your dance."

Snarling, Tsongkha leaped in. He feinted a kick at

Conan's knee but the true attack came from his right hand, which darted toward the Cimmerian's face, fingers spread to spear the eyes from his head.

Swift as was the attack, Conan was swifter. He grabbed the easterner's wrist, stopping the fingers an inch from his eyes. With a mighty wrench, he twisted the arm around and down, and Tsongkha grimaced as bones snapped and tendons tore. His other hand shot up, the heel of the palm aimed to smash Conan's nose, but the Cimmerian batted the hand aside and smashed an elbow into the man's temple.

Tsongkha collapsed upon the ground, and servants came to drag his inert form from the tent. Conan stood relaxed, unwinded. There were cheers for his performance, but not many of those present truly understood the intricacies of unarmed combat. Armed almost from birth, the Hyrkanians considered such things to be the sport of boys.

"The next bout with weapons, *Kagan*," called a chief whose face was covered by a dragon tattoo.

"By all means," said Bartatua. He looked at Conan and graciously waved a hand over the low table before him. It was still covered with food and wine. "Excellent fight, Cimmerian. Here, refresh yourself before your next bout."

"Why?" Conan asked. "Do I look tired?"

Bartatua slapped his thigh in high amusement. "Never have I seen such arrogance! You shall provide us rare sport. What is your favored weapon?"

"The sword." He eyed the chests of weapons, seeking a blade to his taste.

"Then you shall fight with the lance!" said Bartatua. The Hyrkanians rocked with laughter at this example of kingly humor.

Conan shrugged. "It is all one." He picked up a slender lance of Vendhya. It was about seven feet long and made of tough ash wood. At one end was a ten-inch point, razor-edged. At the other end was a steel ball the size of a child's fist. He had handled spears since earliest youth and was expert in their use, but the lance was far from his favorite weapon. Within the confines of the tent, he would not be able to use it to best advantage.

The next man to be led in was a lean Turanian, tall and saturnine.

"Choose your weapons," said Bartatua. The man looked through the chests and came back with a long talwar in one hand and a round steel buckler in the other. The buckler was convex, with four bosses on its face, and was about twenty inches in diameter.

"Begin," said Bartatua.

The Turanian leaned forward and closed with Conan, his shield held well out from his body for best protection from the thrust of a lance. Had Conan been armed with a sword, the man would have held the shield higher, for then the greatest danger would have been a cut to his unhelmeted head. For a spear, though, the prime target area was the torso, and the Turanian knew it.

Conan thrust for the throat. It was a shrewd and unexpected move, but the Turanian turned it with the edge of his shield and replied with an almost simultaneous cut to Conan's leading thigh. The Cimmerian had to abandon the attack and leap back swiftly. He cursed the surroundings in which he had to fight. In the hands of an expert, the spear was a deadly and versatile weapon, but only if the spearman had room to maneuver. Otherwise, it was useful primarily for fighting in formation, shoulder-to-shoulder with other spearmen. Against a disciplined body of spearmen, even fine cavalry could find themselves helpless.

To add to his disadvantage, the Turanian had two weapons, one offensive and the other defensive. As he had shown with his last move, the Turanian could block an attack with one hand while launching an attack of his own with the other. Now the Turanian came in, cutting low at Conan's legs while keeping his shield no higher than before, secure in the knowledge that the Cimmerian's weapon was not useful for an attack to the head.

Conan had to give ground, but he decided to disabuse the man of the idea that he could not be brained in this fight. Grasping the spear after the manner of a quarterstaff, Conan stabbed downward as if to pin the man's foot to the ground; then, as the shield lowered to protect that extremity, he swung the steel-weighted butt at his opponent's temple. The Turanian escaped a shattering blow only by retreating hastily with his shield, held above him like a turtle's shell.

When they resumed combat, both men moved with great caution. Each had the other's measure now, and knew he faced a skilled and wily opponent. Conan, though, was aware of something else: He was here not only to survive, but to make an impression on Bartatua. This was settling down to a protracted fight. He had no doubt that he would win in time, but he had to take the audience into account. A group of Vanir, or Kothians or Aquilonians, if they were themselves experienced warriors, would be enthralled by this display of two experts with mismatched weapons feeling each other out, testing one another's strengths and weaknesses and battling cautiously to a decision—or to the death. This pack of horse-archers, on the other hand, might quickly become bored, and Conan could not afford to bore them.

A decided change in tactics was in order. So far, his opponent's major advantage was in possessing both an offensive and a defensive weapon. Conan had an answer to that. As the Turanian essayed a shrewd offensive attack with the shield, punching with its edge, Conan leaped back as though this maneuver had taken him unawares. Then he placed the middle of his lance in his mouth, bit down hard and snapped it in twain.

"He surrenders!" shouted some in disgust. "He throws himself on the other's mercy and destroys his weapon! Kill him!"

But Conan was far from surrendering. In his left hand he now held the half of the lance that bore the point. In his right hand was the half terminating in the small steel ball. In effect, he held a short stabbing spear, such as certain Kushite tribes of his acquaintance favored, and a light truncheon. The latter weapon was not a true mace, but it was perfectly adequate for braining an unarmored man. He now slid in swiftly and stabbed beneath the shield. As the shield lowered, he swept the ball at the Turanian's head. At the last moment he had to use the right-hand weapon to block the sword, but the Turanian had become unnerved. Conan had gained a slight advantage, for both of his weapons were equally adept for offense or defense.

The Turanian knew that he had to win quickly. To the Hyrkanians it looked an even match, with the Turanian perhaps somewhat the favorite. That wily warrior, however, was under no such misapprehension. He recognized that in Conan he faced an enemy deadlier than any he had known. His only hope was to take swift and full advantage of his shield and sword.

With a blood-freezing war cry, the Turanian rushed in, shield held close to cover his torso, while with his sword he sought to split Conan's skull. He risked an almost certain spearhead through his leading thigh, but that was the sort of risk a warrior was accustomed to.

Instead, Conan dropped to the ground and rolled. The Turanian could not check his rush and fell head-long. Before he could scramble to his feet, Conan was standing behind him. A swift blow of the steel ball paralyzed the man's elbow, and the talwar dropped to the ground. Another blow to the shoulder rendered the shield useless. Conan rolled the man onto his back and presented the spearpoint to his throat.

"Slay him," said Bartatua after the others had finished cheering.

Conan withdrew his spearpoint and signaled for his erstwhile opponent to leave the tent. After the man had gone, he turned to the *kagan* of the Ashkuz.

"*Why?*"

"Why?" demanded Bartatua, his face growing crimson at this defiance. "What kind of warrior leaves a defeated enemy alive?"

"When a man attacks me unprovoked," Conan said, tossing the shattered bits of his lance back into a chest, "I rarely fail to slay him. But why should I slay a fine swordsman who fights me merely because we are both prisoners of a chief who likes to see men fighting?"

As Bartatua sat dumbfounded, the Cimmerian stepped up to his table and said: "I will now trouble you for some of that refreshment you offered earlier. This was a harder fight than the first." He poured a brimming cup of wine and took a long drink; then he picked up a handful of raisins and began tossing them into his mouth. The Hyrkanians stared at him as if at a ghost come to life.

Bartatua broke into hilarious laughter. "This man surpasses all expectation. Such insolence is tolerable only in a court fool! Will you entertain us as a fool, Cimmerian?''

"I am a warrior," Conan reiterated. "Put me to work as a warrior and you shall soon know my value. Fools are those who misuse their fellow men.''

There was deadly silence for a few moments. At last Bartatua said, "Very well, there is more proving to be done. What next, my friends?''

"He says he is good with the sword," said the older of the two flanking chiefs. "Let him prove it. Give him a sword and set him against another swordsman.''

"So be it!" cried Bartatua. "Go choose yourself a sword, foreigner.''

Conan complied. There were many swords in the chests, from many different nations. He preferred the straight sword of the western lands, but all the swords he could see were of the east. At last he found a Vendhyan sword that had a straight blade. The hilt was too short for his big hand, but he could achieve a comfortable grip by looping his forefinger over the crossguard. The blade was broad but light and somewhat whippy. He would not have chosen this sword for battle, but against an unarmored man, it would be adequate.

"Bring in the next," called Bartatua.

The next man who came in was Rustuf. Neither prisoner wasted time on curses or recriminations. Rustuf went to the chests and came back with a sword of Iranistan, slightly curved and single-edged, with a flat, oval guard. Its long handle could be used by one or both hands.

"Begin," Bartatua ordered.

The two faced off and Rustuf immediately started a combination attack, cutting high, low and in between. Conan blocked the cuts efficiently and replied with thrusts. Rustuf backed off to gain room and parried with the strong back third of his blade. The weapon was not well designed for the action, but a good swordsman could make do with almost any blade.

Conan closed in with quick strides and began an attack at the *kozak*'s head. Rustuf blocked efficiently and replied with repeated attacks at Conan's waist. Conan fell into a routine of cutting high and blocking low, and then Rustuf cut yet lower and nicked the Cimmerian's knee, bringing blood for the first time in the fight.

"Hah!" said the *kozak*. "I am not quite the child that the other two were, eh, Cimmerian?"

"Save your breath for fighting, *kozak*!" said Conan.

The pair fell to with a will, and for many minutes steel rang on steel as they advanced and retreated around the fighting space allowed. At one point Rustuf pushed Conan back across a table, both blades crossed under the Cimmerian's throat. With a superhuman effort, Conan pushed him away, and the swords licked back and forth like the tongues of fighting serpents.

The tent resounded with cheers, and warriors from without crowded in to see the spectacle. After one especially vicious exchange, Rustuf threw away his sword and snatched up another that was not hacked into the semblance of a saw.

"Prepare now to die, Cimmerian!" shouted Rustuf as he launched a furious attack.

Conan was driven back until he fell sprawling upon the spread of meats, fruits, bread and wine flasks before Bartatua. Rustuf leaped through the air and fell upon him, cutting furiously. Conan caught his sword wrist and twisted the weapon away from himself, driving the *kozak* across the room and leaping upon him in turn.

With both hands he forced his blade down upon Rustuf's throat.

"Yield, dog!"

"Cut and be damned!" said the *kozak*. "I yield to no man!"

Conan turned to Bartatua. "*Kagan*, I ask leave to spare this man. He is a superb swordsman, and he would be an asset to your army."

In the excitement of the splendid fight, it did not occur to Bartatua that the Cimmerian had not thought it fit to ask of him the disposition of the first two combatants.

"Very well. Spare him." The Hyrkanians acclaimed the *Kagan*'s magnanimity.

Conan straightened, his chest heaving. "Have you any more opponents for me?"

"Nay, this has been a good evening's work. You have proven yourself, Cimmerian. You are slave and prisoner no longer. I name you fifty-leader in my own horde. Does that please you?"

"It pleases me well, my lord," said the Cimmerian. He looked about the tent and saw that most were glaring at him. They had enjoyed the fights, but that was not the same thing as accepting him as a fellow officer. He knew this situation as well. Bartatua was a born general, and he valued nothing but ability in his subordinates. Bartatua's men, however, were different. No foreigner, however skillful he might be, was the equal of a Hyrkanian. He would have to watch his back.

"What would you have of me?" Bartatua asked. "You shall have horses, armor, weapons in plenty. What else?"

"My lord is generous," said Conan, knowing that it was time to be diplomatic. "I would like to have my last two opponents under my command."

"As you will," said Bartatua. "Is there anything else?"

"I would like to have one of your Hyrkanian bows and an expert instructor to teach me in its use."

"What?" asked Bartatua mockingly. "Such a master of weapons, and yet you are not an archer?"

"I had thought so," Conan said, "until I saw your men shoot."

"See?" said Bartatua. "This man is no braggart. He is a master in the fighting styles practiced by our enemies, but he knows that we have much to teach him in the way of the bow. Would that all my men had such honesty. Go, Cimmerian. We shall talk on the morrow."

Conan bowed politely and took his leave. Bartatua eyed his retreating back with approval. From behind Bartatua's dais another pair of eyes, beautiful but pitiless, watched him with much less favor.

Outside, Conan found Rustuf and sat down next to him. "It worked out just as we planned."

The *kozak* rubbed his sore jaw. "A good thing, too. When you fed me that clout on the twenty-third pass, I leaned into it by mistake. By Mitra, but I saw stars! And had you not pulled your leg back on that last exchange, I'd have laid your thigh open to the bone. It was too late for me to stop."

"It worked, so let us not worry about what might have been. We had to make it look real. Now we have positions in his army, and a chance to make our fortune."

"Aye," said Rustuf. "It will be good to have a horse under me again, and a sword at my waist, and all the wide steppe to roam in."

"Spoken like a true *kozak*," Conan said. Unlike the Hyrkanians, who were tied to their herds and pastures, and who seldom strayed from their tribes, the *Kozaki* were raiders pure and simple, and a *kozak* with the wanderlust on him frequently would ride abroad alone, seeking adventure.

The Turanian came up to them, rubbing his elbow. "Is it true what I hear, that you have freed me to join the *kagan*'s army?"

"If it is your wish," Conan said. "I'll have no reluctant soldiers behind my back, though."

"Think you I would rather stay in the slave pit or be chained to a fighter's post? I am your man, and you have my thanks." He put forth his hand, and Conan took it. "My name is Fawd."

A servant arrived with a key and removed their neck rings, and they followed the man to their new quarters.

Six

When Conan arose in the morning, it was in a tent he now shared with Rustuf and Fawd. The structure was round, with a domed roof supported by an interior lattice. There were no ropes or pegs with which to fasten it to the ground, yet he had been told that such a tent would stay firm in the most violent windstorm. He pushed aside the door-hanging and went outside, in time to see a group of soldiers laying out a heap of arms and armor, and tethering a trio of horses to a stake driven into the ground.

"These are for you and your companions," said a servant. "You have nine more horses, and your men five each. When you wish to look them over, I will guide you to where the mounts of your fifty are penned."

Conan examined the three horses and selected the largest and strongest for himself. The saddles were all but identical, mere heavy pads innocent of pommel or cantle. Broad loops of leather served for stirrups. He could find none of the armor to fit him, and he made a mental note to search out Boria and retrieve his mail shirt and his helmet. The Vendhyan sword he had used the evening before was among the weapons and he belted it on, along with a broad-bladed dagger. There was a selection of the felt caps favored by the nomads, with their hanging neck- and earflaps, but he eschewed these. To his delight, he found a pair of the soft knee-high boots, with their upturned, pointed toes. He added a loose tunic with billowy sleeves.

There was even a selection of barbaric jewelry, from which he chose a pair of broad bracelets made of a pale electrum alloy and worked into designs of fighting eagles. Satisfied that he now looked like an officer rather than a ragged prisoner, he examined the bows. There were two for each man, in covered cases that were heavily embroidered. He drew one from its case and studied it.

Unstrung, the bow was an almost complete circle. In design it was similar to bows with which he was familiar. The archers of Koth, Turan and Shem used such bows, but this one was half again as thick and looked to be far more powerful. He itched to take it to the archery range and try it out, but he had other matters to take care of first. He saw a rope such as he had been captured with and added it to his new belongings. This was another weapon whose mysteries he was determined to learn.

He went back to the tent flap. "Rise, you sluggards. We have work to accomplish!"

Yawning and scratching, his two followers emerged. Rustuf's eyes widened. "You have improved in appearance since last I saw you." Then his eyes went wider. "What is this? Loot! And we have yet to fight a battle!"

"Dress and arm yourselves," Conan said. "I want to inspect my new command."

"Already you are talking like an officer," Rustuf

complained as he pulled on a pair of boots. He selected a coat from Iranistan, thickly quilted, with small plates of steel stitched between the layers of cloth. Its collar stood higher than his ears and protected the back of his neck. Fawd found weapons and armor to suit him, and the three men saddled their mounts.

"It is good to be a warrior again," said Rustuf with the air of a man at peace with the world.

"Do not expect to have it easy," Conan warned. "These Hyrkanians think they are the lords of the earth, and they will resent being under the command of a foreigner. You will be proving yourself to them every day."

"That shall not be difficult," Rustuf retorted. "The *Kozaki* are the true lords of the earth, and I shall make these tribesmen acknowledge the fact."

They followed the servant to a small encampment at the edge of the great camp. Near a small fire, a group of men lounged about, drinking and conversing. None looked up when the three companions arrived.

"This is your fifty, lord," said the servant.

"Not yet," Conan muttered, "but they shall be." He dismounted and walked into the midst of the Hyrkanians. His voice tore through the camp with the force of a stone hurled by a catapult. "On your feet when your commander comes among you!"

They looked up curiously. One rose slowly and came to stand before Conan. "Why should we be led by a foreigner?"

"Two reasons," said the Cimmerian. "First, I am the strongest, the wisest, and the best warrior among you. Second, and more important, the great *kagan* has ordered it so. I am a reasonable man. If you do not wish to obey my command, you may try to slay me. It is possible that a few of you may survive. The survivors would be well advised to kill Bartatua, for he does not strike me as a man who takes disobedience to his orders lightly.''

The standing man backed away a pace. ''We meant no disrespect, captain,'' he said. He turned to the men seated behind him. ''You heard our fifty-commander. On your feet.'' The men stood, not hurriedly, but neither with insolent slowness.

''That is better,'' Conan said. ''Listen to me. I am Conan of Cimmeria. I have fought in many wars in the armies of many nations. I have been a foot soldier and a general, and I have held every rank in between. I know how to lead men, and I know how men like to be led. You will never find me ordering you to do that which I would not do myself. I am fair, but I mean to be obeyed. I will give you the best leadership you have ever had. In return, I expect you to be the best fifty in the *kagan*'s horde. Back me to the best of your ability, and I will do the same for you. This I swear by Crom, the god of my people, and by the Everlasting Sky.'' He made the hand gesture he had observed among Boria's band, and the men of his fifty repeated it.

The Cimmerian walked up and down before the fifty, surveying them. They had the features and dress of a number of tribes, and there seemed to be little unity among them. He turned to the man who had first challenged him. ''How are you organized?''

''We were sent over here last night, captain. We have not yet been divided into tens. I am Guyak, and I will be your standard-bearer.'' He pointed to a small tent beside which was propped a pole surmounted by a horse's skull and a pair of spreading yak horns. From the silver-sheathed tips of the horns dangled two black horses' tails.

''Later today,'' Conan instructed, ''I will watch each

of you ride and shoot. I shall then form you into tens, each under a ten-commander. For now, go to the horse pens and care for your mounts. Henceforth, I do not want to see you lounging about at your ease at this hour. At first light, as soon as you have eaten, you are to be caring for your horses. After that, weapons practice. In one hour I shall inspect the mounts. I want to see glossy coats, and woe unto the man whose beast has open sores or a sore mouth.''

The men turned away to do his bidding. Clearly, they resented being told by a mere foreigner how to care for horses, but they said nothing.

"You know how to take charge, Conan,'' said Rustuf when the others were gone. "I think we shall see warm work under your command.''

Conan turned to Fawd. "Can you lead cavalrymen?''

"As well as they can be led,'' said the Turanian. "There are no formations or maneuvers to practice. Ten-leaders make sure that their men are at the right place on the battlefield, and at the right time. They watch for the *kagan*'s signals and deploy their men where they are ordered to.''

"What do they signal with?'' Conan asked.

"Flags by day, lanterns by night.''

"They fight by night?''

"Rarely, but they often make night marches, the better to take an enemy by surprise. These night marches may be done at a gallop, with men changing mounts frequently. It is essential to maintain order during night movements, and the signalers ride in front with colored lanterns.''

"These Hyrkanians do not lack boldness,'' admitted Rustuf grudgingly.

"Let us see what kind of mounts we have been given,'' Conan said.

They rode to the horse pens and found that the *kagan* had supplied them with prime horseflesh. Conan's men were grooming their mounts. The Hyrkanians were not in the habit of currying their horses daily, but his men would learn.

At the archery range he saw a familiar form riding toward him.

It was Boria.

"The wheel of fate turns, foreigner," said his erstwhile captor. "You were my prisoner, now you are my equal. I brought you these." He handed over the mail shirt and the helmet he had taken from the Cimmerian. "I would return your horse and sword as well, but I lost them at dicing."

"I am satisfied," Conan said.

"Are you satisfied with these rogues you have been given to command?"

"They are not pretty," Conan admitted, "but I will make them into something. Tell me, Boria . . . last night the *kagan* said he would give me men from his own horde. Yet these are not all Ashkuz, by the look of them."

Boria laughed, and Conan reflected that the Hyrkanians found humor in the grimmest of situations. "The *kagan* spoke truly, but his personal horde includes any men who are not claimed by another commander. Some of these men have been expelled from their own tribes or are the survivors of hordes that have been wiped off the steppe."

"No matter," Conan said. "I have commanded men of less than illustrious background before this. It does not mean that they cannot be good soldiers." He slipped the mail shirt over his head and buckled his sword belt over it. "Tell me," he said when he was satisfied with its fit, "am I to expect trouble from your man, Torgut?"

"Torgut nurses a grudge and is not likely to forget you," said Boria, "but if he comes for you, it will be from in front."

"That is all I ask," said Conan.

"Then farewell, Cimmerian. Your situation is improved, but I do not envy you your new command." With a shrill laugh, Boria rode off.

Conan took up his bow and called his standard-bearer to his side. "Guyak, I need practice with this bow. Watch me as I shoot and tell me what I am doing wrong."

"First," said Guyak, "you must string it. It is possible to do this oneself, but it is easier to use a stringing harness and the help of a friend. The *kagan* has given you a two-man bow. He himself wields a three-man bow. There should be a harness in your bowcase, and I will help you string the bow."

"Let me try it alone first," Conan said. He hooked the lower limb of the bow around his left ankle and stepped across it. Grasping the upper limb in his right hand, he bent the bow around the back of his right thigh. The extreme curvature of the bow made this maneuver awkward, but he brought the upper limb around to his front. The multiple layers of the bow creaked in protest as he slipped the bowstring loop into its notch on the upper limb.

Guyak was visibly impressed. "You are very strong, captain. Few men can string a two-man bow so easily."

Conan stepped from the bow and thrummed its string with his thumb. The silken cord quivered like a lyre string. In the case he found a horn ring and slipped it over his thumb. It covered the joint and tip of the thumb and would bear the bite of the string.

"Remember that when it is strung, the bow is under great strain," Guyak cautioned. "Never leave it strung for more than two hours. That is why you always carry two bows. If there may be trouble, keep one strung and the other unstrung at all times. In cold weather, always warm a bow before you string it or it will shatter. These are the finest bows in the world, but they are as temperamental as a fine horse or a Vendhyan courtesan.''

"Do the Hyrkanians make their own bows?" Conan asked.

"No, we cannot. The staves are made of many layers glued together, and they must spend years seasoning in special forms. Most of them are made in villages north of Khitai, bordering on the steppes. Some of these villages have no occupation except to make bows for the horseback tribes. I have seen workshops where hundreds of prepared bowstaves lie seasoning in huge wooden forms. There is no way we can carry such forms in our wanderings. Those villages are fortunate, for they lie under our protection and no king dare molest them.''

His men were shooting at long-range targets, arching their shafts so high that they looked like fowlers shooting at birds. "First," Guyak advised, "try that target." He pointed at a cloth-covered bale some one hundred paces distant. "That is one we train boys on.''

Conan selected an arrow and laid its nock to the string. The easterners shot on the right side of the bow, whereas the westerners shot on the left side. Shooting in the eastern way was swifter when riding, for the string hand did not have to reach the arrow all the way around the bow in order to nock it.

He wrapped his horn-ringed thumb around the string and locked it with his forefinger. Slowly, testing the tension of the bow, he drew until the fletching of the arrow brushed his cheek. He loosed, and watched as the arrow sailed high over the target.

"You are not allowing for the power of the bow," Guyak said. "You must hold very low at such close range."

Close range! The Bossonians, best of the western bowmen, would have considered this a fair cast for a good archer. He tried again, and this time his arrow just caught the upper edge of the target. Ten shots later he was putting every arrow into the center.

"You are beginning to get the feel of it," Guyak said. "Now try one at two hundred paces."

The process resumed. By the time the sun was past its zenith, he was hitting the three-hundred-pace targets more often than he missed. Guyak was impressed at such quick improvement by a mere foreigner.

"Enough for today," Conan said, unstringing the bow. "Tomorrow I begin practice from horseback. Gather the men now, and we shall portion them into tens."

For the next few hours Conan watched his fifty ride and perform various feats of horsemanship. All could stand in the saddle at a gallop; many could stand on their heads or hands. Most could grasp their mount's barrel with their legs and shoot beneath its belly or neck. All could unsaddle at a full gallop and transfer saddle, weapons and all, to another mount.

With Guyak's expert advice, he divided the men into five tens, making an equal distribution of excellence in riding, archery and other skills. Rustuf and Fawd each received command of a ten. Two other tens were put under experienced warriors. The remaining ten Conan kept as his personal command, with Guyak as his subcommander.

As the long day drew to a close, the Cimmerian addressed his tired men. "Your riding and shooting please me well, but there is more than that to fighting. Tomorrow, after bow practice, we will drill hard with the sword and lance. All of my men must be proficient with these weapons.''

There were sour looks, but no complaints. The Hyrkanians had little regard for sword or lance, considering them useful mainly for cutting down or skewering enemies who were fleeing and not worth wasting arrows upon.

As he dismissed his men, Conan saw a lone figure approaching. All the Hyrkanians were superlative horsemen. With this one it was difficult to tell where the man ended and the horse began. It was with no surprise that he recognized Bartatua. The *kagan* did not bother with an escort, nor with any weapon save his belted dagger.

''Greeting, *Kagan*,'' said Conan.

''Greeting, Cimmerian. I hear that you have taken charge of your command most efficiently.''

''You have eyes and ears everywhere, *Kagan*,'' Conan observed.

Bartatua grinned. ''Something all do well to remember. A *kagan* who is blind and deaf is of little use to anyone. Attend me this evening at the feast I shall hold for my commanders. There are things I wish to discuss with you.'' The *kagan* wheeled and rode away, leaving Conan to wonder why the greatest chieftain of Hyrkania wished to so honor a mere fifty-leader.

That evening's feast was no such elaborate event as the revel of the previous evening. The chiefs were seated in circles around the dais of Bartatua, and Conan found himself occupying a place at the periphery, his back against the supporting lattice. The food was lavish, though, if not exotic, and the Cimmerian ate well. He drank only moderately, for he knew better than to befuddle his wits when his situation was so precarious.

As a mere despised foreigner, Conan knew that his

neighbors were not inclined to socialize with him. He was not unaccustomed to such social rejection, and he used the opportunity to observe more closely these people among whom he had fallen.

He saw immediately that those of a certain dress or cast of features tended to sit close together and draw away from those of another sort. Whatever unity they shared was the result of Bartatua's will. He saw much evidence of differing customs as well. A plate of steaming meat would be fallen upon with gusto by one group, while another group would turn away from the same food with disgust. Some men were heavily tattooed; others did not practice the custom.

Against one wall sat a band of men who drew his special attention. Their hair was long and unbraided, and their faces were shaven or plucked clean of beard. Their clothes were bizarre collections of rags, finery and even, he was amazed to note, of some elements of women's dress. They were draped about with animal bones and amulets, and many carried drums, flutes and rattles.

Conan did not need to question his neighbors in order to identify these odd persons. They had to be shamans: medicine men and sorcerers, practitioners of the tribesmen's primitive religions. The place where they sat was not that of most-favored guests, and that came as no surprise either. Conan had encountered few nations wherein priests and kings were not fierce rivals for power and influence.

As the banquet drew to a close, a servant came to Conan and said in a low voice, "The *kagan* bids you stay after the others have left, lord."

Soon men arose and walked out, many of them unsteady. Some had to be carried. Drunkenness was the abiding vice of the steppe warriors, and the sight made

Conan more determined than ever to keep a clear head while he was among them. Soon the last of the guests were gone, leaving only Conan and Bartatua.

"Come, Cimmerian," the *kagan* said. "Sit with me."

Conan sat upon a cushion facing the chief and took a bowl of the wine proffered by his host. His eye caught a hint of movement from behind Bartatua's low dais. There was someone on the far side of the silken curtain that screened off Bartatua's sleeping quarters.

"That you are a good fighter I saw last night. Today you have shown that you are a capable officer as well. This is good, but these are the abilities of the hands and the will. The abilities of the mind are also valuable to me, and since you are now my follower, I expect you to put what is in your head at my disposal as well."

"I understand, *Kagan*," Conan said. "What would you have of me?"

"You have traveled widely in the west?" the *kagan* asked.

"I have visited all the western nations, and many of those to the far south. I have sailed upon the Western Sea and upon the Vilayet. From boyhood I have been a wanderer, and never can I stay in one place more than a season or two before I yearn to see new lands."

"Good. I shall wish to hear much about those lands. Most of the information I have of them I must glean from traders. These men know all the mysteries of buying and selling, which kings levy the most oppressive taxes, and which officials are the most amenable to bribery. This is useful information, but when I wish to know how armies are organized, how forts are garrisoned, whether commands are given for merit or for birth, they rarely know aught of value. You have some idea now of how my hordes fight. Where in the western lands would they be the most effective?"

Conan thought for a while, drawing in his mind a map of the world he knew. Few men of his day had traveled more extensively. "The nations west of the Vilayet and north of the Styx are for the most part pastoral lands: Koth, Shem, Corinthia, Ophir and the lesser kingdoms. Zamora, Brythunia and Nemedia are likewise lands with few rivers and broad plains. In those lands your style of warfare will serve you well. Beyond Nemedia and Ophir, though, are Aquilonia, Poitain, Zingara, Argos and other lands that are cut up by broad rivers and are often mountainous, with many deep valleys. They are populous, with a great many towns, each with its fort or castle. I think you would not fare so easily there."

"And south of the Styx?" asked Bartatua.

"First, there is Stygia. No king in his right mind would have anything to do with that land. It is the home of wizards and priest-kings who can call upon the ancient serpent god, Set. South of Stygia lie the black lands. These are countries where your hordes would be all but useless."

"Are the black men so fierce?" Bartatua demanded.

"Fierce enough, but they are few in number, and men are not the true enemy in those places. The land itself is ferocious, with squalling, chaotic jungles so thick that often it is necessary to cut your way through the growth with heavy knives. The rain is incessant and anything made of cloth or leather rots quickly. But worst of all is pestilence. Men die in droves and horses die even more swiftly. If you pressed your hordes into those lands, within six moons you would have half of your men and none of your horses. The only way to subdue those countries is with armies of native troops."

"These things are good to know in advance," said the *kagan*. "It shall be some time before I seek westward conquests, but that eventuality shall come. And when I do reach the western lands, I shall have foot armies of soldiers pressed from the conquered lands. From Khitai I shall have the cleverest siege engineers in the world, with their machines and stratagems. Should I wish to take the black nations, I shall by that time have armies so huge that the loss of half to disease shall be of no consequence.''

Conan sipped at his wine. ''I take it, then, that you intend to conquer the entire world.''

''That is what I will do '' the *kagan* said simply.

Conan studied his face and saw no madman's gleam in his eyes. To Bartatua, his destiny as master of the world was as natural as the daily ascent of the sun above the steppe.

''I was born into a chaotic world,'' the *kagan* said, ''a world in which all mankind was divided into an absurd number of peoples and kingdoms, bickering with one another wastefully, and ruled often by fools whose only qualification was birth, as if kingship were a quality one could achieve by breeding, like swiftness in horses or fatness in cattle.''

''I have never seen much sense in aristocracy of birth,'' Conan said truthfully. ''Among my people, all are equal and all men are warriors. Clan leaders bear the family name, but leadership in war goes to the most-proven warrior, whether chieftain or cowherd.''

''It is much the same among us. So you can see that I am offended by this senseless situation. As there is one Everlasting Sky above the earth, there should be only one supreme king upon it. My destiny is to become that king. Those who help me to realize my destiny shall be great lords. My first step was to unite the steppe tribes. This was a formidable task. You have seen how fractious and feuding they are. Some eat horseflesh, and

others think horse-eaters are blasphemers. The red-haired
Budini are the greatest drunkards beneath the sky, and
most believe that the green-tattooed Geruls eat human
flesh. Only the greatest force of will can make a unified
army of such independent people."

"They seem satisfied to follow you," Conan said.

"And rightfully so. As soon as I have given them
one great victory and much loot, they shall be mine for
life and their petty squabbles will be submerged in
obedience to my will. I shall be *Ushi-Kagan*, the supreme chief, first to hold that title in many generations."

The *kagan* sat back and there was a moment of
silence. "Now," he continued, "on to matters of more
immediate interest. Are you able to read any of the
western languages?"

"I am no scholar," Conan said, "but I can read
several tongues. It is a fool who thinks that books and
reading weaken a man."

"Wisely spoken. Can you read Turanian?"

"I served as an officer in Turan. Only those who can
read may hold an officer's commission."

The *kagan* took a small scroll from within his garments. "This was captured early in the spring from a
courier riding from Khwarism to Sogaria. The courier
died, and none of my followers can read Turanian.
Translate it."

Conan spread the document before him and began to
read. It had been some time since he had coped with
these letters, but the facility returned quickly. "It is a
message from King Yezdigerd to his esteemed friend,
the prince of Sogaria. It states that the king is most
anxious to learn the whereabouts of a renegade Turanian
wizard named Khondemir, who treacherously plotted
against Yezdigerd and fled the country when his plans
were discovered. If found within the prince's domin-

ions, it is requested that the wizard be arrested and held so that agents of the king may come take charge of him and return him to the king's court for punishment. It ends with the usual pleasantries.'' He handed the scroll back to Bartatua. ''This has the look of a message copied many times by scribes. It was probably written up, with words and names changed here and there, and sent to all the neighboring rulers.''

''So,'' the *kagan* said as if to himself. ''Yezdigerd, too, has trouble with the spell-casters.''

Conan said nothing to this. Following a king in warfare was one thing, but he had no intention of becoming embroiled in the *kagan*'s feud with the shamans.

''Sogaria shall be our first target,'' Bartatua went on, ''the opening campaign in my conquest of the world. Can you guess why I have chosen Sogaria, Cimmerian?''

''Like all the cities of the caravan routes,'' Conan said, ''it is very wealthy and will provide much loot.''

''That is a worthy reason,'' Bartatua said. ''What else?''

Conan thought. ''Such a city seldom sees war and should be a fairly easy conquest. It will be good practice for your hordes, who will need to be skillful in the besieging of cities.''

''Excellent,'' said Bartatua. ''Also, it is the westernmost of the caravan cities. Through it pass most of the goods that cross between east and west. That includes information, and thus I shall be able to control what knowledge the kings of the west have of eastern matters. Someday I shall embark upon my conquest of the west, and hence at the outset I will have much influence there.''

Conan nodded understanding. This was very subtle

planning for a simple steppe chieftain. He suspected that besides his own native abilities, which were considerable, Bartatua had expert advice from someone of greater sophistication.

"How shall I serve you in the opening campaign, *Kagan*?" Conan asked.

"You have a few more days in which to drill your men. Then I shall send you on raids into Sogarian territory. Outside the great city lie only small villages, and forts with their garrisons. You shall take some of these forts and harry the countryside, driving the inhabitants into the city, where I may bag them all in a single operation."

As if eager for the victories he dreamed of, the *kagan* grew restless and shifted on his cushion. "Go now. Hold yourself in readiness, and remember that my eye is always upon you, Cimmerian."

Conan rose and bowed. As he turned to leave, he saw once again the slight movement of the curtain behind Bartatua. When the Cimmerian was gone, Lakhme came forth from its folds.

"Why do you spend so much time on a mere fifty-leader, my lord?" she asked. She had shed her voluminous robe and wore naught but a loincloth and jewels. She sat at Bartatua's feet and the chief twined his fingers in her midnight tresses.

"He amuses me. He comes from a far land I wish to learn about. He is shrewd as well, unlike so many of the simple brutes I lead. He owes his position only to my favor and has no friends here. That ensures his loyalty to me."

"Still, you should not reveal so much of your plans to a mere adventurer." She turned her head and nuzzled his hand.

"I make no great secret of my intentions," Bartatua

said. "What is the sense of that? Wise and cautious kings will strengthen their defenses no matter how fair my words are to them. Weak fools will pay no attention to the danger even when I state plainly my intention to reduce them to vassalage. A man's character is his destiny, and a fool will die a fool's death no matter how fully he is warned."

"You are wise, my lord," said Lakhme, "but you should confide the deepest of your plans only in me."

The *kagan* thought for a while. "What think you of this message from Yezdigerd to Amyr Jelair about the wizard—what was his name?—Khondemir? Could this matter be of use to us?"

Serenely Lakhme shrugged her white shoulders. "I cannot see how. We know nothing of what lies between Yezdigerd and this wizard. Nor do we know if he is in Sogaria or some other land thousands of leagues away."

"So it is useless. It is a disappointment."

"As I have told you many times, my lord," she said, "*all* knowledge is useful, and this may prove so some day."

"Enough of such weighty matters," he said with a smile. "I have more pleasant prospects to attend to at the moment." He enfolded his concubine in his powerful arms.

Seven

"The rope," Guyak explained, "is braided of hair from a horse's tail, or from human hair. It is said that the best are made from the hair of your enemy. One end is braided into an eyelet and the rope is passed through it, forming a noose. First you must learn to control the noose, then to cast it for a long distance."

Conan was dividing his attention between Guyak's rope lesson and his men's drill maneuvers. Rustuf had half of them slicing at gourds set atop stakes. The other half were taking lance instruction from Fawd. Fawd had been a Turanian light lancer and was a master of that weapon.

"Slice, you horse-eaters, slice!" Rustuf cried in exasperation. "You need not hack a man from shoulder to saddle to get his attention! Three inches of sharp steel across his neck and he is a dead man. Also, it is much easier on your sword!"

Conan tried a cast with the rope, using the snapping, underhand motion Guyak had taught him. The rope snaked out, the noose spread and settled over the tethering stake he had selected. With a flick of his wrist, he cleared the noose of the post and recoiled it.

"Now try a moving target," said Guyak. "That slave who rides—" But now they could see that the serving man was riding toward them with some manner of urgent business in mind. The man reined in just before them.

"The *kagan* summons you to his tent, fifty-leader," he said.

Conan spurred his horse toward the tall standard with its nine white horses' tails. He found Bartatua outside the great tent, surrounded by minor officers and fifty-leaders. He dismounted and saluted the *kagan*.

"Today," Bartatua announced, "we open the campaign. Each of you will be given either a fort or a section of land, with its villages to pillage. Remember, there are to be no massacres, unless a fort puts up a truly stiff resistance. But neither are you to show too much caution. These city-dwellers must know that we are utterly invincible. Do not let them think that we are either fearful or merciful. If there seems to be some doubt in their minds, slay them."

The *kagan* waved his arm toward a small group of mounted men who were distinguished by black plumes in their helmets and whose standard bore a pair of eagle's wings. "These scouts have just returned from a reconnaissance into Sogarian territory. Each mission leader will be assigned one scout to guide him to his objective. Now come and receive your assignments. You must be riding from camp before the sun begins to go down."

When Conan returned to his men, he found them already preparing for their march. As in military camps everywhere, word of the opening campaign had passed through the horde with the swiftness of the steppe wind.

"What is our destination, captain?" Rustuf asked with a grin.

"A small fort called Khulm, edging a stream of the steppe near the northern border of Sogarian territory," Conan answered.

"With which horde do we ride?"

"We shall be our own horde."

"Just a single fifty to take a fort?" Rustuf queried, nonplussed.

"The *kagan* expects us to show initiative," Conan said. He raised his voice to address his troops. "We march in one hour. I want each man to bring all his horses with the remounts and to pack *all* his clothes."

The men muttered among themselves, convinced that their commander was mad. They had by now learned, however, that such thoughts were best kept to themselves. They packed their belongings, including the clothes, and made a hurried meal. As the sun passed its zenith, they rode out. Nearly half of the assembled horde poured from the camp. For hours they rode together, then small or large groups—each guided by a black-plumed scout—broke away to go to their individual objectives.

As the sun was touching the horizon to the west, the scout attached to Conan's fifty reined off to the left and Conan followed with his command at his horse's heels. Within a few minutes his fifty were riding alone over the darkening steppe.

Conan felt free at last. This was the kind of warmaking he liked best: to have an independent command, without some bothersome superior officer or nosy courtier interfering with his every move. It was something he seldom experienced in civilized armies.

At nightfall he called a halt. The *kagan* had stressed that his commanders were not to risk night gallops.

They could achieve complete surprise without such extreme measures. The scout assured him that the fort at Khulm was still more than a two-hour ride and that the garrison was not sending out patrols. Since they were safe from observation, Conan granted permission to gather fuel and make small fires for cooking their evening meal. Some went out to find wood while others set about skinning and jointing the wild game they had shot during the march. They had sacks of the fermented milk of mares, but the Cimmerian had forbidden anything stronger.

Conan and Rustuf sat at a fire and the soldiers brought them meat as it was cooked. "So," said Rustuf, "our *kagan* plans to be king of the whole world? There have been others with that ambition."

"This one may come closer than most of them," Conan said. "But I do not think he understands how large the world is. He has many horsemen, but spread out over the world, they are all too few."

The *kozak* rubbed his bristled chin. "Still, he could make great gains if he heads west. The *Kozaki* might well join him if he moves against Turan. Koth, Shem, perhaps Ophir and Corinthia also, would fall ere the western nations could cease their squabbling and unite against the Hyrkanians."

"So think I," said Conan. "But he intends to conquer Khitai first, and then Vendhya. Those nations are so vast that it must be ten years before he could even consider a western campaign. By then, much will have changed. I believe that Bartatua will have to be satisfied with such conquests as he has, if he still lives."

They had been moving along at a steady pace for two hours and the sun was just clearing the eastern horizon when the scout halted them. He pointed to a low rise ahead. "Beyond that hill," he told Conan, "you may see the fort."

"Keep the men here," Conan said to Guyak. He rode up the hill but stopped his horse and dismounted well below the crest. He walked toward the summit, then dropped on his belly and crawled the last few yards. Below him was the fort, standing in the bight of a tiny river scarcely more than a stream. Reeds and brush grew along the stream, which looped around the hill and passed near the spot that Conan had posted his men.

On the far side of the stream a narrow road passed before the fort. He watched as a plume of dust appeared in the distance down the road and neared the fort. The fort itself was not imposing, a mere mud-walled enclosure large enough for a garrison of perhaps three hundred. The walls were no more than fifteen feet high, and there was no moat. It was not meant as a strong defensive position, but only as a stronghold for sending out mounted patrols.

The plume of dust soon resolved itself into a force of men on horseback, riding with no haste or urgency. He counted fifty, all of them heavy lancers in gilded armor and with colorful plumes. They rode into the fort and the gate swung shut behind them.

Conan was about to return to his men when he saw another plume of dust, this one small, coming from the road in the direction opposite that of the cavalry's approach. This he could well see was a single horse, hard-ridden. It had to be a messenger bringing urgent news to the fort. He meant to find out what that news might be.

Backing away, still on his belly, Conan rose only when he was well below the crest of the hill and sprang into his saddle. His men were too far away for him to hail, so he left them gaping as he spurred along the flank of the hill and down onto the flat land. By staying along the base of the high ground, he remained out of sight of the fort. When he judged that he was far enough from the garrison to escape detection, he rode over the short spur of hill that remained and down its other side.

The stream flowed along the base of the hill and he waded his mount across it without difficulty. The beast wanted to stop and drink, but he forced it on until he was upon the road. A few hundred paces away, the messenger was still coming at a gallop. The man waved something overhead, above his multiple yellow plumes. He caught sight of Conan, who had taken up his position in the center of the road.

"Make way for the messenger of the prince!" the rider shouted as, perforce, he slowed his horse. "Stand aside, fellow, or feel the wrath of the prince's justice. It is death to interfere with the prince's messenger!"

Then the man's eyes went wide as he realized he was facing a foreign warrior, one equipped with the great bow favored by the nomads. Setting spurs to horse, he sought to ride around Conan, for the road was on flat ground, with nothing to stop a horseman.

As the messenger rode past him, Conan wheeled and gave chase. He caught up quickly, for the messenger's horse was tired. From his saddle he took the rope with which he had been practicing and shook out a wide noose. He rode up within three spear lengths of the fleeing man, whirled the noose a few times and snapped it out underhanded as Guyak had taught him. True as an arrow, the noose dropped over the man's head and settled around his chest and upper arms. Conan pulled the rope tight and rode off at an angle, tugging hard.

The messenger sailed over the rump of his horse and landed in the dirt with a bone-jarring thump. The horse ran on for a few dozen paces and then, with no one spurring it, slowed and halted, its sides heaving. Conan rode over to the fallen man, who was quite unconscious but did not seem to be badly hurt. From the messenger's belt he took a cylindrical case of gold-washed bronze. This was what the man had been waving overhead.

From the case Conan took a rolled parchment. Unrolling it, he saw that it bore a script that he could not read. Cursing, he replaced the parchment in its case, remounted, and caught the messenger's horse. He threw the man across the horse's back and rode to join his men, horse and messenger in tow.

When Conan was within sight of his force, Rustuf rode out to him grinning with relief. "I am glad to see you, Conan. The Hyrkanians were most puzzled to see you rush off like that. They thought you might have deserted the *kagan* to go warn the Sogarians. Things might have gone ill for Fawd and me."

"I should be satisfied to have obedience when I am present," Conan said. "Love and loyalty are too much to expect when I am absent."

"What have you brought us? A prisoner?"

"A messenger," Conan said. "But I cannot read what his message says."

"Oh, we shall have answers out of him, never fear," Rustuf assured him.

The Hyrkanians were equally delighted to see the prisoner, and anticipated some good sport. "First we will see whether the man will talk without coercion," Conan ordered. "No harm is to come to him if he cooperates."

The Hyrkanians were puzzled by such unaccustomed delicacy, but they were willing to humor their commander. After a few minutes, the messenger began to revive. He sat up and looked about and fear spread across his countenance as he saw the fierce steppe hawks who sat in a circle surrounding him.

"Sogarian," said Conan, "you are my prisoner. I wish some answers from you. Speak freely and truthfully and you shall come to no harm. Refuse to speak, or speak falsely, and I must let my men try to persuade you. They are most proficient at the business of loosening tongues."

The man swallowed hard. "Ask what you will. The little I know cannot aid you much."

Conan grinned. "I shall be the judge of that. Know you the content of the message you carried?"

"It is a warning to the commander of the garrison at Khulm. He is warned that the steppe nomads are descending upon Sogaria. This can hardly be news to you."

"As you say. Were there special instructions for the commander?"

"Just that he is to hold his fort bravely and die where he stands rather than yield an inch of Sogarian soil."

"They all say that," Rustuf said with a barking laugh. "What soldier is so foolish as to take such orders seriously?"

Something puzzled Conan. "How long has the prince of Sogaria known that the nomads are coming?"

"Three days ago the city began to prepare for siege. I was sent forth yesterday morning to warn the three royal forts on my route. Khulm is the last."

It seemed, Conan thought, that the Hyrkanians were not quite as swift and invisible as they thought. Or perhaps there was a traitor within the *kagan*'s following who had warned the city. A traitor who knew that

Sogaria was to be the first city attacked. He kept his suspicions to himself.

"How many men garrison Khulm?" the Cimmerian asked.

"Why, the same as any royal border fort, of course. A quarter-wing of cavalry, two hundred fifty men."

Conan knew well the ways in which a frightened man would strive to salve his pride. This one was pretending that since it was common knowledge how many the forts garrisoned, he was giving away nothing.

"Is the commander an experienced warrior?" Conan asked

"He is the son of some courtier, like most of the officers in our army." The man acted as if this, too, were common knowledge.

"Bind him," Conan said. "I may want to question him further." The messenger wore a look of intense relief as he was tied securely.

Conan scanned the landscape. At the place the stream wound around the left side of the hill, there was a stand of small trees. He pointed to the trees and addressed his men. "Go to yonder stand and cut many short poles and gather bundles of reeds. Be careful not to advance past the cover of the hill lest you be seen by the fort. Be quick, now." Mystified, the men obeyed. Surely, they thought once again, their foreign captain was mad.

As the sun was passing its zenith, Conan and his fifty rode around the hill and across the stream. In a few minutes they closed the distance to the fort, and there was much blowing of horns and beating of drums as the gates were shut and barred. Fearlessly the horsemen rode to within a few dozen paces of the walls.

"Commander of the fort!" Conan called. "Come out and parley!"

After a short while, during which time the wall grew

crowded with men, a man in elaborate plumes and gold-chased armor mounted the wall. "Who are you?" he shouted. "And what does this mean?"

"I bring you greetings from Bartatua, lord of the Ashkuz and rightful king of all the world," Conan cried in a loud voice. "My lord has come to take his sovereign place as ruler of Sogaria and all the other cities of the caravan route. I am General Conan, formerly of Cimmeria, and I am here to accept the surrender of this trifling stronghold. Accept my terms and you shall live."

In the silence, an archer atop the wall, too poorly disciplined to wait for orders, drew his bow and aimed at Conan. Rustuf spoke a word and his ten shot as one man. The Sogarian archer toppled from the wall and landed with a dust-raising thud in full view of the defenders. At such short range, the ten arrows had smashed through the man's heavy scale armor as if it were no more than parchment. All ten arrows stood in a space that could be covered by a man's palm, directly over the heart.

Conan acted as if nothing had happened. "I await your answer."

"Can you be serious?" the commander blustered. "You call yourself a general, yet I see you at the head of less than fifty riders. How can you expect me to surrender to so inconsiderable a force?"

Conan smiled grimly, knowing that he had won. The commander had not said that he would not surrender, only that he would not give in to a force so small.

"This is merely my personal bodyguard," Conan said. "I came ahead of my troops so that you would have the opportunity to surrender to someone of suitable rank. *There* is my army!"

The Cimmerian swept his arm upward and to one side in a grand gesture. The heads of the men atop the wall turned to see where he was pointing. On the ridge cresting the low hill from which Conan had spied upon the fort, a file of horsemen could be seen clearly. They rode up the low spur to the left, walked their mounts along the high ridge and descended the right-hand spur, disappearing from view in the clump of reeds and small trees where the stream wrapped around the base of the hill.

Conan saw the lips of the men on the wall move as they sought to count the enemy's strength. There seemed to be no end to the troops, and as they vanished into the reeds and trees, more of them ascended the spur to the left.

"They go to water their mounts and set up camp in that convenient spot by the stream. I tell you that to save time should you wish to come out and fight us in the open, before the siege engines arrive with the sappers. I see that you are too proud to surrender and would rather die nobly in defense of your prince's honor, although your lord did not see fit to warn you of your danger. A quick fight now will spare us several hours of tedious work in the morning, storming your little fort."

"Be not so hasty, good General Conan!" said the commander of Fort Khulm. "In truth, this is not a true stronghold of war but a mere barracks from which we may chase the scurvy bandits of the wasteland. Our real duty is the defense of Sogaria. If you will allow us to march away from here to rejoin our lord in his city, I will listen to your terms."

"Excellent," Conan said. "All of you are to lay down your arms at once. All horses, arms and armor are to be left in the fort. All valuables as well. Each man may keep one tunic, one pair of trousers and a pair of boots. Each will be searched, so I warn you not to try to hide anything on your persons. I also remind you that I could leave you with a good deal less, including bodily parts. My men, for instance, are fond of collecting men's—''

"I accept your generous terms, good General Conan!" the commander gushed. "We comply at once!"

The defenders rushed from the walls, tearing at the laces and straps of their armor even before they could reach the stairways. Within minutes the gates were opened and the unarmed men began filing out. Conan detailed a ten to search them, while the rest of his men sat their horses with bows at the ready.

"You have had a cheap victory, General," said the commander as his men began their long, weary trek toward Sogaria. "Do not expect to have it so easy in the future. Sogaria is strong, and its walls are vast beyond the comprehension of you steppe savages. We found it inconvenient to give you battle today, but you will never take Sogaria!"

"With such defenders as you," Conan said, "I anticipate a spirited and enjoyable fight. Good evening to you, Commander. If you hurry, you and your men may make it into the city before the gates are closed against refugees." Head bowed, the commander trudged wearily off toward his city.

When the former defenders were but dwindling spots on the distant road, Conan nodded to Fawd and the Turanian blew a long note on his silver hunting horn. A few minutes later Guyak came riding in, wearing a broad grin and leading some of the remounts. Others chivied the beasts along, each horse bearing a dummy of wooden poles, reed-stuffed clothes and stick weapons. Guyak had been leading them in an endless procession, circling between the crest of the hill and its base, turning Conan's force of fifty into an army of thousands.

"It worked, captain!" Guyak shouted gleefully.

"Not captain," said a jubilant bowman, "but general! He named himself so!" The men of the fifty were dancing about and singing in exuberance.

"Come," Conan ordered, "let us see what we've won."

Inside the fort they found heaps of armor, many stabled mounts, stores of food, and sacks of personal belongings tied at the foot of each soldier's bunk. In the commander's quarters there were rich furnishings and hangings. He had left behind a table service of gold plate and a great deal of jewelry. "Take all of it into the courtyard," Conan ordered.

By torchlight they packed everything on captured horses. "The *kagan* will divide the spoils," Conan reminded them. "We may take only food and drink. Any man who is caught trying to keep something back for himself is to be executed immediately."

By midnight all was in marching order. "Captain," said Guyak, "we have captured much wine. May we have some in celebration of this fine victory?"

"We'll not encounter enemies as we ride to join the horde," Conan said. "Give each man a skin of wine to drink on the march back. But any who gets so drunk that he falls off his horse is to lie where he drops and make his way back on foot."

He knew that the thought of walking would so horrify his men that they would moderate their drinking. He had neither the manpower nor the tools with which to demolish the fort, and so he had the gate soaked with oil and they rode away as it burned brightly behind them.

Conan's force was the first to return to report its mission accomplished. The *kagan*'s camp was marching upon Sogaria, herding the slaves before it. About half of the total strength of the army was with the *kagan*, and news of Conan's feat spread through the ranks like a steppe fire. The camp rocked with laughter as the men sat about their fires after the day's trek.

Bartatua was vastly amused. "Would that all my officers showed such imagination!" he said. "A fort taken with all its loot and we lost nothing at all?"

"One of the captured armors was damaged when we had to kill an archer," Conan corrected. "And Rustuf's ten had three broken arrows."

"Seldom," said Bartatua, "has any man gone from fifty-commander to five hundred-commander so swiftly."

"Not to mention possessor of a siege train and sappers," added a grizzled officer whose face was tattooed with a stylized eagle. All the Hyrkanians thought this cheap victory won by cunning and deception was a fine thing. They did not have western concepts of chivalry, and they judged courage and honor by different standards.

Bartatua let the merriment die down and then became serious. "Your next assignment, Conan, will not be so easy. Tonight your men rest. On the morrow you will take them and ride southeast. The prince of Sogaria has appealed to his fellow ruler, the satrap of Bukhrosha, for reinforcements. He has asked for a large force of horsemen, and there is little doubt that the satrap shall comply. You are to lie in wait upon the Great Road and destroy this column of reinforcements. This time you shall, of course, have five hundred men."

"How many should I expect to meet?" Conan asked.

"The satrap will not send less than a wing, about one thousand heavy cavalry."

Conan nodded. Two to one was not bad odds when leading warriors of such caliber. "It shall be done, *Kagan*."

As he walked from the tent, he encountered the black-draped woman who had picked him for the fights. He knew now that her name was Lakhme and that she was the *kagan*'s concubine. She stood before him as if she wanted to speak, and he saluted her respectfully.

"A good evening to you, my lady."

"You have risen high in a very short time, foreigner," she said.

"The *kagan* appreciates ability when he encounters it," Conan said, "and he rewards loyal service generously. I shall not fail his confidence."

"See that you do not. I am not so easy to please. The *kagan* is a trusting man who does not realize that treachery can lurk behind a smile and that loyal service is often a stepping-stone to treason."

Conan felt the hot blood rising to his face and he reined his temper. "Should *any* prove treacherous to the *kagan*," he said, keeping his voice steady, "I shall kill him. Or her."

She hissed like a Stygian serpent, and he saw that his barb had sunk into oversensitive flesh. The woman swept around him in a swirl of black robes, and he caught the heady scent of her perfume. It was not only at the civilized courts, he knew, that those closest to the ruler had their daggers ever sharpened for one another.

Eight

"Do not trust him, my lord," Lakhme said.

"I trust the man to perform his duty on the battle-field," the *kagan* told her. "No more than that. What has he to gain by serving me ill? Who can reward him more greatly than I? How can he rise higher than in my service? And surely he cannot hope to seize my power and become *Ushi-Kagan*!" He laughed at the idea. "My vassal chiefs may nurse such hopes, but not Conan. He knows well that the Hyrkanians will accept only a king of their own blood."

Lakhme knew that well also, and it was for this reason that the wizard, Khondemir, must resort to so perilous a spell in order to seize control of the *kagan*. She knew, too, that it was time to turn her lord's thoughts from logical paths and play upon his passions instead. She crossed to the table before Bartatua and poured him a cup of wine. A more worldly king might have seen calculation in her pose, but the Hyrkanian saw only her white, statuesque body, draped in jewels and nothing else.

"There is one thing you possess that he envies and would have," she said as she handed him the cup.

His brows came together in an eagle frown. "What may that be?"

"Your concubine."

"What has he said—"

"He has said nothing," she broke in. "But he has the eyes and the manner of a stallion, and he makes his desires plain for me to see."

The *kagan* sat back and brooded into his cup. "Anyone may look, and envy. But no more than that. For now, the man is valuable to me. Later, we shall see."

"Your welfare is all that concerns me, my lord," said Lakhme. She was well satisfied that the seed she had planted was in fertile ground.

Late that night the Vendhyan woman slipped silently from Bartatua's tent. Inside, the *kagan* slept soundly. As she neared the boundary of the camp, a sentry challenged her.

"It is I, Bajazet," she said. The sentry was he who had accompanied her to Sogaria. Once an officer of Kuchlug's, he nursed a grudge against the *kagan*. Lakhme had carefully subverted him with favors and bribes, and now she owned him fully. "I go without the camp. I shall return before dawn."

"Very well, my lady," he said, bowing as she pressed gold coins into his palm.

She walked eastward until she heard a sound of drums and flutes. In a depression in the ground, she came upon a group of shamans gathered around a small fire, playing their wild, shrill music.

Around the fire whirled two dancers. One of these was dressed as a royal stag, in spreading horns and glossy hides. The other was a slender, effeminate boy clothed in scanty, women's garb. Lakhme watched impassively as the dance grew wilder and quite obscene. When it ended, she stepped into the circle of firelight.

The shaman who had been beating the drum looked up. He had hair and beard like matted cobwebs, and his teeth were yellowed snags. "Why do you interrupt our rites, my lady?" he asked.

"I have a task for you," she said. "There is someone whose influence with the *kagan* waxes daily, and I want an end to it." Never would she plot directly against Bartatua with these repulsive creatures, but there was no risk in using them against another.

"Who is this?" asked the ancient shaman.

"The foreigner, Conan. He has gone from slave to fifty-leader to leader of five hundred in the space of a few days. His ambitions grow vaunting, and I wish an end to them."

The old man cackled shrilly. "Death is the end to all ambitions, whether those of common adventurer or great *kagan*."

"Do not speak to me of the *kagan*," she warned. "It is the Cimmerian who concerns us here. Can you dispose of him for me?"

Again the old man laughed like a screeching bird. "Who may we not dispose of! We commune with the world of spirits. We spy what the future holds and can identify the casters of baleful spells—or cast such spells ourselves. Yes, I shall return the tall foreigner to the obscurity whence he came."

"Good. You shall be well rewarded." She began to turn away.

"With what," the shaman called, "shall you reward us?"

Slowly, she turned back. "With gold. With jewels or silver."

"Those things mean nothing to us," he said with deep scorn. She saw the eyes of the other shamans upon her, and she felt their hunger.

"What would you have?" she asked.

"There is a rite," the old man whispered, his voice like the wind in dry grass. "A very important rite, one that renews our power. We must perform it soon. It calls for a woman. A woman such as you, my lady. Many would be terrified to take the woman's part in this rite, but you have the courage to do what must be done to preserve your influence." The voice was low, insinuating. She saw the effeminate boy as he swayed by, a smile of infinite evil on his painted face. The stag-man loomed beyond the flames, his exaggerated attributes glistening in the crimson light.

"Very well," she said. "Eliminate the foreigner for me and I shall perform in your rite."

As she walked away, she heard the drums and flutes take up their maddening rhythm once more. This would certainly mean Conan's doom should her seed planted with Bartatua fail to bear fruit. She would have tried hiring a simple assassin as well, but she had doubts that any man, or group of men, she might subvert could ever succeed in killing the terrible Cimmerian. She would never leave an important plan to chance by attacking it from only one direction; always she had fall-back plans, and further plans should those fail. As with Conan, so with Bartatua. And also with Khondemir.

Conan and his five hundred rode across a landscape turned chaotic by invasion. They could see that in the distance a column of smoke rose every few miles, marking the site of a burning village. The roads and paths were choked with refugees, their bundled belongings balanced on their heads or borne upon their backs.

"I will never understand villagers," Rustuf said as they surveyed the scene of confusion. "Why, when the countryside is attacked, do they always have this urge to get out on the roads and walk as if somewhere else is safer than where they are?"

Conan had called a brief halt to rest the horses and let an especially large pack of pitiful refugees go by. His men had wanted to clear a way with their swords, but he had reminded them of the *kagan*'s command that there be no massacres, yet.

"I do not know," Conan said. "Perhaps it is because we burn the villages."

"How long does it take to replace a little thatch? If they would stay where they are, they would be fairly safe. They could scavenge food in the countryside after the armies have passed. As it is, they are going to the one place where they are sure to starve and die of pestilence: a besieged city."

"They are afraid of being robbed," said Fawd.

"That, too, makes no sense," said Rustuf. "They have already been robbed, and they had little to be stolen in the first place. What they have left they carry bundled on their heads, where it may be conveniently plucked without dismounting. They are fleeing to the man who robs them on a regular basis: the local overlord. He will use them on the defensive works while they are useful and expel them as soon as there is food enough for only the court and the fighting men."

Conan shrugged. "I do not know. It is the way peasants always behave when there is war. I have never been a peasant, and shall never be one. Let us ride."

The regiment of Hyrkanians rode on, occasionally scattering panicked peasants with their whips. Sometimes they saw other bands of Hyrkanians bound upon

their own errands of destruction. By the evening of their
second day's ride, they were beyond the ring of chaos
and the Great Road was relatively clear. From the
scouts' description of the route, the distance to Bukhrosha
and the condition of the road, Conan did not expect to
encounter the Bukhroshan column until the next day, or
perhaps the day after that. Nevertheless, he had scouts
riding far ahead, to give warning should the enemy
appear untimely. The unexpected was the one thing that
he knew could be relied upon in warfare.

Now that they were past the ravaged land and the
swarming refugees, Conan's main concern was to find a
good spot for an ambush. There would be no negotia-
tion, and he foresaw little chance for trickery or deception beyond the usual feints and false retreats. His
orders were to fall upon the Bukhroshan column like a
thunderbolt and destroy it utterly. That was exactly
what he intended to do.

As evening fell, he found the position he wanted.
The Great Road rose steadily, then passed between two
small peaks as symmetrical as a woman's breasts. Beyond
the pass the way descended, not steeply, to a long
stretch of plain over which the road led to Bukhrosha,
twenty leagues away.

With his subordinate fifty-leaders and ten-leaders,
Conan rode around both hills and along the road beyond
the pass, examining the terrain on which they would be
fighting. The rest of the men were ordered to make a
war camp, to be ready to remount at a moment's notice,
and to light no betraying fires.

Before darkness fell he had made his dispositions and
issued his orders for the coming battle. He would use
no complicated maneuvers, but he needed careful control of his forces in order to make the best use of their

mobility and archery and to minimize the enemy's superiority in numbers. The Hyrkanians sneered at the suggestion of a mere two-to-one advantage, but Conan was acutely aware that those were the best odds he could expect. The numbers he faced might be far greater. All depended upon the satrap of Bukhrosha, upon whether he felt goodwill toward Sogaria, and especially upon how much of his military strength he was willing to part with in anticipation of attack against his own land.

Two hours after sunrise the next morning, the scouts rode in with word that the Bukhroshan cavalry were coming. They would be within sight in an hour.

"Were you able to count them?" Conan asked.

"No, lord," said the chief scout. "Your orders were not to be seen, so we kept our distance. I can say that there are more than the one thousand you were expecting."

"Each of you has his orders," Conan said to his officers, "and you know the signals. Take your positions and await the enemy. It may be that we face far more men than we anticipated. That is no matter. Our tactics will remain the same."

With two hundred of his men, Conan rode to the hill that flanked the road to the north. Rustuf took another two hundred and led them around the southern hill. The remaining hundred, under Fawd, stayed where they were, about five hundred paces from the pass.

Once they were in place, neither of the larger bands would be visible to the approaching Bukhroshans. Conan rode near the top of the hill, accompanied by Guyak. The standard-bearer brought a case holding a number of colored flags. The two sat and waited.

"They come, captain," Guyak said. In the distance a dust cloud announced the arrival of their prey. As the force neared, his vantage point allowed Conan to get a

rough count of its numbers. He cursed as he saw the
length and breadth of the column.

"Three thousand at least. And we have five hundred.
Six to one instead of two to one."

Guyak shrugged and grinned. "What matter, captain? Each of us has more than six arrows."

Conan laughed and clapped the standard-bearer on
the shoulder. "So we have! What are mere odds to
heroes such as we, eh? Be ready now, and keep your
flags loose in their case."

At the head of the Bukhroshan column, no more than
five hundred paces before the main body, rode the
advance guard. Conan had been fairly certain that this
would be the case. In civilized armies, outlying forces
were loath to lose sight of the main force. An advance
guard so near was all but useless. The advance body of
a Hyrkanian host rode hours, or even days, ahead of the
main horde, keeping contact by relays of scouts. An
ambush such as Conan had devised would have been
useless against a truly efficient cavalry.

After the advance guard, at the very head of the host,
was a band. Conan marveled at the sound and the sight:
mounted drummers, flute-players, musicians with horns
and tinkling instruments, even goatskin bagpipes, all
splendidly mounted and draped with colorful horse trappings, as if they rode to a parade instead of to a battle.
The satrap of Bukhrosha seemed determined to impress
his brother-monarch.

Guyak gaped at the approaching host. "Are these
really warriors, captain?"

"Some of them are," Conan acknowledged. "And
do not be lulled by the sound and the glitter. I have
known some very fierce peoples to like music to accompany their war-making. There are up-country Bossonians

who have pipes that set up a snarling fit to curl your hair, and the knights of Poitain go into war with fiddlers playing stringed instruments as if at a dance. They fight none the less fiercely for the music.''

"If you say so, lord," said the standard-bearer doubtfully.

They lowered themselves as the enemy drew nearer, and then the forward elements were entering the pass.

"Red flag," said Conan.

Guyak stood below the crest of the hill, unfurled the banner and waved it above his head vigorously. Below, Fawd and his one hundred mounted and began to ride toward the pass as if they were merely out hunting loot. They slowed and then halted as the advance element of the Bukhroshan force came through the pass. Fawd and his men stood uncertainly, watchful as the enemy cavalry began to pour, rank after rank, from between the hills.

Conan had given strict orders that they were not to turn tail until a clearly overwhelming number of the foe were within sight. A too-hasty flight would seem suspicious and might cause the Bukhroshan commander to scent a trap.

In the pass, horsemen shouted back over their shoulders, and one or two wheeled from the rear rank of the advance guard and hastened back to the main body to report that the enemy had been sighted. They were forced to ride around the musicians in the narrow confines of the pass, and they went straightaway to a splendidly armed man who sported a formidable mustache and side-whiskers. He shouted out orders and waved a ceremonial mace glittering with jewels. The scouts returned to the advance guard, which was then beginning to deploy at the mouth of the little pass. Conan noted that this maneuver was accomplished efficiently. These men were not show-soldiers, despite their swagger and excessive display.

Fawd's men began to grow restive. So expert were they with their mounts that they made the horses appear nervous, dancing from side to side and seemingly difficult to control. Fawd screamed a few nonsensical orders, as if trying to egg on half-mutinous troops, and a few of his men made halfhearted but stinging bowshots into the Bukhroshan host.

A Bukhroshan officer shouted a high, clear command, and a trumpet sounded a brief call of ascending and descending notes. As one man, the forward element began to advance, the horses' hooves striking the earth in unison. The first rank of the armored mass rode with lowered lances, the riders slightly crouched behind their shields as they bore down upon the Hyrkanians.

Fawd and his men held fast until Conan feared that it was almost too late; then they turned tail and fled, a few of them twisting and firing over their horses' rumps at the advancing enemy. The archers made their casts seem panicked and hasty, but Conan saw that almost every shaft dropped into the massed horsemen with deadly effect.

Conan had hoped that the enemy would go charging after the fleeing Hyrkanians heedlessly, but this disciplined pursuit was acceptable. He knew well the folly of expecting an enemy to behave foolishly. As the armored troops thundered through the pass, he made a count of ranks, of banners and formations. At length he judged that half of the enemy force had gone through the pass.

"Black flag!" Conan called.

At the signal, the Hyrkanian horsemen came riding around the two hills. They halted on the hillsides, fifty paces above the Bukhroshan host. Immediately they began pouring a deadly, plunging crossfire into the horsemen milling in the pass. The scene below disintegrated into panic and confusion as some tried to ride on through, others to go back out of the pass. A few bold riders sought to charge uphill against their foemen, but none made a score of paces before being brought down by a shaft.

Within a few minutes the pass was a ghastly morass of inert armored forms. At Conan's command, Guyak waved a yellow flag. The Hyrkanians poured off the hillsides and charged against the Bukhroshan soldiers who had already cleared the pass. The steppe warriors rode against the rear of the column, raining arrows into the confused mass as they came.

The Hyrkanians split right and left and rode around the cavalry procession, riddling it from both flanks and then converging at its front, bringing down warrior and musician without distinction. They re-formed, now joined by Fawd's detachment, wheeled and rode back. The remaining Bukhroshans tried to fight or sought escape, but were successful at neither. The arrows poured in again, piercing man and horse, passing through mail and scale and hardened leather as if they had been cobwebs.

The marauders did not slow but kept riding toward the twin hills, though they did not attempt to use the corpse-choked, narrow pass. Again they split into two forces and took opposite routes around the bases of the hills. Screaming their wild war cries, they fell upon the rear half of the Bukhroshan column, which was still trying to force its way into the pass. Conan watched as the two pincers of his force closed on the foe like the claws of a gigantic monster. Futilely the city troops tried to change from marching order to order of battle.

They succeeded only in throwing their ranks into greater disorder.

The Hyrkanians rode up and down the lines of Bukhroshans, raining their shafts into the helpless, stymied mass of packed soldiery. The rear guard had had enough. In twos and threes, then in squadrons, they broke away from the slaughter and galloped down the road leading back to Bukhrosha. Some of the Hyrkanians pursued, shooting mercilessly at the fleeing soldiers.

"White flag," Conan ordered. As they saw the signal, the horse-archers gave up pursuit and wheeled their mounts to return. Conan descended from his vantage point. It had been a great victory, but he could take little pride in it. For all their numbers, the city men had had no more chance against the steppe warriors than unarmed children. Conan relished battle, but he could not enjoy a massacre.

As he reached the foot of the hill, his men were moving among the bodies, retrieving arrows and stripping the dead of arms and valuables. The smell of blood was strong, and already the flies were gathering. Overhead, the vultures soared in broad circles. Rustuf rode up to him, looking uncharacteristically solemn.

"Your plan worked," the *kozak* said. "But this is not a manly way to fight."

"Aye," said Conan. "Sword to sword is better. These men will not have it so easy when we camp around the walls of Sogaria. Never have I taken part in a siege where the besiegers did not suffer. You cannot take a fortress with arrows."

The *kagan*'s camp was a two-day march from Sogaria when the Cimmerian and his five hundred rode in and deposited their loot before the great tent. Conan dismissed his men with orders to erect his quarters while he went within to tender his report. The space before the tent was filled with the loot of other expeditions, and commandeered carts were being gathered to transport the goods.

His report concluded, Conan sought out his quarters. He found his men gathered near his tent, jabbering excitedly and with looks of fear upon their countenances. He wondered what could instill fear in these men, and felt sure that it boded ill.

"What is it, Rustuf?" he asked.

"These fools set up your tent," Rustuf said, "then their own. Come look at this."

The *kozak* led him to the entrance of the tent. A pole had been thrust into the ground, and from its top a bundle of some sort dangled on a leather thong. Conan leaned close and studied it. He recognized the feathers, beaks and claws of birds. There were bones and herbs as well, and things that looked somehow unnatural, all bound in skins and colored cords.

He snorted in disgust. "What means this trash?"

"You have been cursed, captain," said Guyak. "This is a shaman's curse. If it is not lifted, you cannot prosper. All your undertakings must fail, and you will sicken and soon die." The other men nodded and muttered, eyeing Conan fearfully.

"What!" said Conan scornfully. "Are these the men who just slew six times their number of enemies, now standing in fear of a bundle of filth?" He glared at them, and they would not meet his eyes. "Which shaman did this?"

"We saw no one, captain," said Guyak. "The shamans can make themselves invisible. But in this camp, none can work magic without the permission of Danaqan."

"Where is the snag-toothed old villain?" the Cimmerian demanded. "I shall wring his scrawny neck for him."

The men would say nothing. With a blistering curse, Conan seized a flaming brand from the nearest fire and strode to the pole. He held the brand beneath the bundle, which began to smoke and catch flame. Then his hair rose as the bundle began to twist and writhe. From inside came a hideous screaming, and the thong burned through, dropping the thing to the ground where it ceased to burn.

Slowly the bundle unfolded into a bat-winged homunculus, as black as the midnight sky and perhaps two feet tall. It hissed at Conan, baring a double row of tiny, needle teeth. It was entirely hairless, with eyes like burning black coals. Smoke continued to rise from the thing as it advanced. The Hyrkanians jabbered in fear and backed away.

The creature squalled and launched itself at the Cimmerian. Conan ripped out his sword, slicing upward and cutting through the little demon, splitting it in twain as easily as if it had been made of smoke. The sundered halves rejoined and once again the thing came toward him. He slashed it in two sideways. This time, as it sought to re-form, he speared the still-smoking bundle on the tip of his sword and jammed its tattered remnants into the fire.

The winged homunculus hissed loudly and began to spin in ever-tightening circles in midair. As the last bits of the bundle were consumed by the flames, the creature faded into black smoke, then disappeared entirely.

"The thing was naught but a phantom," Conan said contemptuously. "It was a conjurer's trick, no more substantial than fog."

"No, captain," said Guyak. "It was an *ulu-bekh*. A

spirit of the air, it obeys the shaman. Shamans have great powers over the spirits.''

"You are like children!" Conan barked. "Your shamans are nothing but mountebanks and frauds who keep you cowed with their trickery." He saw that his words were having little effect. Efforts to convince them would be of no avail. Once men were persuaded of anything supernatural, mere facts and demonstration would accomplish nothing.

"Go to your beds," he ordered. "The magic show is over for this night."

Slowly, muttering among themselves, they obeyed. Rustuf and Fawd joined Conan in the tent they shared. Fawd passed Conan a wineskin as the three sat cross-legged upon the floor and the Cimmerian washed the day's accumulation of trail dust from his throat.

"On the morrow," he said, "I shall cut down the whole pack of these shamans. Bartatua should promote me for it. They are no friends of his."

"It is an attractive idea," Rustuf said. "But what wizard ever lived who did not let it be known that his death would bring a curse on everyone nearby?"

"It is true," said Fawd. "Ask these tribesmen and they will all tell you that if a shaman dies by violence, disaster must befall the horde. Shamans must have it so for they have many enemies. If you move openly against the shamans, the tribesmen will kill you."

"But how can I control my men if they believe I am accursed and unlucky? And what have I done to earn the enmity of these filthy conjurers? I have not attacked them." The Cimmerian grew more morose by the minute. He detested sorcery at the best of times, but it was especially galling to be stymied by such petty, contemptible medicine men.

"I think," Conan said, "that it is time for me to pay these bone-rattling magicians a visit."

"You may not have to go far," said Rustuf. "Unless I am much mistaken, I hear the drum of a shaman thumping nearby."

The three rose and walked noiselessly from the tent. The drum was being played quietly, but it was no more than a score of paces away. They trod lightly to a spot where a knot of Conan's men sat in a circle around a fire. Close to the fire sat the old shaman, Danaqan, behind him an effeminate boy. With his fingertips the boy was softly tapping on a drum made of human skin stretched over the open top of a human skull. The eye sockets of the skull were inlaid with silver and they glinted evilly in the firelight.

"Woe to you all!" the old man was saying to the assemblage. "It is an evil thing that the *kagan* has elevated a foreign slave to the rank of officer among us. This man has no family, clan or tribe. His ancestors are not entombed in a sacred burial place on the steppe. His gods are not our gods. The spirits of the endless steppe grow angry. They will bring the storms of hail and lightning if you continue to follow the foreigner. They will bring the great grass fires, and the smoke will darken the Everlasting Sky. You must not—"

The shaman's voice faltered and died away as a hand fell heavily upon his shoulder. It was a very large, battle-scarred hand, and he tried to shrug it off, but the thumb was curled around the back of his neck and began to squeeze. A terrible pain shot up the old man's neck, although the hand had barely flexed.

"Friend Danaqan," said Conan heartily, "there seems to be some misunderstanding between us. I wish only to serve the *kagan* as best I may. If I have inadvertently given offense to your gods, please tell me how I may make restitution to them. You are a mighty shaman, one who speaks directly with the spirit world. Surely you can settle things between the gods and me.''

The shaman tried to rise, but another squeeze of the powerful fingers caused him to cease his struggle. ''It may be,'' he said hesitantly, ''that something could be arranged. My magic is strong and the spirits listen to me.''

''Good!'' Conan approved. ''Come, walk with me and we will discuss this privily. There should be no enmity between reasonable men of goodwill such as we.''

The fingers dug into the old man's shoulder and hauled him erect. ''Yes,'' Danaqan managed to grate out, ''let us speak together, foreign captain.''

Conan smiled at his men. ''Now get you to bed, for we are off again upon the *kagan*'s business on the morrow. This good shaman and I shall settle matters and all shall be fair again.''

His men looked relieved, but the boy with the skull-drum had a countenance full of fear. Conan favored him with a bone-chilling glare, and the kohl-outlined eyes rolled up in his head, the drum fell from his hands, and the boy keeled over sideways in a dead faint.

''He seems to be in a spirit trance,'' Conan said. ''Do not wake him lest the spirits be angered.''

He led the old shaman from the firelight until they were at the very edge of the camp, near the line of sentries. There Conan placed his palm in the middle of the shaman's back and thrust him forward, sending him sprawling upon his face. The old man sprang to his feet and began to gesture at the Cimmerian, growling out spells in a deep, sepulchral voice. Conan slapped him with his open palm, sending the shaman flying several paces through the air to land in a rattle of bones and amulets.

"Who was it?" Conan demanded. "Who bought you, shaman? Who paid you to place your piddling curses on me? I'll have the answers out of you, so you might as well speak now."

"Cursed foreigner! You shall die—" The old man's evil eyes bulged as Conan ripped his sword from its sheath and slashed out and down in a single motion too swift to see. The ragged, filthy clothes began to shred away from the Hyrkanian's body. Strings of charms and amulets dropped to the ground, and the old shaman looked in horror for signs of damage to himself. The moonlight revealed that his withered flesh was untouched.

"It could have been through flesh and bone, wizard," Conan said. "I could have hewn your filthy, cowardly heart in twain. Think upon that while I decide where next to strike."

"It was the Vendhyan woman," Danaqan said in a defeated voice. "The *kagan*'s concubine came to us, desiring your life."

"And secret murder is your trade," Conan said. "She came to a poor craftsman. Why does she want me dead?"

The man shrugged. "She is jealous. You have risen too far too fast. The *kagan* favors you, and she would that he has no other favorites, only herself."

"Then I must speak to her as well. I hope that she will see reason as readily as you, shaman. I know now that your paltry spells cannot harm me. I suspect that you will next try poison. I urge you to reconsider. Even a powerful poison can take hours to kill a strong man. The moment I feel a bellyache, I shall come and kill you, along with the rest of your scurvy breed. Go now, and be glad that you found me in a merciful mood."

As he walked back to his tent, Conan was satisfied that he was safe from the shaman for the moment. He was glad that he had decided to handle the problem himself instead of taking it to Bartatua. The difficulty had originated in the *kagan*'s very tent. He shook his head. King, priest, concubine. It was deadly to stand within such a triangle. Here things were as corrupt as in any civilized court.

As he entered his tent, Rustuf and Fawd looked up from where they sat passing a wineskin back and forth.

"How went it?" Rustuf asked.

"He saw wisdom at last. However, I think it would be a good idea if we three were to keep fast horses close at hand from now on."

"I always do," Rustuf said.

Nine

As the sun began to lower, the city of Sogaria shut its gates for the final time, not to be reopened until the enemy were no longer in Sogarian territory. Trumpets brayed and gongs tolled out their thunder as the huge wooden valves closed and the great locking-beams slid across to settle into their iron-bound brackets. Masons began to sheathe the gateways with dressed stone. From now on only small sallyports, each capable of admitting a single file of horsemen, would be permitted to remain, for they were easy to defend against enemy incursion.

Atop the walls, citizens impressed into the defense forces stood shoulder-to-shoulder with the soldiers who readied the engines that would drop hot oil and weighty missiles upon the attackers. From the highest towers of the city, lookouts kept watch for the terrible raiders from the steppes.

At last a cry arose from those atop the wall. To the west, a column of horsemen advanced along the crest of a low range of hills. Then, to the south, another, wider

column advanced up a broad highway. Fingers pointed
to the north, where countless horsemen stood looking
down from the great escarpment that defined the beginning of the steppe country.

The innumerable mounted savages were a terrifying
sight, but the wiser and more-experienced of the city
people knew that they were not the greatest threat. The
real danger would be in the innocuous-looking rabble of
siege workers, who would slowly, laboriously, undermine the walls of Sogaria, fill in its ditches and carry
the ladders to scale its walls.

And many there wondered where was the wing of
Red Eagles that had left the city some days before, led
by the Turanian wizard, Khondemir.

At that moment Khondemir and his escort were crossing the Steppe of Famine, an aptly named stretch of dry
plain where water was rare and grazing was sparse. The
pack train slowed progress, but it carried the grain the
horses required, else every day hours would be lost
while the mounts scattered wide in search of forage.

The Princess Ishkala rode in her lurching carriage,
thoroughly miserable and frightened. She wondered what
glorious plot her devoted but foolhardy lover, Manzur,
had hatched to rescue her. She knew him better than to
expect him to do her bidding and remain in Sogaria
until she should return.

Her thoughts on that prospect were no less troubled.
The wizard, Khondemir, was remote and cold, and his
manner toward her was little more than civil. She heard
strange sounds from within his tent each night. In the
mornings he released a pigeon, a small tube attached to
its leg. Each evening a different bird would arrive and
he would carry it into his tent. No one ever saw what
messages the birds carried. Messenger pigeons were

common enough, she thought, but what manner of bird could find its way to an ever-moving column?

She leaned from her carriage and signaled to Captain Jeku, commander of the escort. The glittering officer rode to her side and saluted with his short silver-mounted whip. "Yes, my lady?"

"Captain, what think you of the Turanian, Khondemir?"

"Think, my lady?" He frowned as if at some utterly alien concept. "Why should I think about him? I have been given orders to escort him to a destination that he shall choose. That is what I am doing."

"Of course," she said impatiently, "I realize that you must obey my father's orders. But does it not seem odd to you that Khondemir keeps sending out and receiving messenger pigeons?"

The captain looked away uncomfortably. "I know naught of the ways of wizards, my lady. As long as he does nothing treasonous to my prince, I'll not interfere with him."

Resignedly she sat back within her heavily padded carriage and shut the curtain. She had been raised in a palace, and her new surroundings appeared decidedly odd. The carriage was luxurious compared to the circumstances endured by the troopers outside, but she had not even a single maid here. She missed the company more than the help, for her requirements were very few on this trek.

It was on the sixth day of the slow journey that she heard the troopers shouting, and the sound of trumpets and drums. From earlier drills she knew that the trumpet call was the alert, signifying enemy in sight. The troopers outside were not behaving as if this were a drill, but were forming battle order in deadly earnest.

"What is it?" she called as Jeku rode past her carriage.

"The savages come, Princess," he called. "Stay within your carriage. We shall protect you."

From what she had heard of the Hyrkanians, she doubted that even the bravest of Sogarian cavalry would be much protection. She got out and climbed to the top of the carriage, taking a seat beside the driver. Near her were Jeku and his staff. The Red Eagles were formed up in four ranks, facing the approaching horsemen. At a call from Jeku, all lances were lowered toward the enemy.

"There is no sense in standing here and awaiting their arrows," said the captain. "As soon as they are within bowshot, sound the charge."

"Stop!" The voice was that of Khondemir. The mage rode up to Jeku and his staff. "These are not Hyrkanians."

"Say you so?" said Jeku, glowering fiercely. "Then who may they be, pray?"

"They are allies, friends of mine. From Turan. We are not in Sogarian territory any longer, Captain."

"And why are they joining you here? My prince gave me no instructions concerning this situation. This is quite irregular."

"Irregular or not, Captain, I have need of these men. The reasons for that need not concern you. Suffice it to say that they are allies. They will strengthen our band should we face the Hyrkanians. I assume that you have sufficient control over your men to prevent ugly incidents?"

Jeku's face darkened like a thundercloud. "My men are perfectly disciplined, sir. You may rest assured of it. I shall expect you to keep rein on these men who seem to belong to you. We have been at peace with Turan for many years, so there is no cause for enmity.

However, when we return to Sogaria, I shall report this
. . . peculiar circumstance.''

"The prince will have no cause for complaint,"
Khondemir said.

The Turanians were now within bowshot, but they
made no hostile demonstration. They rode to within a
few-score yards of the Sogarians, then halted at an order
from a leader. A small group detached itself and rode to
the small band of staff surrounding Khondemir. A black-
bearded man bowed deeply to the mage.

"Greeting, my Lord Khondemir. We, your followers, stand ready to escort you to your rightful place,
the—''

"Very good, Bulamb," said Khondemir, cutting off
the man's words. "Have your men fall in beside our
esteemed allies, the Sogarians. We ride for a place deep
within this arid plain, and we are now near our
destination.''

The one named Bulamb regarded Jeku and his staff
with an expression of insolent irony. "I am always
delighted to meet . . . allies, my lord. I shall relay your
orders.''

"Excellent. We make camp an hour before sunset.
Attend me in my tent this evening," Khondemir said.
The Turanian rode off.

Now that they were closer, Ishkala studied the foreigners. She knew by the style of their dress, arms and
horse trappings that these were Turanians. She had little
experience of military men, but these seemed to lack
the smartness and fine discipline of the Red Eagles.
There was no uniformity in their equipment, and many
had the raffish, brutal look of common adventurers
rather than the mien of respectable, professional soldiers. In number they roughly equaled the Sogarians.
All were mounted, a necessity on the empty plain.

The Turanians had a sizable pack train, presumably loaded with forage for the horses and waterskins for man and beast. The Sogarians eyed them askance, the way that professional military men always regard amateurs, especially those who bear more the aspect of bandits than that of soldiers.

Ishkala resumed her seat in her carriage, but when next she saw Captain Jeku riding past, she beckoned him to her again. "Well, Captain, what think you of the Turanian wizard now?"

Jeku frowned furiously. "This surpasses belief! Not only does the man drag us out into this wasteland when our city lies in danger, but he foists upon us a pack of . . . of Turanian riffraff! Your father shall hear of this, Princess, never fear!"

Manzur leaned on his spear and stared gloomily over the host encamped around the walls of Sogaria. Already he had found out that a siege had a single, all-pervasive quality: boredom. He wore his sword, an old shirt of bronze scales from the city armory, and a spired helmet won at dicing with a city guard. He had felt quite soldierly upon taking his assigned post atop the city wall. That had been two nights earlier. The excitement of the novelty had not outlasted the first night.

He had tried to compose verses full of the clash of arms, the neighing of war-horses, the bray of trumpets and the thunder of drums. Unfortunately, what was happening around Sogaria had no such stirring aspect. During the day there was only the occasional whisper of an arrow as the Hyrkanians amused themselves by taking potshots at the guards atop the wall. At night he could hear the digging of the slave train as it sought to undermine the great walls of the city.

A breeze from behind brought him the stench of a

massive overcrowding of man and beast within the restricting walls of the city. The old poems had never mentioned that aspect of war, he thought. The siege could drag on for weeks, or even for months. The thought was unendurable. Manzur was certain that he was made for better things. He was also frantic with worry over the fate of Ishkala. But how might he escape inevitable death from boredom and join his beloved?

A sound from below drew his attention. He leaned over the parapet between the newly erected arrow shields of thick wicker. From the gloom below, came the creaking sound of one of the sallyports as it was opened. The thudding of muffled hooves came up to him; then the hoofbeats faded into the distance. Once again the sallyport creaked and he heard its bars slide back into place. He resumed his sentry post and turned to a companion.

"Another messenger off to seek reinforcements," he said. "I wonder how many ever pierce the lines."

"Few, I would wager," said the man, an old veteran called back into service for the emergency.

"But if they capture our messengers," Manzur said, "why do they not display them before the walls and mock us for our efforts?"

"This savage is too clever," said the veteran, gnarled hands locked about his spearshaft. "This way, we never know who has made it through and who has not. Also, if we grew discouraged, we might stop trying to send messengers. As it is, every one he captures he can torture to learn about the conditions within our walls."

Manzur nodded. A thought formed in his mind.

"The messengers must be very brave. I would like to speak with such courageous men. Know you where they may be found?"

"The Messenger Corps frequents the tavern called

the Weary Horseman, near the cavalry barracks,'' the older man replied.

At midnight Manzur was relieved. Instead of going home, he went in search of the Weary Horseman. The streets were crowded with refugees lying on pallets. He stumbled in the gloom, for since the rationing of oil had been instituted, only one streetlamp in four was lighted at dusk.

The inn was not difficult to find, for there were a half-score of horses tethered at its forecourt. This was a rare sight within the walls of the city, but this tavern had leave to keep the beasts unpenned, for the messengers had to be ready to mount and ride on a moment's notice.

Inside, Manzur found the mood subdued. The patrons ate and drank desultorily, and conversed in low voices. The depressing atmosphere of the besieged city had spelled an end to the carefree roistering of the city's taverns. He saw that on a long table amidst the men there rested a casque bearing the yellow plumes of the Messenger Corps. These men were never truly off duty, and all were dressed in the light armor of their highly mobile service.

Soon Manzur saw what he was looking for. In a corner by himself sat a man who silently and gloomily stared into the lees swirling at the bottom of his wine cup. Manzur knew the situation well: a man with a flat purse, a man who had spent his last coin on wine and whose companions seemed disinclined to advance him the price of more. Manzur crossed to the table.

''Excuse me, sir,'' said the youth.

The man looked up at him with red-shot eyes. ''Yes? Who are you, another summoner from the palace with a suicide mission for the only soldiers doing this city any good?''

Manzur paid no attention to the man's sneering belligerence. It merely meant that the fellow was already half-drunk, which would make his task that much easier.

"Pray forgive my intruding upon your privacy," Manzur said, "but I have heard wonderful things about you men of the Messenger Corps. I would be most honored if you would allow me to buy you a cup or two of wine. I would greatly enjoy hearing of your adventures. I am a poet, and I intend to compose an epic about this war when we have driven away the savages."

At the mention of wine, the man brightened somewhat. "There may be few ears to listen to your verses when this is over, but have a seat anyway. Yes, we are the finest service in the army, all picked men, mounted on the finest steeds, and this," he slapped the goldwashed message tube at his sash, "is our passport to anywhere in the allied nations. If I encounter a duke when I am on duty and my horse is tired, I may demand that he exchange mounts with me and he can do no more than ask restitution of the prince."

The pitcher of strong wine arrived and Manzur poured generously into the messenger's cup, stingily into his own. "Tell me more," he urged.

For the next two hours the man regaled Manzur with tales of his adventures. Toward the end he grew incoherent and took to repeating himself. At last he began to slump forward onto the table. Manzur grasped him and hauled him to his feet.

"Time for you to return to barracks, my friend," Manzur said. "Let me help you."

No one bothered to look up as Manzur half-carried the drunken man from the tavern. Apparently his companion was not popular among the other messengers. Instead of guiding him to the barracks, Manzur stepped into the alley separating the inn from a back wall of the military stables. When he reemerged, he was dressed in the uniform and armor of the Messenger Corps. He had retained only his own sword and dagger, for these weapons were not standardized within the corps, each man instead bearing such arms as he fancied.

Hurriedly Manzur examined the mounts hitched before the tavern. He did not wish any of the messengers to see him leaving the establishment. Then he found the name of his erstwhile companion stamped upon a saddle skirt. He unhitched the horse and led it away by the bridle. As soon as he was a distance from the tavern, he mounted and picked a careful way through the refugee-clotted streets.

At the north gate, the small contingent of guards looked up to see the yellow plumes nodding above the rider's head. "Another message to go out tonight?" asked the senior guard. "Where do you ride, messenger?"

"You know better than to ask such questions," Manzur said, bluffing.

"Your pardon," said the guard. "You are right. We shall have the sallyport open in a moment. You had best ride like the wind if you would be well beyond the savages by daybreak. Will you dismount now?"

"Dismount?" Manzur said, puzzled.

"Yes, so that we may muffle your horse's hooves. The ground is hard-packed just beyond the walls and you may hear a horse for half a mile."

"Of course," Manzur said. "It had slipped my mind. Difficult to get used to, the idea of Sogaria being under siege." He hoped that his airy tone was sufficient to deter suspicion, and he fretted silently while the guards tied clumsy shoes of thick-plaited straw over his mount's hooves.

When they were finished, he remounted and waited as they opened the sallyport. The horse stamped impatiently, trying to shake off the unfamiliar, muffling shoes. Slowly, trying to make as little noise as possible, he rode through. Tensed for the impact of innumerable arrows, he let out a long sigh of relief when none greeted his exit.

In the distance he could see the low-burning fires of the encamped Hyrkanian army. As he heard no patrols nearby, he sat his horse for a few minutes, getting his bearings. Then he began to ride to the northwest. As a boy, he had often visited a modest farm owned by a kinsman near the edge of the cultivated land surrounding the city. The farm was no doubt in ruins, but the land was bisected by the dry bed of an ancient stream and the gully might provide him with a path through the enemy lines unseen.

An hour's easy trot brought him to the edge of the farmland. A brief excursion to the right should bring him to the dry wash and a path to freedom. With his attention on the ground just before his horse's hooves, he was caught by surprise when a voice to his left hailed him. "Who are you? What horde?"

Manzur could barely understand the words, spoken in the barbarous dialect of the steppes. He did not want to run until he knew where the gully was, and he preferred not to be pursued. Feverishly he tried to remember all that he had heard of the tribesmen. For one thing, they were notorious drunks. Manzur slumped over his saddle, humming an ancient sheepherder's song.

"I said who are you!" barked the voice. Then Manzur heard the hooves of two horses approaching.

"Another drunk," said a different voice disgustedly. "Fool, the *kagan* will have the hide from your back for this."

A hand grabbed Manzur's left arm and roughly jerked him erect. "This is no—" But before the tribesman could finish, Manzur was drawing his sword and cutting upward. The blade caught the man below the chin, cleaving up through the teeth and into the brain. Only with a powerful wrenching could he free the sword from his enemy's skull. In the dimness he barely saw the other Hyrkanian thrust at him with a lance. Manzur leaned back and let the point pass before him. With his left hand he seized the shaft and jerked the Hyrkanian forward. His right hand swept the tip of his sword across the man's throat in a move as precise as his years of training could make it. The Hyrkanian toppled from the saddle with little noise.

Manzur found the gully a few paces away and rode into it. He had to restrain himself from shouting in triumph. He had slain two enemies with two blows of his sword! What a poem he would be able to write when he had the leisure! He felt that if he were not the greatest warrior in the world, he had at least made a good beginning and would probably hold that title before the war was over. He rode on through the night in a state of high exaltation.

By sunrise the city was far behind and Manzur risked riding out of the gully. A quick scan of his surroundings told him that no one was near him and that he must be far past enemy lines. He began to quarter the land before him. Sooner or later even the veriest amateur should be able to find the trail of a thousand mounted men.

By midday he had found the tracks of the Red Eagles. Somewhere in their midst would be his beloved, Ishkala. He began to ride on their trail. This was far more exciting than sitting atop a wall in a besieged city. The fact that he would almost certainly be hanged upon his return did not bother him. Something would happen to prevent it, no doubt. In any case, he intended to return as a hero.

Somewhat more unsettling was the state of his provisions, or rather, his lack of them. He had a large skin of water and a small bag of dried fruit and parched grain. The water would last him for several days, but no more than two if he had to share it with his horse. He would have to find a stream or water hole, no easy task in this arid steppe. He refused to worry. The gods always provided for a hero.

He deliberately avoided the thought that in most poems the hero came to a bad end, eventually.

Ten

Conan rode into the *kagan*'s compound in the late afternoon, when the sun was past its zenith and the shadows of the skull-and-horses'-tail standards grew long upon the ground. His day had been busy. The *kagan* had given him orders to assess the state of the siege and its prospects for success, and to investigate untoward incidents. As a man with no clan affiliation, Conan was a natural to investigate disputes between tribesmen, leaving the *kagan* to adjudicate.

To aid in his assessment, he had obtained permission to take a well-educated prisoner with him to interpret. He also made use of the man to improve his own skill with the dialect spoken in Sogaria. To a man with Conan's wandering urge, a facility with many tongues was a matter of survival.

Conan dismounted and tossed his reins to a serving man, then entered the tent. He found the *kagan* surrounded by his higher officers. He seemed not to notice the Cimmerian's entrance, but by now Conan knew that the *kagan* missed absolutely nothing that happened around

him. Before the *kagan* was a model of the city fashioned by an artisan prisoner, complete with walls and
the buildings within the walls.

"Conan," said Bartatua when he had finished another conversation, "what are the prospects of con-
structing siege towers?"

"None," Conan replied. "There is no timber to
speak of in all of Sogarian territory. The only trees are
in the orchards, for the growing of fruits, olives and
nuts. They are small, and much of the wood is unsuitable in any case. Fruitwood is too soft. Olive wood is
strong but so oily that one fire arrow would transform a
siege tower into a funeral pyre. Besides, the destruction
of the orchards would devastate the city."

"What care we for the woes of city people, foreigner?" asked a haughty chieftain whose face was a
snarl of tattooed serpents.

Conan stared him in the eyes. "It will devastate the
kagan's city, not the Sogarians'." The chieftain looked
away, grumbling.

"The timber is also little good for mine shorings,"
Conan continued. "And we can't even use cut stone for
the purpose, since all the outlying structures are of mud
brick. The only cut stone is in the city itself. The lack
of good timber also rules out a battering ram."

"I had not known that timber was so important to a
siege!" the *kagan* said angrily. "What do you propose,
Cimmerian?"

"There are three courses we might take," Conan
suggested. "One is a masonry ramp. Nearby are quarries from whence the city gets its stone. There is an
abundance of rough stone, and we can set the slaves to
hauling it. Under cover of hide and wicker shields, we
could build a ramp to the top of the wall. The whole
army could then assault that single spot. It is certain

victory but slow and laborious, and large numbers of the slaves will die.''

Bartatua flicked a hand deprecatingly. "No matter. We have plenty of slaves. What else?''

"We can make ladders. There is sufficient wood for that. Without the support of siege towers, though, the casualties among the soldiers would be terrible. It is the riskiest way to storm a fortification, especially when the walls are so high. The third way is to sit here and do nothing. Soon starvation and pestilence will force the city-dwellers to capitulate. By then, though, there may be pestilence among ourselves as well.''

"You have not mentioned the fourth possibility," said the *kagan*. "We might suborn traitors within the city to open the gates for us.''

Conan could guess the source of that suggestion. "That is not my realm, *Kagan*. If you have agents within the city who can do this, well and good. By now, though, the Sogarians have sheathed the great gates with brick or stone and left only small sallyports. We cannot enter the city in sufficient numbers that way.''

Bartatua wasted no time in discussion. "It is the ramp, then.'' He turned to a small man who stood nearby. Conan recognized him: a Khitan who had been on a caravan bound for Sogaria. He had presented himself as an expert engineer and had offered his services on the siege works, for suitable compensation. "Can you build it?'' the *kagan* asked.

"Lead me to the quarries and give me the slaves,'' the man said, "and you shall have the ramp.''

"It is done, then,'' said Bartatua. "See that you fail me not.'' He turned back to the Cimmerian. "Now, Conan, what of the two men found dead this morning?''

"They were killed by a messenger who left the city

last night," Conan reported. "Near their bodies were the marks of straw-muffled hooves, and whoever slew them was an expert with the sword. It was as neat a bit of bladework as I could have done myself. His tracks led to a dry wash and thence northwest. There was no sense in pursuing since the man had such a wide lead."

"Very well," Bartatua said. "He will have no city to return to anyway, so our men will be avenged. Have you anything else to report?"

"Just one curious matter," Conan said. "My fifty-commander, the *kozak* Rustuf, took out a patrol yesterday to the northwest. He found the trail of at least a thousand horsemen. From the spoor, he estimates that they must have passed that way a day or two before we arrived around Sogaria. For some reason, they are headed into an empty waste called the Steppe of Famine."

Conan was astonished at the shouts of surprise from Bartatua and some of the assembled officers. He noted that all of those who were agitated belonged to Bartatua's own people, the Ashkuz.

"The Steppe of Famine!" barked one. "That is—"

"We will discuss this later!" snapped Bartatua with a ferocious glare. Now what, thought Conan, does this mean? "All of you leave me now," said Bartatua, "except for the Cimmerian. You have your orders."

The others filed out of the tent, many of them glowering at Conan. He glowered back. He was resigned to being unpopular with these clannish men. He had lived with worse.

"Pour us some wine, Conan," said the *kagan*. Conan poured two cups from a golden ewer and handed one to his chief. The *kagan* took a long draught and said, "You tell me that your Cimmeria is a country of mountains and rock, Conan?"

"It is that, *Kagan*," Conan said, wondering where this might be leading.

"I suppose that a Cimmerian lad must learn to climb at an early age, not so?"

"Very true. I climbed many a rocky spire to rob bird nests of eggs or warm down. And I descended many a cliff to find a broken-legged ewe or to ambush a wolf's lair."

"Excellent," said Bartatua. "Tonight I want you to climb the walls of Sogaria and bring me news of what goes on inside."

He might have known. It was like the *kagan* to shower a man with favors and then send him on a suicide mission. A clansman might have resentful kinsmen, but a wandering adventurer such as himself had none to protest on his behalf. He did not hesitate. "Of course, *Kagan*. Had you a particular destination for this reconnaissance?"

Bartatua pointed at a large structure in his model. "Here, the prince's palace. With the city packed with refugees, you should have little trouble in making your way there once you are over the wall. If you can sneak within the premises and find a good point of vantage, you might overhear much that would be of value to me."

Conan wondered whether the man had the slightest concept of how deadly this mission was. He decided that the *kagan* knew, but did not care. Other lives were mere counters in his game of power. Conan was a very small counter indeed.

"Anything else?" Conan asked drily.

"A survey of the defenses would not come amiss, as well as an estimate of the number of horses in the stables. I would also like to know the state of morale among the troops and refugees, but that may wait for another night, another mission."

"Another mission, as you say. Well, *Kagan*, I should go to prepare myself for this night's work."

"Do so," said Bartatua, turning his attention to his model. "And Conan—"

The Cimmerian turned back. "Yes, *Kagan?*"

"Fail me not."

"This is madness, Conan!" said Rustuf. The two men sat in their tent. Fawd was away on a patrol. "Do not do it," urged the *kozak*. "Let's you and I take our best horses and be away from here. This siege will drag on for months, and probably nothing will remain but a heap of ashes to loot at the end of it. Come, I have laid by some emergency stores and a bag of dice winnings. Let us go find some sensible army to serve in, where there is no mad leader who wants to wipe out the whole world in order to own it. I want to do my fighting in an army that values the important things: loot and women and good wine."

"I have laid by some stores as well," said the Cimmerian, donning a belted tunic he had taken from a prisoner. "And I may make use of them yet. But it is not my habit to desert a leader under whom I have taken service. Should he play me false, it will be different, but thus far he has dealt fairly and raised me from prisoner to high rank."

"And now gives you an assignment that is certain death!" the *kozak* said.

Conan shrugged. "What war leader does not send his men into danger? If it were something whimsical or needlessly cruel, I would not hesitate to mount and ride away, but it is not. He needs intelligence of the enemy's condition within the city, and it so happens that he has a man skilled at scaling walls and with a knack for languages. It is a sensible plan. And do not be so sure that it is certain death. I am not easy to kill."

Rustuf threw up his hands in exasperation. "There is such a thing as carrying courage and loyalty too far!"

* * *

Conan stood at the base of the city wall and reached high into the night over his head. His fingers found purchase in the crack between two courses of great stones, and he began to climb. To one not raised among the rocky slopes of Cimmeria, the wall might have seemed unscalable. Years spent as a thief in the rich cities had honed his skills to such an extent that an ancient, wind-scoured wall such as this was nearly as climbable as a ladder.

The true trick was in not being seen or heard. He had chosen a dark tunic for this purpose and had further stained his skin with soot. To avoid the likelihood of noise, he was unarmed except for a dagger thrust through his sash in back. His sandals were hung by a lace around his neck as he climbed, and every so often he stopped and listened for sounds from above.

He had spent the evening observing the walls and had chosen a spot where the guards seemed to be fewest and least vigilant. As he had anticipated, there was a place where the wall was high and the nearby terrain was rough and rocky. Because nobody expected a serious attack across such ground, there were only a few sleepy guards atop the battlements, and such attention as they devoted to duty was given over to the far encampment of the enemy.

As he neared the top of the wall, he paused. Just above him was a guard leaning on a spear and talking to a distant comrade. Suddenly, to his right, a swarm of fire arrows arched over the wall and the guards on that sector cried out in alarm. One of them drew back from the battlement, snatching at a burning shaft embedded in his shield.

With a sublime disregard for proper discipline, the guards above Conan left their post and rushed to see what was happening. He had counted on just such unprofessional behavior from drafted civilian troops. The soldiers would be reserved for the points of likely attack.

The instant the post above him was vacated, Conan was over the parapet in a tigerlike surge of perfectly honed muscles. Once on the wall-walk, he crouched for a moment, getting his bearings. The fire arrows were still causing a commotion to his right. He had instructed several of his men to fire the blazing shafts for a few minutes after he reached the top of the wall. To his immediate left he saw a stair leading down to the streets below, and he darted silently to the top step and descended. Halfway down he paused at the sound of voices from above.

"They've stopped shooting," said a guard.

"Any fires?" demanded an authoritative voice.

"All out," reported another voice. "Shall we raise the alarm, sir?"

"Nay," said the voice of authority. "It was just harassing fire. They want to keep us sleepless and wear down our nerves. And just what are you two rogues doing away from your posts? Get back to your places or I'll have you flogged at sunrise for dereliction of duty!"

Conan grinned. He knew well the woes of an experienced soldier forced to command untrained louts. He faded into the twisting lanes of the city. There were many people in the streets, most of whom were rolled into blankets and robes, seeking the relief of sleep before the dawn of another monotonous day.

The sound of gushing water drew him. At a corner, a fountain poured from a shell-shaped pitcher, held by a little goddess, into a marble basin. Hurriedly he washed the soot from his face and limbs.

With his appearance restored, he was able to walk

more openly. There was no great risk of attracting attention. The city was packed with people, many of them foreigners from the caravans, and Conan bore not the slightest resemblance to any of the Hyrkanians. With plenty of time before sunrise, he made a leisurely progress in the direction of the prince's palace.

The welcome sounds of a tavern drew him and he stooped through the low doorway, brushing aside a silken hanging as he entered the single, spacious room. The patrons were foreigners for the most part, caravaneers from a score of nations. Among them were a small number of city men. In rich Sogaria, even this comparatively humble establishment was luxuriously appointed, displaying walls of fine stone and furniture of exotic woods. Everywhere there were hangings of the intricate embroidery for which the city was famed.

A serving wench placed a platter of bread, fruit and cheese before him, and he ordered a pitcher of wine. It seemed that these foodstuffs were not rationed yet. Joints turned on spits over a charcoal fire, but that was to be expected. The rule in a siege was to slaughter and consume livestock first, the better to save on fodder and grain. Fresh fruit, greens and olives and other perishables went next. Last to be eaten were cheese, dried beans and peas, and the grains, which would last indefinitely if the rats and weevils could be kept from them. On no more evidence than this room around him, Conan could report that the city of Sogaria was confident and of no mind to surrender. The city was also certain that the siege would last no more than a few weeks. Inexperience could explain this surety, but he wondered about it.

A group of young men entered, swaggering in armor they plainly were not accustomed to. They looked about for an empty table and spied the one at which Conan sat. They took seats at the table without asking permission and called for the serving wench.

One of them glowered at Conan. "You look able-bodied," the youth said. "Why are you not in arms for the defense of the city?"

Conan put on the look of a simpleton. "I stranger. Not speak your tongue well."

"Shouldn't be allowed," said another young man. "Foreigners taking refuge within our walls and not taking part in the fighting."

"Leave my customer alone," said the serving wench. "The difference between him and you is that he is paying for his fare, whereas I must feed you layabout knaves for free as long as you wear the city's colors."

"Only fair," said a young hero, "since we risk life and limb for you helpless civilians. Bring us your best food and wine."

"Food, yes," she said, "but wine you must pay for. The prince wants you healthy for battle, but he will not pay for your drunken revels. Pay up or drink water."

"Water!" said a young man with a drooping brown mustache. There was true horror in his voice. "I had heard that a siege was hell on earth, but I had not imagined anything so ghastly."

Conan gestured toward his pitcher. "I share," he said.

Instantly the four young men were his close friends.

"I always said that it was a fine policy, protecting the strangers within our gates," said the one with the mustache.

They helped themselves to the pitcher and agreed that the foreigner was a fine and upstanding man. Conan knew that this joviality would last until the wine ran out. They conversed, paying little attention to him, a mere ignorant foreigner.

"Did you hear?" said one. "The authorities think that it was Manzur who got that messenger drunk and left the city with his horse and apparel."

"I always knew he would do something like that," said another. "After all his boasting and his poems of war and heroism, as soon as he has a chance at glory, he leaves his post and deserts."

"I for one do not think he has turned coward," said the one with the mustache. "A fool, yes. A coward, no. He probably hatched some scheme to go out and assassinate the Hyrkanian leader all by himself."

"Aye," said another. "Riding alone into enemy lines was not the act of a coward. And for all his boast and bluster and awful verses, Manzur is probably the finest swordsman in the city."

"Little matter," said the one who had first spoken. "Coward or hero, the poor fool is undoubtedly dead by now."

Conan remembered the prints of muffled hooves and the two men dead from two expert sword blows.

"That stands to reason," said one. "I think we should drink to the shade of our dead friend. Is there anything left in that pitcher?"

The one with the mustache peered into the vessel. "Empty as poor Manzur's head. Foreigner—" But when they looked, Conan had gone from their midst as silently as a wisp of mist.

Outside, he made his way to the palace. There was a chance that people would be up and talking and that he might learn something of interest. This early in the siege, the inhabitants would still be excited and restless. They had yet to learn the deadly tedium of siege warfare.

He crossed a public garden full of refugees from the country, huddled in makeshift tents and shacks, looking forlorn and miserable. Rustuf was right, he thought. If the siege were to be a long one, these people would suffer terribly. They would soon wish they had stayed in the countryside.

With the eye of an expert, Conan scanned the low wall surrounding the palace. Climbing would be no problem, as his first glance revealed. The stones were large and rounded, not cut flat and polished. There were vines and other growths as well. He saw no guards patroling the top. That was to be expected. Most of the guards would be defending the city walls now, and would fall back to the palace only if the enemy gained the city.

The plan of the wall was irregular. Over the centuries, new wings of the palace had been built and sections of the wall had been demolished and expanded to accommodate them. The result was a great many angles and corners. He explored until he found an apt cranny, well away from the nearest crowds and gloomy enough to hide a climber from casual observation. With a final look around, he removed his sandals and hung them around his neck.

Swift as a lizard, Conan climbed the wall. Within a few seconds he had gained its crest and lay atop the parapet on his belly, eyes and ears sharp for sign of guards, strolling courtiers, or lovers seeking privacy. All was silent. Crouched low, he ran along the top of the wall, seeking a part of the rambling structure where the city's most important men might be planning their defense.

He passed wings of servants' quarters, stables, guards' barracks and sweet-smelling harem apartments. At last he found a broad, low structure from which poured bright illumination. After the fashion of the eastern lands, it had thick walls and small, high windows, against the blazing heat of the semi-desert surrounding the city. It was from these high windows that the light poured. In the center of the building's tiled roof there was an opening to admit light and whatever rain might fall. Conan guessed that there would be a pool beneath the skylight. This had the look of a council chamber, and by the light coming from the windows, it was in use.

One side of the structure abutted the wall that Conan was traversing, and he silently stepped onto its tiled roof, moving cautiously lest he disturb a loose tile. He considered going to an edge of the roof and hanging head-down over one of the windows, but the skylight seemed more promising. He edged his way up the gently sloping roof to the rim of the opening and cautiously peered within.

As he had anticipated, there was a rectangular pool in the center of the room. He could just make out the knees of a line of figures seated along one side of the chamber. They were obviously facing a person or persons seated on the opposite side of the pool. All of the knees were richly dressed in silks except for a few that were armored. The armor was gold-chased and elaborate. These were important men. Clearly, he had come to the right place. They were apparently wrapping up a lengthy argument concerning the number of horses within the city walls.

"We wrangle over nothing here, sire," said a voice that seemed to come from behind a pair of the armored knees. "The question is not the beasts. We can always eat them should they prove too numerous. The problem is that we have taken in every two-legged creature within a score of leagues!" There were murmurs of agreement. Thus encouraged, the speaker went on. "I mean no disrespect, sire, but it is madness to allow so many useless mouths and bellies into a city facing siege! Not only able-bodied men who can help with the defenses, but women, children and foreigners, who have no stake in preserving our city.''

"And on top of that, sire," said an elderly voice, "there is no rationing either. Should the siege not be lifted within a single moon, the people shall suffer grievously.''

"Gentlemen," said a voice from the other side of the pool, "what would you have me do? I am the sworn protector of my people. Should I deny them the refuge of Sogaria's walls after they have obediently paid their taxes all their lives? Should I cast out the caravaneers who have made this city rich, perhaps thereby leading them to take their goods and beasts to some city other than Sogaria? I wish to keep the reputation of our splendid city stainless so that east and west may know that this is the safest route by which to transport goods. Without the caravans, we will wither and die like a vast grapevine once the single stem has been cut.''

There were ritual murmurs that this was, indeed, wisdom.

"Besides," continued the man who, Conan guessed, was the prince, "you worry too much about this siege. Any day now I anticipate word from the mage, Khondemir, that he has reached his destination, and shortly thereafter the savages will be in full pursuit.''

"He has been gone for many days, sire," said the armored speaker, "and we have seen none of his messenger birds. A thousand picked cavalrymen of the Red Eagles away when we most need them! All off chasing into the Steppe of Famine after this supposed City of Mounds. I for one have no faith in this Turanian mountebank, sire.''

"Enough," barked the prince. "I have chosen our course, and it is for the rest of you to follow. Now, my treasurer, let us speak of the loans by which the unfortunate landowners and peasants may restore their ravaged homes and farms.''

Conan edged back from the skylight. The foregoing conversation had been enigmatic, but he was certain that it was important. He remembered the consternation of the *kagan* and the other Ashkuz when he had mentioned the enemy excursion into the Steppe of Famine. Now he had another location: the City of Mounds, whatever that might be.

A few minutes later he was in the streets of Sogaria once more. So that was why the Sogarians were taking few of the usual measures common to sieges. Their prince expected some sort of sorcerous aid from Khondemir. He remembered the name from the Turanian message the *kagan* had given him to translate. What the connection might be was a mystery, but he had come here to gather intelligence, not to interpret it. He made for the nearest city wall.

When Conan returned to the camp, the *kagan* was away on one of his ceaseless inspections of the far-flung units of his horde. The sun was up and Conan visited one of his unit's cookpots for breakfast, then inspected the men at their daily weapons practice. Satisfied that all was in order, he went to his tent to get some long-delayed sleep.

Rustuf woke him in early evening. ''Get up, Conan. The *kagan* wants your report.''

Conan sat up and stretched. ''The *kagan* will not hear my report for hours. First I will have to sit through a banquet for his allied chiefs while they ignore me. Then I shall render my report after the rest have left. I do not know why he does not just summon me when he is ready to listen.''

"Perhaps," opined Fawd, "he desires that your beauty be an ornament to his banquet." Conan cast a malodorous saddle blanket at the Turanian, who ducked adroitly.

As he had expected, Conan had to endure the lengthy banquet while the *kagan* flattered his more-important allies and listened to the reports of his horde leaders and that of the Khitan engineer. The Khitan spoke at some length of how he would construct sidewalls for the ramp, filling the interior with earth and rubble. His assessment of the enemy's firepower at the most auspicious site for the ramp indicated that the construction would cost approximately five hundred slaves per work day. The *kagan* decided that this was reasonable attrition.

The horde commanders, whose concept of masonry was limited to a circle of stones around a campfire, were forced to sit through this dry, technical summary. They fought hard to hide their boredom, unaware that the *kagan* wanted the siege of Sogaria to be a lesson for them, that they might serve him better in the future conquests they would undertake for him.

Conan stifled his yawns and endured. He ate mightily, drank moderately, and awaited his chance to give his report and be away. At length the banquet broke up and he stood as Bartatua dismissed his guests.

"Now, Conan," said the *kagan* when the others were gone, "what did you learn in Sogaria?"

"They expect a short siege," the Cimmerian said.

"What makes them so—" But the *kagan* was interrupted. A sound of drumming and chanting came from without the tent, accompanied by rhythmic rattling and the high, wild skirling of pipes.

"What now?" growled Bartatua.

The evil, snag-toothed countenance of Danaqan appeared in the tent's doorway. With a demented leer, the old man shook his rattle and cast colored powders about the interior. When the powders touched the flames of torch or brazier, they exploded into brilliant light and evil smell.

"What is it, shaman?" Bartatua demanded.

"*Kagan*, with my fellow shamans I have detected evidence of a dire plot being drawn against you. We devote ourselves wholeheartedly to your welfare, and this night we have found that someone within the camp seeks your life. Come join us without, and by our arts we shall detect who this might be."

Bartatua glowered at the old man from beneath lowered brows. "Very well, shaman, but you had better have better proof than just a pointing finger. If you seek to discredit some loyal man in order to weaken me, I shall have your filthy hide flayed from your body."

The old man grinned and nodded. "Fear not, *Kagan*. When we find the guilty one, there will be no doubt of his iniquity. Our gods will not be mocked."

As the *kagan* walked to the doorway, he turned to Conan. "Cimmerian, stay you here. I still want your report. This ancient mountebank should not keep me long."

Conan paced for a few minutes, then threw himself on a low divan of wool-stuffed leather. With the thumb of his left hand he pushed his sword guard, loosening the blade in its sheath. He did not know but that this event portended some assault upon him by the shamans, and he did not wish to be caught unaware. His swiftest horse was tethered outside, but he regretted that he had not taken the precaution of tying his provision-stuffed saddlebags behind his saddle before coming here. This evening's doings might end in an urgent need for sudden flight.

"I see you prosper yet further, barbarian." The voice came from the curtain behind Bartatua's seat. Conan rose as the Vendhyan woman came around the arras. She wore fluted silver breast cups with large, smoky-red rubies in their centers, and a similar ruby cast its red glare from her navel. A silver belt rested low about her hips, and from it depended an ankle-length skirt of sheerest black silk. Her feet were bare except for numerous rings upon her toes.

Conan bowed. "In this camp, my lady, to be called a barbarian is no distinction. And if I prosper, it is because I serve the *kagan* faithfully and he rewards such service generously."

"You are a careful man, Cimmerian," she said. "I had thought you a mere brainless oaf, a swaggering bravo with a strong sword arm and little else. It seems I was wrong. You and I got off to an ill start, Conan. I would like to make things easier between us. You serve the *kagan* with your warrior skills. I serve him not only as concubine, but as advisor. Let us have an end to this enmity. It serves no purpose and harms only ourselves."

"I too, would see an end to these disputes," said Conan cautiously. "I have no wish to take part in the feuds that surround the *kagan*. I have no ambitions beyond those of a serving soldier. How could I, when the Hyrkanians treat a foreigner at best with grudging tolerance?"

"That is wise," she said. "A man should know the limits of his ambitions as well as those of his capabilities." She came closer to him and her heady perfume rose to his nostrils. Instantly the Cimmerian was on his guard.

"You are cautious, Conan," she said. "You do not commit yourself except to voice your loyalty to the *kagan*. You should have been a courtier." She poured two cups from the *kagan*'s flask and handed him one.

Conan took the wine and sipped lightly. "I hope not,

my lady. I have no taste for the games and subterfuges of the court. I had trusted that there would be no such doings among the Hyrkanians. I find that I was wrong.''

"So you were," she said, coming so close to him that he could feel the animal heat from her body. "Wherever kings play for power, there will be those who do the king's bidding and seek a share in the power. Those servants keep their knives ever sharpened for each other. A wise man learns which of these vassals will rise in the ruler's service and sides with them.''

"I am not interested," Conan said. "Let the *kagan* value my service by my deeds on the field of battle.''

"Yes," she said, "you are not one who manipulates the power of another. You are like one of the great tigers of the eastern forest, strong and solitary. I am much like you, Conan, but I use different weapons.'' Abruptly she wound her arms around his neck and pressed herself against him.

Conan was stunned. She had succeeded in arousing his passions, but even further had she aroused his caution. It could be death to be found thus with the *kagan*'s woman. Her right hand went beneath his heavy hair and he felt a pricking at the back of his neck. With her other hand she snapped the thin chain that held her breast cups together in front. As they fell away, she ripped her skirt from its jeweled belt, laughing.

"Vendhyan slut!" Conan thrust her from him to sprawl upon the divan. "What do you—" He began to lurch toward her, but he was struck by a wave of dizziness. He remembered the pricking at the back of his neck. The woman had poisoned him! He fumbled for his sword hilt, but found that he could not get a proper grip.

"My lord!" the woman screamed. "Save me!"

Conan turned to see the *kagan* standing in the doorway of the tent. Next to him was Danaqan. The old man chortled in obscene glee. "See, *Kagan*? It is as we foretold. The foreigner has brought evil among us. Now, in his drunken lust, he seeks to have your woman!"

"*Kagan*," Conan said, his tongue barely answering his bidding. "I do not—" But a blow from Bartatua's fist struck him sprawling upon the carpet. Inwardly he cursed his unwariness. He saw the *kagan* draw his dagger and raise it high, but then the shaman gripped Bartatua's wrist.

"Nay, my lord, nay! Do not slay him yet. I have a use for him!"

"What manner of use, shaman?" asked the *kagan*, his face still twisted with fury. He resheathed the dagger.

The shaman squatted beside the inert Cimmerian. He took the black-haired head in his hands and stroked it lovingly. "I have certain rites to perform, rites that require a strong victim, one who will not die easily. This foreigner should last far longer than any of your other prisoners."

"Give him to the shaman, my lord!" hissed the Vendhyan woman.

In a display of false modesty, she had wrapped herself in a cloth-of-gold hanging. "He is a treacherous beast who betrayed your trust, after you raised him from slavery to high rank and showered him with favors. He deserves the most degraded of deaths."

"Very well, Lakhme," said the *kagan*. "Take him, shaman. I wish never to lay eyes upon him again."

Danaqan gave a high-pitched call and two of his minions came in. Between them they carried a yoke of thick wood. They placed the yoke behind the Cimmerian's muscular neck and stretched out his arms upon the wooden limbs. His wrists were made fast to its ends with iron manacles, and a heavy wooden U was fastened in place to encircle his neck.

Conan began to regain use of his legs, but his tongue was still paralyzed. The shaman's henchmen grasped the yoke and hauled him to his feet. Bartatua thrust his face within a few inches of Conan's own.

"I would have made you a great general, Conan," he said. "In time, when I came into my empire, I might have made you a king under me. Now I see that I was foolish in trusting a man of alien blood. I should have left you a slave. Better for you as well had you remained a slave. You might have lived longer that way, and your death surely would have been more pleasant."

Conan sought to speak, to tell Bartatua of the treachery of his shaman and his concubine. All he could manage was an inarticulate growl.

"Take him from my sight!" shouted the kagan in disgust.

The group of shamans grasped the yoke by both ends and half-dragged Conan from the tent. Warriors looked up curiously as the Cimmerian was driven through the camp, helped along by lashes from Danaqan's riding whip. His mind still reeled with confusion under the influence of Lakhme's drug. Rage and hatred surged through him at each new indignity.

A final shove from Danaqan sent Conan to his knees. He knew that they were no longer within the camp. He managed to raise his head slightly within the confines of the yoke. Before him was a rough stake set into the ground, and somewhere near a great fire was burning.

"Enjoy these hours of oblivion," said Danaqan. "I want you fully aware for your death. When the moon is past its zenith, we begin our ritual. Never has even the strongest of my victims kept his sanity until death!"

Conan fell forward and the black wings of unconsciousness closed over him.

He awoke to vicious pain in his shoulders and wrists. There was fiendish music playing somewhere. He opened his eyes and saw bizarre forms whirling about a fire that burned with unnatural colors. They moved so swiftly and with such lizardlike suppleness that he could not quite make out what they were doing.

He saw Danaqan, and the youth in women's clothing. He also saw Lakhme. The Vendhyan woman was nude, and she seemed to be the focus of the hellish rite. He was not certain whether it was the aftereffects of the drug affecting his vision, but some of the things she was doing were not only obscene, but looked to be physically impossible.

At last the music slowed and the frenzied participants began to encircle Conan. The Cimmerian hung by his wrists from the crossbar of his yoke. Its neck piece had been removed and the bar hauled to the top of the stake, and Conan dangled by his wrists from his manacles. He tried to close his fingers but found that his hands were numb.

From the circle around him, Danaqan stepped forth, and beside him was Lakhme. The shaman's wrinkled hide and the Vendhyan woman's alabaster skin were glossy with unguents and sweat. Both were streaked with blood, but Conan could not guess its origin, nor did he wish to.

"Are you awake now, foreigner?" Danaqan demanded, cackling lewdly.

"He is conscious," said the concubine. "He is ready to play his part in our rite." Her smile belonged on the face of nothing in human guise.

Conan took stock of himself. He had as yet suffered no severe damage. His armor and other clothing had been removed, and he wore only his loincloth. He calculated that a perfectly timed kick of his feet would snap the neck of both woman and shaman, only to find that his ankles were bound to the stake.

"Let us begin, then," said the shaman in high glee. "The gods are waiting."

An acolyte handed the old man a curved knife with a hideously serrated edge and he reached high with it, waving the blade suggestively before Conan's eyes as the woman hooked her fingers into his loincloth. Then the hellish scene before the Cimmerian halted suddenly, as if a spell of paralysis had been laid upon all present.

Conan saw that instead of a right eye, the shaman now wore the hawk-feathered fletching of a Hyrkanian arrow. At the back of his skull protruded the red-stained head and shaft of the arrow, studded for most of its length with bits of brain and scalp and tiny white bits of bone. Silently the old fiend collapsed in a heap. A panicked screeching arose as the woman-clothed youth threw himself upon the corpse, wailing in crazed grief.

Another shaman spun and fell in a rattling heap, an arrow in his chest. The youth in women's dress looked up at Conan with a glare of maniacal ferocity and snatched up the knife from the shaman's relaxing fingers. He sprang at Conan with the weapon raised high, foam flecking the corners of his screaming mouth, but before he could strike, something described a glittering silver arc across his throat. The youth's eyes went wide as his hand flew to his neck, but he could not prevent the flow of blood that fountained for two yards, splashing the corpses that were beginning to fill the area illuminated by the fire.

The youth staggered away and collapsed as a horse brushed the stake and its rider shook the blood from his curved sword. "Always in the midst of trouble eh, Conan?" said Rustuf. The *kozak* sheathed his blade and cut Conan's ankle bonds with a dagger. The Cimmerian saw Fawd, mounted on a fleet mare, thrust his lance between the shoulders of a fleeing shaman.

"Did you get the Vendhyan woman?" Conan managed to choke out.

"Be still," said Rustuf. He took a heavy hatchet from his saddle and chopped through the chain that bound one of the Cimmerian's wrists. "We are still in great danger, Conan. No, I did not slay her, and it is very bloody-minded of you to be thinking solely of vengeance in your position." He chopped through the other chain and caught Conan before he could fall.

"Of course," the *kozak* went on, "had she been about to do to me what she was going to do to you, I might want to hack her pretty form in twain as well. But no, she slipped away, supple as a serpent."

Fawd came back, leading a large stallion that Conan recognized as his favorite horse. The two helped him to mount, and Rustuf tied his reins around his wrist. His hands were still too numb to grasp them.

"We must ride like the wind now," Rustuf said. "If we are swift enough, we might gain sufficient distance on the *kagan*'s pursuit to get away. We go northwest."

"Why northwest?" Conan asked, the words painful in his throat.

"Because the sky was red and black in that direction this evening," answered the *kozak*. "I know the signs. There is the very grandfather of duststorms brewing there. If it does not kill us, the storm might hide us and wipe out our tracks."

Fawd rode up to them, a string of remounts at his left hand. Conan ignored the agony in his arms and kicked his mount to a gallop. "I will not forget this, my friends. Now, let's ride!"

Eleven

Ishkala brooded in her tent. Two nights earlier they had arrived at their destination in the featureless Steppe of Famine. The mixed column of horsemen, now some two thousand strong, had been following a tiny stream, one barely adequate to water the mounts each evening. The land was so flat, so utterly without points of reference, that the mind reeled and grew disoriented. Only the sun, moon and stars provided any sense of direction.

Blindly, they had followed the directions of the Turanian mage, Khondemir, and unerringly he had guided them to this place, the City of Mounds. This was the sacred burial ground of the Ashkuz, where the clan chiefs and *kagans* had their funeral mounds. The sides of her tent were rolled up for the sake of ventilation, and she studied the eerie scene around her with dread. This was an uncanny place.

A high, earthen rampart enclosed a burial ground many acres in extent. The entire area was filled with the mounds. Some were as tall as a man, but many were three or four times that height. A few were immense, towering to crests eighty or more feet above the level of the steppe.

Atop many of the mounds were standards bearing the skulls of beasts and men and varying numbers and colors of horses' tails. From many depended banners of bright silk, most of them ancient and rotted. These standards were not fashioned of wood, such as those carried by the nomads on their migrations, but of imperishable bronze. Everywhere were the skeletons of men and horses. In some places skeletal warriors, still helmed and armored, sat upon equally skeletal steeds, ready for some ghostly battle, bound to stakes or frameworks to keep the semblance of life.

"Awesome, is it not?" said a voice near her side. She looked up to see the wizard, Khondemir.

"It is an evil place," she said. "Raised by live savages to the memory of dead savages. I would be away from here."

"Ah, but our work here is not yet finished." The day before she had seen the mage walking about the City of Mounds, making some sort of sketch. That evening he had released two more of his messenger birds. "Now is a time of waiting, while I prepare my spells that shall save our beautiful city of Sogaria."

"I wish you well, then," she said. "I would be away from here as soon as possible." She looked at the huge mound before her tent. "Did the savages truly build this place?"

"They did," he assured her. "While the nomads have little liking for manual labor, they are capable of prodigies to do honor to their dead chiefs. When one of the greatest of them dies, they will import many slaves to do most of the work. Last night I communed with the spirits of this place and learned much of its history. The

City of Mounds is old, even more ancient than the Ashkuz themselves dream.''

He gestured broadly, taking in the whole of the necropolis. ''What we see here are the most recent tombs, most of them less than two thousand years old. But mounds far more ancient once stood here, only to subside back into the earth in the fullness of time. This place is richly imbued with magical force. It is a nexus of powers that no ordinary human can feel, but one readily detectable by a sorcerer of high ability.''

She shivered, but not because of the cutting steppe wind. ''I have no love for such things.''

''When last the tribe rebuilt the rampart,'' he went on as if she had not spoken, ''its people raided the border towns for months, taking all the slaves they could catch. That was more than a hundred and fifty years ago. They gathered more than twenty thousand and began driving them here. More than half of them died of hunger and thirst on the trek. Many died in rebuilding the earthen wall with only the crudest of tools. When the work was done, all of the survivors were slain as a sacrifice and to preserve the secret of this place.''

''I can believe it,'' she said. ''The savages are inhuman to all who do not belong to their nation.''

He smiled thinly. ''They are no more merciful toward themselves.'' He pointed to a mound a hundred paces distant. It was three times the height of a tall man. ''That is the resting place of a mighty *kagan*. When he was slain in a far war, his body was preserved with herbs and embalming and brought to this place, along with tribesmen and slaves to do the labor. The mound was raised and consecrated, and the *kagan*'s body laid therein. When the obsequies were over, his wives and concubines were strangled and placed in the mound with him, along with fifty of his horses.

"Last of all came fifty young warriors, all of them volunteers. A framework was built for each man and his horse. The horse was slain and then transfixed through the body from tail to neck with a wooden stake. This stake was placed across the framework so that the horse's hooves dangled a few inches from the ground. Then the youth was strangled and likewise impaled, the stake holding him upright and its lower end fitted into a socket in the stake running lengthwise through the horse. Then horse and man were harnessed and armed to stand guard for eternity. This was done to fifty young men of good family. Is this not the mark of a mighty race of conquerors?"

"I think you admire them, wizard!" she said scornfully.

"Indeed I do," he said. "Once my people, the Turanians, were such a race, savage and ruthless, holding only contempt for lesser breeds. In time, though, they became weak, absorbed by the softness of the civilizations they conquered. Yes, these Hyrkanians are crude, but they have the virtues of the uncivilized. They respect only strength: the power of arms and the power of magic. Their way with enemies is to crush them utterly. They honor their dead with blood sacrifice and think nothing of slaying other peoples by the thousands, simply to be rid of them. Such a people, with proper leadership, can shake the earth."

"Then let us hope," said Ishkala, "that they never have that leadership."

That night Ishkala grew restless. There were faint sounds from the camp around her. The nearby Sogarian Red Eagles were subdued, conversing in quiet voices by their small fires. Their spirits were oppressed by the eerie surroundings, the ghastly mounted skeletons, and the brooding mounds of the *kagans*.

Somewhat louder were the villainous Turanians, encamping by themselves in a different sector of the City of Mounds. More adventurous or merely more irreverent, they did not seem to be so suggestible. A few of the hardier souls had had a go at breaking into some of the mounds in search of rich funeral goods, but soon gave up after a few hours of unaccustomed manual labor.

Ishkala rose from her pallet and dressed in her darkest robes, with a black veil wound about her head and face. She knew not what she sought, but she did not want to attract attention to herself. She extinguished her candle and pushed aside the curtain that served her for a door. The Sogarians did not look up from their fires or their conversations, and she slipped silently from their midst.

She was not certain why, but she wanted to find out what the Turanians were up to. Since leaving the city, nothing that had happened to her had made any sense. Why did the mage need her here for his magic-making? Why had they been joined by a thousand Turanian rogues?

Carefully she picked her way around the countless human bones that gleamed white in the moonlight. They were merely dry bones, she knew, but she avoided them as if they bore some defilement. She walked around the looming mounds and shuddered at their tall, skeletal standards. Her imagination peopled the uncanny scene with a ghostly horde of horsemen, *kagans* and their hideous retinues of strangled concubines and their impaled horses and guards.

Preoccupied with her hyperimaginative thoughts, Ishkala collided with a wooden framework and set a skeletal horse swaying as if with unnatural life. She barely suppressed a scream as the beast's skull shook at her, and she looked up to see a human skull leering from beneath a widespreading helmet of antique design.

She hurried past the dead sentry and circled the titanic mound he guarded, the final resting place of an *Ushi-Kagan* of generations past. Ahead she heard the raucous sounds of the Turanian encampment. Everywhere there flickered fires of brushwood and dried dung, gathered from the steppe. She had heard Jeku complain that at this rate, the Turanians would exhaust all the available fuel within a few days.

She skirted the Turanian camp, listening to the rough songs and brawling voices. Once she stumbled over something lying on the ground and found that it was a corpse. The dead man wore Turanian garb, and there was a gaping wound in his flank. A trail of blood glistened in the moonlight, revealing that he had been dragged thither and left. Evidently the Turanians did not consider their late companion worth the trouble of burial.

Somewhere in the sprawling camp she hoped to find the command group. Perhaps she might overhear something of use. She had little faith in Khondemir's powers of magic and hoped that she might find evidence to persuade Jeku to abandon this mad venture and return to the city.

She saw a large and ornate tent a little apart from the others. Next to its entrance was a small shrine of Mitra, a lump of gummy incense smoking in its brass bowl. Before it burned a fire, and in the light of the fire sat a circle of men. All were Turanian, but these had the dress and aspect of highborn men, unlike the bulk of the force. Even so, they bore a general brutality of look and manner, suggesting that they were embittered exiles, or disinherited sons of the aristocracy.

"It will not be long now, my friends," said one. Ishkala recognized him as Bulamb, the leader who had greeted Khondemir when the two columns had met. "Soon the weary years of exile will be over and we will be great lords again, as is our right."

"I wish I had your sanguine confidence in the mage," said another. His beard was dyed crimson in the fashion of an obscure Mitran sect from northern Turan.

"Have you no faith, Rumal?" Bulamb asked him.

"I believe in Lord Mitra and in my right to the lordship of Sultanapur. The wizard showed signs of great power when first he raised his rebellion against the usurper, Yezdigerd." At mention of the hated name, all spat upon the ground. "But two years ago the insurrection failed and we fled to such refuge as we could find. I follow him because we have no other claimant to the throne, but I cannot share your confidence."

"You should show more spirit," Bulamb admonished. "Two years ago we were forced to act before we were ready. The revelations of a turncoat betrayed us, and Khondemir's carefully prepared spells came to naught. Great wizardry is as much a matter of timing as is that of a military campaign. Even so, the spell of pestilence by which he prevented the royal army from pursuing us saved our lives. Do any here deny that?" He glared about fiercely.

"It is true," said a graying man in splendid armor. "They would have had us between the mountains of Jebail and the Lake of Tears had it not been for the foul-breathed spirit the mage sent among the cavalry as they slept in camp. Not a man fit to ride by morning, and two thousand of them dead within ten days. It was a fell working of magic, but it bought us time to get away with our lives."

"And a starveling life as bandits ever since," said the red-bearded Rumal.

"That is now almost over," promised Bulamb. "Here, in this place of ghosts and powerful spirits, our lord shall work such a spell as no wizard has performed in a thousand years. With the powers he shall summon and the reinforcements he shall procure for us, we will ride into Agrapur in triumph!" His black eyes burned with fanatacism combined with a near-maniacal greed. "We shall seize back the purple towers and fertile lands of our nation from those who reviled us and cast us out. Our Lord Khondemir shall deliver into our hands those who mocked us and drove us from our rightful inheritance, that we may slay them, or torture them, or put them to use as chained slaves, whatever our pleasure may be!"

Ferocious cheers greeted Bulamb's tirade, and even the most downcast of the group seemed to take renewed spirit. A slave went among them, refilling their jeweled cups with rich Turanian wine. While they were preoccupied with their talk of greed and vengeance, Ishkala slipped away.

Now she had something to take to Captain Jeku. Somehow, she had no idea of just how, Khondemir planned to seize the throne of Turan. What all this could have to do with the siege of Sogaria she could not guess, but she was certain that her father wished to maintain peaceful relations with King Yezdigerd. The mad schemes of Khondemir must be abandoned.

"Where are you going, my pretty?" Her heart rose into her throat as someone grasped her arm. She was whirled around to face an ugly, pockmarked Turanian, reeking of wine. He favored her with a spittle-laden grin as he jerked away her veil. His squinting eyes widened at the beauty thus revealed. "I thought to find some spy sneaking about our camp. I never thought to catch such a prize.''

The man dragged her within the light of the nearest fire. The others looked up in wonder and drunken stupefaction. ''Look,'' crowed her captor, ''at what I, Hazbal, have taken captive.'' He ripped away her dark robe, revealing her pale limbs for all to appreciate. She wore only the brief tunic of sheer fabric that she had donned for bed.

''Let me go, you Turanian swine!'' she said. ''I am the royal Princess Ishkala, and the Red Eagles will flay you to the bone for this!''

The man threw back his head for a great gap-toothed laugh in which the others joined. ''Princess, is it? Think you that your father's rank means aught to us? Not a man here can keep count of his death sentences. We'll hang no higher and burn no longer for having a bit of sport with a princess!'' He grasped her tunic and ripped it from neck to waist.

''That's too fine a prize for the likes of you, Hazbal,'' said a huge man as he leaped to his feet. The speaker was shaven-headed and bare to the sash around his thick waist. Great muscles bulged beneath his fat, and scars laced his face and torso. ''I claim her,'' the man grinned, ''by right of rank.''

''Say you so, Kamchak?'' jeered Hazbal. ''You think because I ride in your squadron that you may claim my booty? Well, have her you shall, when I have finished with her but not before, by Mitra!''

The shaven-headed man flushed scarlet. ''You would defy me, you petty, crawling carrion worm? I will not endure this!''

Hazbal shoved Ishkala, causing her to fall in a sprawl of shapely limbs amid the pack of grinning bandits. In an instant her wrists and ankles were pinioned.

"Hold the stakes while this game is settled," cried Hazbal. From his sash he drew a short, curved dagger, shaving-keen on both edges and tapering to a needle point.

"Yes," said Kamchak, "let us dance together, my friend. A little exercise sharpens the appetite for finer things." He drew a similar dagger and advanced on Hazbal, crouched low and balancing on the balls of his bare feet.

"Save your breath for you will not draw many more of them, you great tub of pig's offal," Hazbal warned. The smaller man darted in, his dagger sweeping up to gut his opponent. But Kamchak, despite his bulk, was nimble, and he easily evaded the attack by springing back.

As the dagger passed by his belly, Kamchak whipped his blade sideways, missing Hazbal's throat but taking a tiny piece from his earlobe. Kamchak smiled broadly as the blood flowed from the trifling wound. "First blood to me!" he taunted.

"It will be last blood for me," said Hazbal with an equally wide smile. His blade described a swift, broad X in the light of the fire, a double feint that caused Kamchak to draw back slightly. As the bulky torso withdrew, Hazbal's dagger plunged downward to slice at the advanced thigh.

Kamchak's trouser leg parted and blood flowed, but the huge man paid it no heed. As Hazbal's blow carried him forward, his shoulder was exposed for an instant, and Kamchak's blade drew a scarlet line from the tip of the shoulder to the elbow.

Both men sprang apart to take stock of their wounds and to plan their next attack. The spectators cheered their delight in the blood and the excitement, in the glorious spectacle of two men fighting to the death to be first with the beautiful captive.

The smiles were gone now and the combatants snarled as they slowly circled one another, crouched like beasts, arms spread with knives ready to cut and stab. They had forgotten the woman and wanted only to kill. Hazbal slid forward and stabbed toward Kamchak's belly. As the bigger man brought his left hand down to block the blow, Hazbal's dagger flicked up and over the blocking arm to lance toward Kamchak's neck.

Kamchak had not been deceived by the feint at his belly. As Hazbal's knife darted toward his throat, he leaned far to the right and grasped his opponent's sash. Jerking Hazbal forward, the shaven-headed man buried his dagger to the haft in the smaller man's belly, twisting the blade in the wound to thoroughly eviscerate his opponent. As Hazbal fell with a ghastly grimace, Kamchak jerked his knife loose with a sickening sound and laid the edge beneath the other man's ear. With a powerful slash, he severed jugular and windpipe, sending a fountain of blood arcing into the fire, where it burst into a cloud of foul-smelling steam.

With an evil laugh, Kamchak cleaned his blade on his late opponent's vest as he accepted the plaudits of his companions. They praised his excellent dirksmanship and slapped his back with sycophantic good fellowship.

Ishkala stared in wide-eyed horror as the huge man advanced upon her. His torso, slick with sweat and blood, gleamed in the lurid firelight. His right arm was red from elbow to fingertips as he resheathed his now-clean dagger. He leered dementedly, ignoring his wounded thigh and reaching for the woman.

"Haul that carrion away," he said, grasping Ishkala's jeweled girdle and pulling her to him. The overpowering reek of him turned her stomach, but she took a deep

breath, preparing to voice the most powerful scream of
her life. Surely someone would hear.

"Stop." The order, quietly spoken, resulted in instant stillness. Even Ishkala abruptly ceased in mid-
breath her effort to scream. Khondemir stepped into the
firelight, and a shudder of superstitious dread shook
even this hardened pack of killers.

"Release her," the mage ordered.

The group of men around the fire fell back, leaving
Ishkala and her Turanian bandit-captor standing alone.
She expected Kamchak to obediently let her go, but
the man was in no mood for any such action. He had
just slain a rival in hand-to-hand combat for this woman,
and he was not going to surrender his prize at the behest
of some posturing sorcerer.

"Release her?" The Turanian's voice rose to a shriek
and his head shook uncontrollably, showering Ishkala
with sweat and spittle. "I took this woman by my own
hand, wizard. Get thee elsewhere with your chantings
and spells! Or else get a dagger and fight with me for
her, as Hazbal did." The powerful arm tightened around
Ishkala's waist, squeezing the breath from her.

"The knife, is it?" said Khondemir. "Very well, the
knife it shall be."

The wizard raised one long-fingered hand, and light
flashed in a multitude of colors from the lacquered nails
as the fingers performed an unearthly dance. Ishkala
watched closely, but she could not quite credit her own
eyes, for surely human fingers were not capable of such
contortions. So hypnotized was she by the uncanny
motions that she barely noticed when the arm fell from
her waist, releasing her.

Kamchak stood as if stunned, body and face slack.
Slowly one hand went to his sash and closed around the
handle of his dagger. He drew it, an inch at a time.

Ishkala thought the man was preparing to attack the mage, and she could not decide which of the two she would rather see dead. When Kamchak had the dagger drawn, though, he stared at it as if he had never seen it before. As he held it high before him, his eyes opened wide with horror, and Ishkala realized that the man's body was no longer under his control. With torturous slowness, Kamchak reversed the dagger in his grip and took its handle in both hands.

The wizard's fingers continued their unnatural dance as the Turanian placed the tip of the knife against the flesh of his lower belly. With a look of utter madness upon his sweating face, the bandit began to thrust the blade in. He screamed bloodcurdlingly as the tip of the weapon disappeared beneath his skin, and continued to scream as the blade slowly penetrated. As he thrust, there was little blood, no more than a trickle beneath the initial cut. Then he twisted the dagger, bringing its convex edge upward. Gradually he began to drag the blade toward his breastbone.

As the weapon made its ghastly path up the capacious belly, the cut below widened and a mixture of blood and entrails spilled out. For a moment the knife was halted by the solidity of the breastbone. Then, impossibly, it continued its progress with a clearly audible rending of bone, separating sternum and collarbones and splitting the larynx. When at last Kamchak fell backward into the fire, sending up a shower of sparks together with a cloud of foul smoke, the dagger was lodged in his lower jaw.

There was utter silence except for the sizzling and popping noises the fire made. The men dared not move as they eyed the wizard with horror. Khondemir stood as still as a statue, his fingers now at rest, although their tips still glowed faintly. Behind him now stood Bulamb, drawn by the commotion.

"What has happened here, lord?" said Bulamb.

"There has been a slight breach of discipline," said the mage. "I trust there will be no more such lamentable lapses."

"There shall be none, lord," Bulamb assured him.

"Princess," said Khondemir, "come with me." He beckoned with his still-glowing fingers and she obeyed. She was not under compulsion, but she had just seen demonstrated the utter futility of defying the wizard. From the nerveless hand of a Turanian onlooker she took her robe and veil and resumed the garments, then followed the wizard from the firelight.

They passed through the camp to an open space near the earthen rampart, where Khondemir had pitched his tent. The wizard said nothing as he went within, and the princess meekly followed. The interior of the tent was unexpectedly lavish, with low, folding tables, carpets and hangings. A small brazier cast up scented smoke, and several finely wrought bronze lamps illuminated the scene. She saw many books and parchments spread upon the tables, and a number of curious instruments of bronze, silver and crystal, some of them glittering with gold and jewels. These she took to be wizardly paraphernalia. Gratefully she noted that there seemed to be no spirits, familiars, or other supernatural creatures about.

"Why, Princess, were you in the Turanian camp in the dark of night?" The wizard's look was severe, but Ishkala determined not to be intimidated.

"And wherefore not? I am a princess of royal blood, wizard, and I am not accustomed to explaining my actions to any but my father, the prince." She hoped that her regality hid her fear.

Khondemir favored her with a faint smile. "And yet

it was an act of the sheerest folly. Those men care nothing for your high pedigree. You found that out to your great discomfort. No, my lady, do not play the haughty princess with me. There can be only one reason for your irregular behavior: You were spying. What was it that you wished to learn among the Turanians?''

''Spying? How can one spy upon *allies*, Khondemir? Surely such friends as we cannot be holding secrets from one another.''

''Do not try my patience, Ishkala,'' said the wizard. He raised a hand and his fingertips began to glow.

''I wanted to know what we are doing here,'' she said hastily. Clearly, defiance was out of the question. She decided to settle for cold dignity. ''I found by listening to your Turanian rogues that you plan to seize the throne of Turan for yourself. I know that my father knows nothing of this. With the Hyrkanians besieging Sogaria, the last thing he would want is a war with Turan. You cannot embroil us in your mad scheme, wizard, whatever the services you have promised our city!''

Khondemir waved a calming hand. ''Have I asked Sogaria to support my claims upon the Turanian throne in any fashion? Of course not. Please, Princess, take your ease and we shall discuss this.'' He poured wine from a ewer and handed her a goblet. He gestured toward a low hassock, and she seated herself.

''Explain, then,'' she said.

''My dispute with King Yezdigerd, the usurper, is a just one, but I have no intention of asking my adopted city of Sogaria to take my part in what is a civil war. I am the true heir to the throne of Turan. My mother, Princess Konashahr, was the first wife of King Yildiz of Turan. Some months before I was born, certain political considerations caused Yildiz to put my mother away and take another wife, the daugher of a northern satrap whose aid he needed in order to secure his own claim to the throne. That woman is Yezdigerd's mother. She wished to assure that no impediment would stand between her son and the throne of Turan, so she had my mother strangled and ordered that I be slain as well, though I was but a babe of less than two years. Whether Yildiz knew of these things I know not. He was a weak man, and easily led by clever advisors and wives.''

The sorcerer gazed broodingly into his wine, as if descrying the future in its depths. ''But I was not slain. Among the men sent to carry out the foul deed was a guardsman who was a distant kinsman to my mother. He was unable to save his kinswoman, but he managed to slay the assassins before they reached the nursery. He spirited me to the family lands, bordering the desert north of Samara. There I was placed with obscure relatives and given an education in the arts of true power, while slowly, over the years, my family was stripped of lands and possessions, accused of plotting against the throne, and weakened by the drafting of its young men into military units destined for suicide missions in hopeless wars.

''When Yezdigerd assumed the throne, he continued these persecutions until nothing remained of my family but a few isolated, terrified households in the desert lands . . . and myself. I swore that I would use the dark arts I had mastered so as to take my rightful place upon the throne and restore the fortunes of my family. I will expunge even the memory of the usurper, Yezdigerd, from the histories of Turan!''

''I see,'' said Ishkala judiciously. She did not bother to give the story either credence or denial. She was wise enough in the ways of nations to know that with the accession of each new monarch, other claimants sprang from the ground like mushrooms. Long-lost sons and brothers of the dead king appeared in abundance, each with a little following of fortune-hunting lackeys prepared to swear to the legitimacy of the claim.

"Excellent. You will appreciate, then, that my meeting with my supporters here has nothing to do with my services on behalf of your father. It merely provided me with a convenient opportunity to carry out certain policies of reorganization without these actions coming to the attention of Yezdigerd. Meanwhile, our numbers are doubled, always an advantage in perilous times when attack may take place at any moment."

"Very wise, Khondemir, and very efficient." She sought to refrain from sounding sarcastic. Khondemir seemed satisfied, but she suspected that his attitude was more that of disdain than of concern. This gave her much food for thought. If he was little concerned with whatever report she tendered her father, was it because he did not expect her to live long enough to see her father again? A sudden chill seized her. "Will you tell me why I am here?"

The mage waved a hand airily, and streaks of colored light hung for a moment in the space through which his fingers had passed. "A mere . . . linkage, my dear. I labor on behalf of your distinguished father. Since he cannot be present at the time the major ritual is performed, I must have an . . . assistant who is of his near blood. He needs his sons in the defense of the city, so his eldest daughter was a logical choice. Do not be alarmed, child. I shall only require your aid briefly, in one short but crucial phase of my ritual. After that, the threat of the Hyrkanians shall be no more and you may go as you please."

Ishkala was well aware that the wizard's words, even if true, carried a double meaning. She was in deadly danger. "When," she asked, "is this ritual to take place? I am anxious to return to my city."

"On the fifth night from this," Khondemir said, "the moon shall be waking, the stars shall be in their proper order, and all shall be ready. Then we shall dispose of the Hyrkanian threat."

"Very well, Khondemir," she said with her best attempt at regality. "I wish you had told me these things ere now. It would have saved us both much trouble and embarrassment this night."

"Trouble, Princess?" Khondemir echoed, his eyebrows arching. "What trouble?"

As Ishkala returned through the dark, brooding night to her tent, she knew that her danger was intense. Where was Manzur? Just now she needed a rescuer, however unrealistic he might be.

Twelve

Conan awoke when his horse started, jerking the rein tied around the Cimmerian's wrist. He sprang from the ground where he had been sleeping, his hand on the hilt of his sword. What had disturbed the beast?

As Rustuf had predicted, they had ridden into the duststorm with the pursuing Hyrkanians visible in the distance behind them. In the storm they had managed to shake pursuit, but they had also become separated. As the wind subsided, Conan saw no sign of the Hyrkanians or of his two companions. He had spent the last hours of darkness in fitful sleep, ever ready to leap up and ride at the first sign of the Hyrkanians.

The dawning light of day paled the sky above the eastern horizon, and against that light Conan saw the silhouette of a lone horseman. Was it Rustuf or Fawd, or perhaps a Hyrkanian separated from his fifty? He decided to await the rider's arrival. If it were an enemy, a single man was not sufficient threat to give Conan cause for flight.

As the man neared and the light grew, Conan saw

that the horseman wore the uniform of a Sogarian messenger, complete with light armor and yellow plumes. The man appeared to be dejected, staring gloomily at the ground as his mount ambled along at a leisurely pace. What might this apparition portend?

"Good day to you," said Conan as the man drew near. The rider, whom Conan could now see was a very young man, looked up in great astonishment.

"What manner of savage are you?" he demanded.

"The best kind, a Cimmerian. And what might you be doing out here on the steppe? Surely there can be few recipients for messages in this desolate waste."

"I am not a messenger. I am Manzur Alyasha, poet and hero. By my own hand, I slew two Hyrkanians with two strokes of my sword."

So this was the mad poet and swordsman of whom the youths at the inn had spoken. Conan smiled grimly. Every youth thought himself the mightiest of warriors after his first blooding. The boy, thin-skinned and touchy, saw the smile and took it for an insult.

"I see that you do not believe me. Trifle not with Manzur the Poet, foreigner. I was trained by the greatest of Sogarian swordmasters. Doubtless you are some caravan guardsman and think yourself to be a warrior, but do not confuse yourself with the likes of me." He stared down haughtily, but the effect was somewhat spoiled by his helmet, which sat slightly askew.

"I do not," Conan replied. "I have served in a dozen armies, in every rank from spearman to general. I have commanded fleets of raiding ships on the Western Sea and the Vilayet. I have fought in every kingdom west of Khitai. And I have slain far more than two horse-archers who were not handy with swords."

"And what is so mighty a warrior doing out here on

the steppe with naught but a single horse?'' the young man asked sarcastically.

"Until recently I was an officer in the horde of Bartatua, the Hyrkanian. A misunderstanding arose and I had to flee. Just now—''

"Bartatua!'' Manzur exclaimed. "You have been serving with our enemies! No enemy of Sogaria's may live in my presence!'' The youth sprang to the ground and whipped out his blade.

"I no longer—'' But before he could finish his sentence, the lad was advancing on him. Muttering an oath, Conan ripped forth his own blade. All he needed, he thought, was a fight with a vainglorious young fool. He had no doubt over who would win, but even the greatest of swordsmen might be wounded by an ardent amateur, and a minor wound could prove serious in this isolated place.

With a distracting stamp of his foot, Manzur feinted a cut to Conan's knee, only to flip his point up and drive a full body lunge toward the Cimmerian's throat. Conan recognized the move; it was a lunge taught by Zingaran swordmasters, modified for the curved blade of the east. He batted it aside and clouted the youth beside the head with his open palm. Boy and helmet went flying.

"First lesson—''Conan said—''never extend a lunge that far in a real fight. It takes too long to recover when you miss. Your leading knee was so far forward that I could have shattered it with my pommel.''

"I shall remember,'' Manzur said, flushing crimson as he picked himself up from the ground. "Now, defend yourself!'' He launched a flurry of blows, bewildering in their complexity, and for a few moments Conan found his hands full in dealing with them. He had to admit that the boy was swift and skillful.

But Conan was swifter and more skillful. He was, in

fact, dazzlingly swift, and he had the advantages of tremendous strength and many years of experience. At almost any time during the fight he could have killed the lad easily, but he found himself reluctant to do anything as drastic. He was not certain why, but perhaps it was because Manzur reminded him of a much younger Conan, who had been just as conceited and unworldly.

Manzur, tiring fast, essayed a cut to Conan's leading knee, a blow to sever tendons and bring his enemy crashing to the ground to be finished off at leisure. But Conan had other ideas. As the keen blade licked toward his knee, the Cimmerian drew his leg back and the blade passed through empty air. Manzur was left leaning far forward and off balance, and Conan brought his pommel down sharply upon the lad's unhelmeted scalp.

The Sogarian dropped like an ox at slaughtering time. He was blinded by pain and dizzy from the force of the blow, and he could feel blood streaming down his face. As he lay moaning upon the ground, Conan carefully relieved him of sword and dagger. Leaving the lad to recover by himself, Conan went to the horse Manzur had been riding. It was placidly munching the tough, wiry grass and paid him no heed as he examined its burdens. A sloshing skinbag drew his immediate attention, and he sampled its contents. It was the yellow wine of Sogaria, mixed with an equal amount of water, a wonderfully refreshing drink to a man who had been breathing dust for most of a night.

"Have you anything to eat?" Conan asked. "I am starving."

"There is a little parched grain and dried fruit in the left saddlebag," Manzur said. He was sitting up now, rubbing his scalp. It had stopped bleeding, but a lump of heroic dimensions was forming there. He winced at the touch. "Where did you learn to fight so superbly?"

Conan ate a handful of the dried provisions, washed down with the watered wine. "Well, I suppose it is better than starving," he pronounced. He walked over to where Manzur still sat and suffered. "Here," said the Cimmerian, proffering the wineskin. "This will make you feel better."

Manzur took a pull at the wineskin. "It does make the world seem a better place at that. Where are you bound, foreigner?"

"To the west, through Turan and beyond. That is where I was headed when I was captured and ended up in Bartatua's army. Since the *kagan* now wants my hide with which to decorate his tent, the time has come for me to continue my interrupted journey."

Manzur drank more of the wine. "I left my city," he said, "hoping to find my love, Princess Ishkala. Many days ago she was taken from the palace by the Turanian sorcerer, Khondemir. Along with an escort of Red Eagles a thousand strong, they trekked into the northwestern steppe upon some mysterious errand for the prince. I feel in my bones, though, that the wizard's plot is something baleful. I go to find my Ishkala and bring her back safe to Sogaria."

Khondemir. The name seemed familiar to Conan. Then he remembered the message he had translated for Bartatua. It had stated that King Yezdigerd urgently sought this mage who had been involved in treason, or in an insurrection of some sort. And hadn't he heard the name mentioned again on the night he had eavesdropped on the prince's councillors as they sat about the pool in the palace of Sogaria? Conan did not like to deal with wizards, but this had possibilities. "Are you still on their trail?"

"Nay," said Manzur sadly. "In the duststorm I lost the broad trail I had been following. The signs left by a mounted force of a thousand are plain even to a town-raised scholar. But the storm obliterated most of the signs, and I am no hunter to detect the passing of beasts in a bent blade of grass."

"I will ride a way with you," Conan said. "I have been a scout and tracker, and I have hunted all my life. I will know it if we cross the path of a thousand horsemen, even after a storm."

"Splendid!" said Manzur. "And will you also help me retrieve Ishkala?"

Conan thought for a while. "Perhaps. I will know better after I have had a look at the situation."

"Her father will reward you greatly," Manzur said, ignoring that it was the prince himself who had authorized Ishkala's journey with the mage.

"I have no intention of going to Sogaria," Conan said, "for any manner of reward. In the first place, I was but recently leading raids into Sogarian territory. I have encountered few kings who did not value a fort more highly than they valued a daughter. Second, your prince is likely to take a dim view of any who thwart whatever mission the wizard has undertaken."

"Then why are you willing to help?" Manzur asked.

"I have heard somewhat of this man, Khondemir. He has earned the enmity of King Yezdigerd by indulging in a bit of insurrection. It may be that if I take him or at least his head back to Turan, I might make peace between Yezdigerd and myself."

"For a man lacking even a skin of wine or a bag of food," Manzur observed, "you seem to have traveled in exalted circles. Few men have kings as diverse as Bartatua and Yezdigerd thirsting for their blood."

"I wish those two were the only ones," Conan said ruefully. "But we waste time here. Are you ready to ride?"

"I think so," said Manzur, rubbing his head again. "But I do not think I will wear my helmet for some time. By all means, let us go. My heart will be desolate until I am reunited with my Ishkala."

"My stomach will be desolate until we are united with some game," Conan said.

"How will we locate the column?" Manzur asked.

"First we must find a stream," Conan told him. "A thousand horses drink a great deal of water, and streams are few on these plains. Where we find water, there we will find the cavalry."

It was full morning as they rode away. The Cimmerian kept his eyes on the ground. The steppe seemed empty, but Conan knew that it teemed with life. Because of the lack of natural cover, the steppe animals were smaller than those of the woodland, or especially swift, or otherwise adept at flight. Many were nocturnal so as to escape the keen eyes of predators. But all needed water, and Conan knew that when he saw many game tracks converging, water could not be far away.

At a signal from Conan, the two men halted. The mounts were restive and did not want to stop. Their nostrils flared, and they strained westward against the taut reins.

"Stay here for a while," Conan said, his voice barely above a whisper. Slowly he drew his strung bow from its case behind his right leg.

"What is it?" Manzur asked. "Enemies?"

"Better than that," Conan said. "Dinner." He pointed to a slight rise of ground three hundred paces away.

Manzur squinted in the direction indicated and saw nothing. Then he caught a hint of movement just above the crest of the rise. It looked as though someone were waving a small stick back and forth.

"What is it?" he asked. "An animal?" His mouth began to water.

"Some breed of antelope, I'll warrant," Conan said. "There will be more than one, and they are drinking at a stream over there. That is why our mounts are eager to run. They smell the water. I have been smelling it myself for the last two miles." He selected an arrow with a broad hunting head and fitted it to the string. "Wait here."

Silently he kicked his horse to a swift gallop. The beast bolted readily, the smell of water making it nearly frantic. This close to water the grass was thick, and the horse's hooves made little sound. As he surged over the crest of the rise, Conan saw perhaps twenty small fork-horned antelope drinking from a little stream. The animals stood in startled paralysis for a split second before they went flying in all directions.

In huge, graceful leaps the antelope fled, their criss-crossing, diverging paths bewildering to the eye. The Cimmerian, though, had picked his target in the moment when the animals had been frozen in surprise. It was a small, fat buck, and Conan drew his bow as the beast slanted off to his right. He released the string at the moment the antelope began its fifth leap. Animal and arrow intersected and the creature went down with the shaft buried deep behind its shoulder. It kicked for a moment, then was still.

Conan replaced the bow. He patted his now-quiet horse between the ears. "That was a difficult cast," he told the indifferent mount. "Guyak would have been proud of me."

When Manzur rode up a few minutes later, Conan was busily butchering the antelope. "There is plenty of brush growing here by the water," he told the young man. "Gather us some dry wood and we shall feast."

An hour later the two sat by a smoking fire as ribs and forequarters sizzled over the low flames. Manzur's stomach rumbled as he sniffed the savory aromas, but he could not suppress a twinge of guilt.

"It seems improper somehow," he said, "that we should be sitting here indulging ourselves while we have yet to find the trail of the Red Eagles."

"We would do little good riding our horses to death and starving ourselves," Conan pointed out. "There is forage and water in plenty, and we can fortify ourselves with this meat. Besides, we've found the column. It passed by here a few days ago. The signs are all around. They have been following this stream."

Manzur gazed about in the dimming light. He could see nothing by way of signs. "Truly?" Instantly he cheered up. "Then soon our task will be accomplished."

"Do not be so confident," Conan warned. "Snatching your ladylove from the midst of a thousand fighting men may prove no easy task. Not to mention the wizard, who may have other plans for her."

"No matter," Manzur said. "You and I are heroes, so what may we not accomplish?"

Conan lifted a skewer from the fire and began attacking a rack of ribs. "I cannot share your sanguine complacency, but perhaps I shall feel better with a full stomach."

Manzur slipped a hand beneath his tunic under his armor and withdrew a sheaf of parchments. "What you need is inspiration, Conan. Let me read to you some of my heroic verses."

"Verses?" Conan echoed apprehensively. The songs and poems of his own people he knew by heart, but he had heard few poems of the civilized lands that were to his barbaric taste. Manzur began to read.

The next morning they rode along the tracks made by the Red Eagles. About midday Conan called a halt, dismounted and examined the ground closely, puzzlement writ large upon his features.

"What is it?" Manzur asked.

"They were joined here by another band of horsemen, about equal in number."

"More Sogarians?" Manzur hazarded. "Or do you think they were attacked by the Hyrkanians?"

"Neither," Conan said. "The horses were shod in the Turanian manner. Some wore the reinforcing bar used by the Turanian cavalry. It was not an attack, but a peaceful merging of the two bands." He remounted and the two rode on for a little way. The Cimmerian pointed to the ground, where Manzur could make out little save a chaotic jumble of hoofprints.

"See," Conan said. "The two bands remain separate but ride along a parallel course divided by a half-score of paces. It may simply mean military discipline, but it could also indicate mutual distrust."

"I cannot imagine why Sogarian cavalry would be meeting with Turanian forces in the midst of this wilderness," said Manzur, shaking his head.

"There is much here we do not know," Conan said. "It behooves us to proceed with caution. And these men are not Yezdigerd's cavalry, although some of the mounts are cavalry-shod. Turanian cavalry ride by squadrons in double column, with forward guard and flank security out at all times. These rogues are straggling along in a ragged file any way it suits them, and they have posted no security forces. The cavalrymen among them may well be deserters."

The two men could make better time than the two thousand, and soon the signs of passage were far fresher. The land began to roll gently and they moved into an area that would have seemed flat in most parts of the world but was hilly for the steppes.

"I like not the feel of this place," Conan said.

Manzur looked about. All seemed much as before, save for the slight rise and fall of the terrain. "Wherefore?"

"The grasses and shrubs do not look right," the Cimmerian said, "and the sky is not the right color, somehow. It smells of sorcery to me."

"Then your nostrils are more sensitive than mine," Manzur said. "Perhaps your primitive upbringing, your wide wanderings and frequent conflicts with supernatural enemies, have rendered your senses more acute in such matters. Do you think that some dire wizardry is being wrought near here?"

"It may be so," Conan said. "After all, we trail a wizard. But in some way I feel that it is the quality of this place. I have felt it before, and always in one of those strange, out-of-the-way parts of the world, where other worlds are nigh."

Manzur remained silent, enthralled by this uncharacteristic speech from a man who had seen such things as it is given few men to behold.

"This world is ancient," Conan continued, "far more ancient than the wildest dreams and fancies of philosophers can speculate. I have wandered into places deep in the squalling jungles of the south, and high in the snowy mountains, and in the baking deserts, where things of ancient times survive. In these places I have found buildings of strange green stone, single structures the size of whole cities. I have found races of men and half-men that disappeared elsewhere long before the rise of Acheron, before even Atlantis reared itself from the waves. I have been on an island where bronze statues came to unnatural life."

It began to penetrate Manzur's mind that this Cimmerian was not the inarticulate savage he had at first judged him to be. For a change, he kept his mouth shut and listened.

"Wise men have told me that this earth is covered with strands of sorcerous power as if trapped in a gigantic net. As in a net, there are places where the strands cross and are knotted together. Where these strands cross, there is a point of great power. There are some places where more than two of the strands converge, as when an armorer builds a shirt of mail and brings many rows of steel rings together to expand or taper the garment. At such spots there are truly great concentrations of power.

"There are other worlds besides this one, and they are as distant as the stars. But at the points where many lines of power converge, they may be brought close. I feel that we are approaching such a point. It lies ahead of us, and not far."

"Mitra aid us then," said Manzur, deeply shaken. "And may he aid my poor Ishkala, wherever she is."

The two men crawled on their bellies to the crest of the little rise. They had picketed their horses near the stream, which in this place ran through a gully somewhat deeper than the height of a tall man. They had circled far to the west so they could make their reconnaissance with the setting sun directly at their back, thereby lessening the chance of detection.

"A good thing the land is rolling here," Conan said. "Out on the flat, they could have seen us coming half a league away."

"I have always held," Manzur said, "that the gods have a way of preparing things in the favor of heroes." He tried to match the silent, sinuous grace of Conan's progress through the grass, but could only scramble awkwardly, scraping his knees and elbows in the process.

"Then I must not be a hero," said the Cimmerian, "for the gods have always made my path notably rough. No idle talk now. We are at the crest. Raise no more than your eyes above it. Even with the sun at our back, a sharp-eyed man might see us."

Slowly they elevated their heads and soon they were gazing down upon a startling sight. A high, earthen rampart enclosed a huge, irregular space covered with mounds of varying sizes, some of them truly immense. Within the rampart were established two separate camps. One was an orderly array of identical tents, lined up in military fashion, with a somewhat larger command tent in their midst. The other camp was a haphazard assortment of tents in varying sizes, from simple cloth lean-tos to elaborate pavilions. Some of these tents were pitched directly upon mounds. Smoke rose from many small fires.

Near the entrance to the enclosure two corrals had been established, and all the horses were kept therein save those that were in use. They spied some men in Turanian garb who were flying hawks outside the ramparts, trying to bring down the geese that flew high overhead, their broad wedges arrowing toward the north with the waxing summer.

"What manner of place is this?" Manzur asked.

"A burial ground," Conan said. "Great kings and chiefs have been interred here. Think of the labor that must have gone into rearing those huge mounds."

"What people put their dead to rest here?"

"Those are Hyrkanian standards atop some of the mounds. This must be where they bury their great *kagans* and *Ushi-Kagans*."

"But why," Manzur wanted to know, "has Khondemir come to this place? And why are those Turanians there? You can see that there is little love between the two bands. The Red Eagles have made camp as far as they can get from the Turanians.''

"We know too little to guess," Conan said. "But from the mage's choice of a site, and in consideration of its remoteness, I think he plans some mighty work of sorcery here. I have told you of the great power that converges upon such a place. As to the Turanians, I have told you also that Khondemir was involved in an insurrection against Yezdigerd. Perhaps these are supporters of his.''

"How can we find out?" Manzur asked. "And how can we learn where Ishkala is being kept?"

"Tonight, very late," Conan said, "I will enter that camp and learn all we need to know.''

Manzur gazed at him in open admiration. "Sneak down into that place, where two thousand men guard Ishkala and the wizard? Surely you must be a man without fear! I shall go with you, for I cannot have Ishkala thinking me your inferior in courage.''

"Manzur," Conan said seriously, "those two thousand men are a daunting prospect, and I detest the thought of seeking out a powerful wizard. But there is one thing that fills me with far greater dread.''

"What could place fear in the heart of such a hero as you?" the younger man asked.

"The prospect of spending another night having to listen to your poems.''

Thirteen

Daily the immense ramp climbed higher on the great wall of Sogaria. The gangs of drafted slaves toiled beneath the blazing sun while, above them, the brazen gongs thundered and a deadly hail of missiles rained down. Flimsy barriers of hide and withes were erected for their protection, but these were soon pierced or crushed, and a constant shower of stones, javelins, arrows and other deadly objects took a continuous toll. The slaves who fell were left where they lay, either on the ground beside the ramp or amidst the rubble used as fill between the stone walls of the structure. In the heat of summer, a fearful stench of death soon blanketed the city, as well as the camp of the besiegers.

Bartatua gazed over the site with satisfaction. The ramp was rising by the daily increments the Khitan engineer had predicted, and the wastage of slaves was no greater than he had foretold. At this rate, the supply of slaves should last easily until the ramp was completed.

Even as he watched, a slave was transfixed by a short javelin cast from the rampart above. The wretched man

202

fell screaming onto the growing pile of bodies next to the wedge-shaped structure. Another slave was driven to the place of the newly slain by an overseer dressed in heavy armor. All along the ramp such overseers plied their whips, protected not only by heavy armor, but by broad, rectangular shields borne by slaves.

Stationed near the foot of the ramp was a line of horsemen whose task it was to shoot down any slave who sought to flee from the work site. The archers sat in their saddles, arrow on string, eagerly scanning the area. A shot at a fleeing slave was a welcome diversion from the monotony of the siege works.

"I do not like this way of making war," said a *kagan* who sat his horse next to Bartatua. His swart, eastern-featured face was a mass of scars. "When men cannot ride and shoot, they cannot feel their ancestors riding with them. This kind of war-making," he waved a contemptuous arm toward the ramp, "is no better than farming."

"And yet if we would conquer widely," said Bartatua, "we must master these skills. Fear not. When we have taken the city and the loot is divided, the men will feel well requited for the tedium of this siege. That city," he extended his arm and pointed to the walls of Sogaria, "contains treasure in greater measure than most of our men can imagine. Gold and jewels, silks and spices, and beautiful women, all there for the taking by men who are fierce and bold. Why should the dwellers in cities have these things when we are strong enough to seize them?"

A broad grin appeared between the scarred cheeks of the other. This was the kind of talk a Hyrkanian could understand. "Aye, *Kagan*, when we have those things in our hands, the hardships of this siege will be forgotten indeed! However," he turned somber, "all of us can smell the foul stench from the ramp and the city. This stench portends pestilence. A plague within the city is no matter of concern for us, but how long before a pestilence afflicts our camp? Out on the broad steppe, where the air and water are clean, we rarely suffer from such things. Here, in the midst of all the foulness of a siege, we could lose half our men in the turning of half a moon.''

Bartatua nodded somberly. ''Those are wise words, my friend. This night I shall send out a slave gang to douse the bodies of the dead with oil and set them alight. In this way, the work site will be cleansed and the city-dwellers will be discomfited by the smoke. Should pestilence break out within the city, we shall know it when they begin casting the corpses of men and women over the walls. Should it be a truly terrible plague . . .'' He thought for a moment, then shrugged. ''It would grieve me to burn the whole city in order to cleanse it, but that would be better than taking the plague ourselves. There would still be much gold to salvage, and there will be other cities.''

The other man's narrow eyes twinkled. ''There may be no need for such drastic measures, *Ushi-Kagan*. Let me tell you of an expedient used by my great-grandsire when he took the city of Hiong-Nu, in northern Khitai. Things had fallen out much as at this siege, and pestilence appeared within the city. Of course no man or woman of the city was allowed to come near the forces, but was shot down as soon as within bowshot.

''In time, inevitably, the elders of the city sued for peace. My great-grandsire bade the citizenry come forth, bringing out their dead with them. Then all were marched a half league away and surrounded by mounted bowmen. After that, slaves were sent within the walls to affirm that there were no inhabitants, living or dead, inside the city. Those same slaves were then sent to join the city people. Then all were slain by arrows from a safe distance. The horde waited a full moon, lest the pestilence be lurking for a while in the goods or in the water, after which time they went in and despoiled the place, and the army was never touched by the plague. Was this not a clever way to solve the problem?''

Bartatua laughed loud and long and slapped his fellow *kagan* on the shoulder. ''Would that all my allies give me such good advice, my friend! That is exactly how we shall handle it should things take such a turn at this siege.''

Inwardly his heart exulted. The advice was good, but the address had been better. The man had addressed him as *Ushi-Kagan*, supreme chief! This was the first time one of his allies had saluted him so, and the man was the most powerful of the eastern *kagans*. It meant that they all acknowledged him as the supreme war leader of the Hyrkanian peoples. He knew they would need some time to understand that he was to be their leader in peacetime as well. There was no such concept among them. They would learn, though. They were already beginning to learn. He gazed at his ramp and smiled. The Everlasting Sky was showing all that he, Bartatua, was its favored son!

The Khitan master of engineers came up to them, riding on a camel. The *Kagan*'s horse tried to shy at the foul-smelling beast, but he kept the mount under taut rein. The Khitan was a mere foreigner, but he was a valuable man and Bartatua was already making plans for him to organize a corps of engineers and sappers for future sieges.

''Greetings, *Kagan*!'' called the Khitan.

''Greetings, Soong-Tzi. The ramp proceeds apace, just as you predicted. I am pleased with the work.''

"I live only to please my *kagan*," said the Khitan. From another man the words would have sounded obsequious, but the Khitan was never less than arrogant. It was just the customary floweriness of his nation's ways. The *kagan* cared not in the slightest whether a man was swaggering or humble as long as he delivered results. For a moment he remembered the Cimmerian with regret. He would have been willing to make such a warrior second only to himself, a general and commander of kingdoms, perhaps even a friend. Why had the man been so undisciplined as to attack the *kagan*'s own woman? Almost any other offense would have been forgivable.

"Now that the work has been so well begun, *Kagan*," said Soong-Tzi, "and the surviving slaves are experienced, we can carry on at night if we but have the light. This will shorten the delay in mounting the first storming of the city."

Bartatua eyed the great piles of bodies next to the ramp on both sides. "Yes, master engineer, I think I can provide you with all the firelight you and your teams need." Beside him, his fellow *kagan* whooped with laughter.

The flames from the oil-soaked corpses cast a bloody glare upon the walls of Sogaria. The clouds of billowing black smoke, towering above the groaning and shrieking men who labored on the ramp, were shot through with crimson streaks. The beautiful city had become an analogue of hell, as certain philosophers and religious sects described that undesirable afterlife.

Bartatua and his subchiefs admired the unprecedented sight as they stood outside his great tent. Many drank wine from golden goblets or the skulls of slain enemies. The spectacle of the nightime work on the ramp, illuminated by the lurid glare of the corpse pyre, was matched by the defenders of Sogaria, lined atop their wall and shouting futile defiance at the hated foe.

"This siege will make your name immortal, *Ushi-Kagan*!" shouted a tattooed subchief of the Budini.

"It is a fine sight," Bartatua acknowledged, "but I hope to be remembered for yet better things. When other cities hear of the fate of Sogaria, they will be more amenable to reason."

"Where do we march next, *Ushi-Kagan*?" asked a Gerul chieftain, his green serpent tattoos writhing weirdly in the flickering red light.

Bartatua smiled inwardly. Already his men were looking forward to new conquests. "My plans shall be known only to myself, my friend," he said. "But it will be soon. We shall not tarry long in this place. Only long enough to gather our loot. Slaves will carry the loot to a place I have chosen, far out on the steppe near a great lake. There I shall establish a capital such as the world has never seen. It shall be a great metropolis where the warriors of all the tribes may come and enjoy the loot of the whole world!"

The men growled their enthusiasm for this new idea. Bartatua knew that he had them in the palm of his hand. They would follow him anywhere, and would make his slightest wish their command.

"My capital," he continued, "will not be a mere marketplace for farmers and herdsmen, merchants and artisans. It will be a gathering of all the booty and tribute of the world for the greatest warrior race beneath the Everlasting Sky. Besides the warriors, it will have no inhabitants except the pick of the world's most beautiful slaves, whose only purpose will be to do the bidding of the warriors!"

The growls now changed to wild cheering as this

extraordinary vision took form in their minds. At that moment they truly believed that they would soon be lords of the earth and that the *Ushi-Kagan*, Bartatua, would lead them to that conquest.

"Come, my friends," Bartatua said. "The feast is laid within, and we have many years of triumph and feasting before us."

Laughing and shouting, they went into the tent. The slaves began placing platters before the chiefs, filling their wine cups and bestowing whatever services were called for. At last the commanders were beginning to realize that this was their due, that soon even every humble warrior of Hyrkania would live like a lord, and the chiefs would be kings. The *Ushi-Kagan*, Bartatua, would be a god.

It was with this cheering thought that Bartatua held out his cup—the gold-mounted skull of an enemy—to be filled with wine. As he brought the exotically worked golden rim to his lips, he felt that at last his destiny was at hand.

A sudden silence swept over the tent. Bartatua looked up to see a bird flying in circles beneath the roof. In whispers the superstitious tribesmen speculated upon the meaning of this omen. Bartatua frowned at this trifling incident that threatened to mar his moment of triumph.

The creature seemed to be an ordinary pigeon, but as it flew above Bartatua's table, it stopped and hovered like a hummingbird. Men gasped and snatched at their weapons as the bird began to change form. Others grasped amulets and yammered protective spells.

Bartatua sat calmly sipping wine from the skull. Above him now floated the ghostly form of a man swathed in strange robes. He wore a turban, and his beard was forked. Within the phantom Bartatua could just discern the shape of the hovering bird.

"*Kagan* Bartatua of the Hyrkanian horde of the Ashkuz," intoned a booming voice, "know that I am the great mage, Khondemir of Turan. I now occupy your City of Mounds with a strong force of cavalry. If you would save the sacred tombs of your ancestors, come and do battle, else we shall raze your mounds to the level of the steppe. If you would have proof of what I say, see that which the bird bears. Come and give battle, or be accursed as a sacrilegious coward forever!"

With these words, the image began to fade and the bird dropped dead upon the table before the *kagan*. The chiefs leaped to their feet and began to babble excitedly. Those who were of the Ashkuz were especially agitated.

"*Kagan*," shouted an Ashkuz chief, "what does this mean? Can this unclean creature truly hold hostage the holy place of our ancestors?"

Bartatua raised a hand and when there was silence, he spoke calmly. "I know something of this Khondemir. He is a rogue who is wanted by King Yezdigerd of Turan for treason. Doubtless he has taken refuge within Sogaria. This is some trick, a casting from the city. The wizard knows that the only thing that might cause us to lift our siege would be a threat to our holy place. This is a ruse, nothing more."

"Still," said a Gerul chieftain, "there was that column of cavalry that left the city before we laid our siege. They went north; the signs were there for all to see. And they never returned."

Bartatua remained impassive, but inwardly he was in turmoil. He looked at the dead bird before him. Slowly he detached the message tube tied to one of its legs. He would have preferred to do this when he was alone, but there was no way now to avoid the attention of his chiefs without arousing suspicion. From the tube he drew a tightly rolled coil of parchment. He unrolled it, then spread it to its full size. It was the very finest and thinnest of parchment, made from the dried and stretched intestine of an unborn lamb. It was nearly transparent, and so light that a square four palms in extent could be rolled into the message tube of a pigeon.

As Bartatua puzzled over the parchment, he frowned, then turned deathly pale. "It is true!" he said at last. "This is a map of the route the wizard has taken to the City of Mounds. He has even sketched in the location of the greater mounds so that we would know that he has indeed arrived there."

The assembly erupted into chaos. "What must we do, *Kagan*?" shouted someone. It did not escape Bartatua's notice that the *Ushi* had been dropped.

"We must lift the siege," he said. "This catastrophe takes precedence over all other concerns. Pass the order that the men must mount and ride immediately. There will be plenty of time to come back and resume the siege when we have taken care of this threat to our ancestors."

"But my ramp!" cried the Khitan engineer. "They will demolish it while the army is away. When you return, there will not be enough slaves to build another."

"Aye," said a green-tattooed Gerul. "My people will not like this. They have put much effort into this campaign, and you would have them abandon their loot to save your holy place. It will not sit well with them."

Before his eyes Bartatua could see his carefully built alliance breaking up. And along with the breakup was the destruction of his position as *Ushi-Kagan*. If he would save his nascent empire, it would have to be by a powerful act of will, and it would have to be accomplished before his chiefs left this tent.

"Silence!" he bellowed. In the shocked stillness he went on in a lower voice. "Think you that this is more than a trifling setback on our march to the lordship of the world? Our ancestors are testing us, to see whether we are worthy of our destiny! They wish to know that our reverence for our honored dead comes before all else, and we shall prove to them that it is so.

"Sogaria is merely one city. I shall give you the whole world! Somehow this wizard from Turan has learned of our only vulnerability: that we will abandon any enterprise at any time to protect the resting place of our ancestors. Never again shall this thing be done to us. When we began this siege, it was my plan to deal gently with the Sogarians, to spare all those who would surrender, pay tribute and acknowledge me as their master, but no more."

He glared at the assembled chiefs who had fallen silent, intimidated and impressed by his intensity. "I swear by the spirits of our ancestors, and by the Everlasting Sky, that when Sogaria is taken, every surviving man, woman and child of that city shall be driven barefoot across the steppe to the City of Mounds. There they shall repair the desecrated mounds and build new ones for those who fall in this campaign. When the work is done, they will be crucified there, that their spirits may serve our dead through all eternity. Thus shall the whole world learn the fate that befalls any who would desecrate the holy place of the Hyrkanian race!"

He was well satisfied with the ferocious cheers that erupted from his hearers. He had successfully deflected their wrath from himself and turned it against Khondemir, Sogaria and the non-Hyrkanian world in general. His path to world conquest still lay clear before him.

"Now go to your hordes and tell them to mount. We ride within the hour!"

As the chiefs stormed from the tent, the *kagan*'s concubine came from her listening place behind his throne.

"This is an ill business, my lord," said Lakhme. "But for your quick thinking and powerful speech, our plans might have come down in ruins."

"Aye," he said, glowering, "it was a near thing. I cannot fathom how this could have happened. How did this wizard know of our burial customs? How did he learn the way to the City of Mounds?" The *kagan* took his armor from its peg on a tent post and began to strap it on.

"The Turanian is a sorcerer," Lakhme said. "What can be kept secret from such a one? Perhaps he learned from the spirits of the air, which fly about the steppe, seeing all under the sky. Ask your shamans."

Bartatua allowed himself a mirthless smile. "I am sorry that the Cimmerian escaped my vengeance, but even in his escape he did me a service. He and his two friends slaughtered half of those bone-rattling frauds. I would no more ask them for advice about a true wizard than I would ask jackals how to fight a lion."

"How will you deal with the sorcerer when we reach the City of Mounds?" she asked, anxious to steer his thoughts away from the night of the Cimmerian's escape. She lived in continual fear that one of the surviving shamans would betray her part in that night's activities. She was plotting a way to poison them all at once.

"I know not," he said. "His force of cavalry I count as nothing, although if he truly holds the City of Mounds itself, he has a certain advantage."

"What might that be?" she asked. She knew the

answer, but she could not admit it lest Bartatua suspect her collusion with Khondemir.

"No matter," he said. "We shall kill all the foreigners, at whatever cost to ourselves. Now prepare yourself. We have a hard ride ahead. This time I'll not be able to spare your ivory skin."

"Do not think of such trifles, my lord," she said. "My only concern now is that you maintain your position as *Ushi-Kagan* of all the Hyrkanian hordes."

As she made her preparations for departure, Lakhme felt the satisfaction of a plotter whose every plan is coming to fruition. Only one minor factor remained to disturb her confidence. What had happened to the Cimmerian?

Fourteen

Manzur watched with puzzled fascination as Conan made his preparations for their night's foray. The Cimmerian had reserved some charred sticks from their last fire, and now he began to shave finely powdered soot from their ends. The soot he mixed with rendered fat from the antelope he had killed. When he was satisfied with the mixture, he smeared it over his face and exposed limbs.

"Surely you cannot expect me to cover myself with that nauseating concoction," Manzur said, wrinkling his nose.

"If you wish to accompany me into that camp, you will," Conan told him. "With odds of a thousand to one, our best plan lies in not being seen. We must be as stealthy as Picts. With water and sand, it washes off in minutes. Wounds last far longer, and death longer yet. Also, you will wear no armor. Carry only your sword and dagger, and see that they do not rattle."

Shuddering, Manzur began to smear the foul stuff on his face and arms. To his surprise, the experience was not all that distasteful. In fact, the act brought with it a feeling of taking part in some ancient battle ritual, long lost to civilized peoples. He took out a small looking glass and admired the white flash of teeth in his blackened face. He began to feel very fierce indeed.

Conan caught the look and cautioned the younger man. "Do not think you can take them all on and spirit your Ishkala from their midst. What we seek is knowledge. Once we know their strength, their plans and the state of alliance between the two bands, we will be able to gauge our actions."

It was a disappointment, but Manzur knew that Conan spoke good sense. Still, he continued to spin fantasies in which he snatched Ishkala from the grasp of her enemies, slew the sorcerer, fought his way from the midst of the host against insuperable odds, and made their escape across the trackless steppe. He even began composing a lengthy epic poem lauding his own feat.

They set out as soon as it was dark, but Conan called a halt while they were still on the rampart surrounding the City of Mounds.

"We wait here until the sounds of revelry are well advanced," the Cimmerian explained.

"Why are we here on the Turanian side?" Manzur asked. "Ishkala is almost certainly with the Red Eagles."

"We are not here for her," Conan said. "She is probably safe with the Sogarians for the moment. The wizard must be with the Turanians. Besides, the Red Eagles have posted sentries, and they act as if they know their trade. Soon most of the Turanians will be drunk, asleep or both. Wizards do much of their work at night. This will be a good time to pay the mage a visit."

"Very well," Manzur said. "But this waiting tries my patience."

"Patience is a virtue you must cultivate if you would be a warrior," the Cimmerian told him. "Too great a thirst for battle has been the death of far more warriors and armies than has the reluctance to fight."

Manzur was growing weary of these barbarian preachments. "True glory should be a matter of inspiration, not cold calculation," he said.

"Learn from me," said the Cimmerian, "and you might live longer. I gained my knowledge at a high price. Wounds, chains and slavery were the cost of that learning. If you would temper your rashness with a little thought, you may live to inflict your verses upon your countrymen for many years to come."

Manzur grumbled, but he sat back and rested against the grassy rampart. The sounds of revelry were loud and continuous, mingled with the noise of quarreling. He closed his eyes.

The Sogarian hero-poet awoke with a start as Conan shook his shoulder. "Awake, mightiest warrior of the age," said the Cimmerian. "We go in now. Keep close behind me and make no sound, no matter what you see. If there is any killing to be done, leave it to me. I can do it silently. Keep your blades loose in their sheaths, but do not draw them unless I draw mine. Now, let us be off."

Once more Manzur had cause to marvel at the Cimmerian's amazing stealthiness. As they progressed through the camp, Conan moved swiftly, yet his bare feet made no sound, and he had an uncanny ability to avoid obstacles in the darkness. Manzur had never heard that such serpentlike grace and silence were praised as warrior virtues. They were qualities he associated with the savages and the dark forests of far lands. Whatever else he was, the barbarian was accomplished in many arts.

Manzur had always believed that besides courage, a warrior needed only skill with his blades, his lance, his bow and his horse. He was beginning to realize that the warriors of his world were amateurs compared to this barbarian. He was thankful to note that his own awkward attempts at stealth were sufficient. The Turanians around the fires were too absorbed in drink, tale-telling and quarreling to take much note of the darkness surrounding them.

For, after all, what had they to fear? For all they know, they were in the midst of the empty steppe, with no enemy for hundreds of leagues. Any who approached would be detected from afar, leaving plenty of time to prepare. In consequence, the Turanians made free with their rations and their wine. Some already lay in drunken stupor, and others had broken out musical instruments. The night resounded to the reedy skirl of pipes, the thump of tambour and the wavering twang of stringed instruments.

Conan came to a halt a half score of paces from a tent much larger than the others. With his palm out, he signaled for Manzur to lower himself to the ground. When both men were flat on their bellies, Manzur crawled up even with the Cimmerian, who whispered in his ear, "Do as I do."

Conan took his sword belt from his waist and slung the sheathed weapon across his back. His dagger he tucked behind a leather bracelet on his left forearm. With his weapons out of the way, he began to slither toward the tent. Manzur emulated him, pleased that he managed the slither with something approaching the Cimmerian's skill. He was getting better at this.

Voices came from inside the tent, but they were too muffled to be understood. With hands widespread, Conan thrust the tips of his fingers beneath the edge of the tent wall. With infinite care he raised the cloth a fraction of an inch at a time. Yellow light poured from beneath the opening to play across their blackened faces.

They could see that several men were seated on cushions within. More important, they could now hear clearly what was being said.

"My Lord Khondemir," said a voice, "we must know now what your plans are. Our men grow more quarrelsome by the day, and if we cannot soon show them some action, I fear that our army may break up. The Sogarians grow restive as well. Princess Ishkala has been speaking overmuch with Jeku, their captain. They are of a mind to pick up stakes and return to their city which is under siege."

"Peace, Bulamb," said a voice that had to be Khondemir's. "Within a day, all shall be changed. Before the sun sets on the morrow, our men will no longer give us trouble. Further, the Sogarians will not be returning to their city. By tomorrow eve, a great host of Hyrkanians shall have this place utterly surrounded and outnumber us by at least forty to one."

Shouts of dismay shook the meeting, but the one called Bulamb quieted them. "Let us hear what the master has to say," said the second in command.

"My friends, what gives the Hyrkanians their great power when they are purposeful? I will tell you. It is their matchless horsemanship and mobility, along with their equally splendid archery. What are they without those things? They are a pack of primitive, superstitious, filthy, unwashed savages. They have always been masters of the steppes, but they have never been able to unite for a great foray into the civilized world.

"That is because their chieftains are as stupid and unimaginative as the poorest tribesman. When they attack, it is mere raiding for tribute, loot and slaves.

When they take a piece of territory, they do not exploit it but merely slaughter the inhabitants and turn it into more pasture for their goats. The hordes would be a fine instrument in the hands of a true conqueror.''

"I hear that this *kagan*, Bartatua, is different," said one.

"It may be so," acknowledged Khondemir. "He seems to possess gifts, at least by Hyrkanian standards. But I have something he does not suspect: I am in control of his concubine!''

There was a brief silence. Then the one called Rumal spoke. "My lord, I rejoice that you have found such comfort in your exile, but I fail to see how—''

"Mitra give me relief from such dullards!" cried Khondemir, his composure slipping for once. "I did not cultivate the woman for her beauty and charm, great though those are. In order to wield magical power over a rival, one must get close to him, and how closer than through a mistress?''

Conan and Manzur saw the pacing feet of the wizard as he explained as much of his plans as he thought fitting that his followers should know. "When the Hyrkanian horde reaches this place, the woman shall slip from their lines and join me here. She shall bring me that which shall give me power over this Hyrkanian kinglet.''

"That is all very well," came the voice of an older man. "But how are we to resist this Hyrkanian horde in the meantime? Forty to one odds are daunting at the best of times. Out here, with no cover and no city walls, they are suicidal. This earthen rampart will not hold for long, and our men may perish beneath the arrow storm before the Hyrkanians begin their assault.''

"I chose this place," Khondemir said, "for reasons other than its magical possibilities. I have told you how primitive and superstitious these steppe horsemen are. This place is surrounded by their taboos. According to the rules of their barbaric religion, no Hyrkanian may ride his horse into the City of Mounds. More important, none may fire an arrow toward it. Do the Hyrkanians now sound so formidable?''

The men assembled thought this over for a while. ''It may be,'' said one, ''that we can hold them at bay for some time, dismounted and without their bows. Our own bowmen will be under no such obligation, and a flying squad of horsemen can be appointed to go to whatever part of the rampart the Hyrkanians may be breaching and reinforce the defenders at that spot. How long must we hold out thus?''

''Only a brief while,'' Khondemir said. ''It is not my intention that there should be much bloodshed. With that which the concubine shall bring me, and with the aid of the Power which I shall summon, I shall gain complete mastery of the soul of Bartatua. He shall become my puppet, to do with as I wish. The savages would never follow me, or any other who was not of their blood. But they will follow Bartatua, and I shall control him. After his campaign to take the caravan cities, he plans to conquer Khitai. Who knows whether or not he could take that vast land? But he could take Turan, and that is where I shall cause him to direct his hordes.''

The wizard paused, waiting to be certain of the effect of his words. When he heard no objections, he resumed. ''That is my plan, my friends. We shall let the steppe tribes take Turan for us. They shall do the dying while we reap the conquest. When we are firmly in power, with myself on the throne and Yezdigerd chained as my footstool, I shall have the puppet, Bartatua, lead his hordes away, toward Khitai or Vendhya or into the black lands south of Stygia, what does it matter? They shall have performed their task: putting us back in our rightful place as lords of Turan!''

There were loud shouts of approval now. The men seemed well satisfied with Khondemir's arrangements. "A bold plan, my lord," said Rumal, "but only bold men may hope to seize and wield power. And what of the princess? Why is she here with her escort?''

"A trifling business," Khondemir explained. "In order to summon the Power, I must have a sacrifice. For complicated and abstruse reasons concerning history and bloodlines, princesses make superior sacrifices. I requested the escort in order to expand our numbers and to emphasize the importance of my mission. The Red Eagles can bear the brunt of our defense and take most of the casualties in such fighting as takes place before I have complete control of Bartatua.''

At mention of Ishkala's fate, Manzur began to start up, only to find an irresistible pressure at the back of his neck, bearing him inexorably down until his face was pressed against the grassy turf. Only by keeping perfectly still was he allowed to breathe. When he had calmed, Conan removed his hand from the back of the youth's neck and signaled for him to back away from the tent.

"Ishkala!" Manzur whispered urgently when they were removed. "We must go to the Sogarian camp and warn her, immediately! Nay, we should rescue her!''

"Rescue her?" Conan said. "From the midst of a thousand defenders? You would earn scant thanks.''

"Then at least let us inform the Red Eagles of what awaits them! They are to be sacrificed to the mad ambitions of Khondemir, just as she is to be sacrificed in his hellish ritual!''

Conan leaned close. "Lower your voice, idiot! You'll

have the whole band upon us! Your Red Eagles are nothing to me, and your princess has no call upon my loyalties. Until a few days ago, I was leading forays against Sogaria. Your prince would skin me an inch at a time in the city square if I rescued his whole family from the *kagan*'s own tent. Do you think his children are more important to him than his territory?''

''You lie, Cimmerian!'' said Manzur hotly. ''We will be received in Sogaria as saviors.''

''I would laugh if it would not bring the Turanians down upon us. Suppose you were able to convince the captain of the Red Eagles to take Ishkala and return to Sogaria. What then? They would encounter the Hyrkanian host that comes hither and they would be destroyed in minutes!''

''Then let us kill Khondemir,'' Manzur said, mad with frustration.

''Now you are beginning to think,'' Conan said. ''That is a sensible idea. I came here with the intention of taking his head to begin with. There remains a problem. The Hyrkanians come apace. I do not give Khondemir's magic great credit, but I am certain that without it, this camp will be overwhelmed and destroyed in no great time, even if the Hyrkanians are denied their horses and bows. If we slay the mage now, panic will ensue and all will try to flee. They will be slaughtered.''

''What care we for that?'' Manzur asked. ''A pack of scurvy Turanian gallows bait? Let them die!''

''That will leave only a thousand Red Eagles between your Ishkala and certain death. I have seen already what happens when the heavy cavalry of your cities encounters even a small band of Hyrkanian horse-archers. Against such a host, it would not even provide amusement.''

"I'll not allow her to be sacrificed in that fiend's foul rites!" Manzur protested, his hand reaching for his sword. He fumbled at his waist for a moment before remembering that the blade was still slung across his back. He reached for it awkwardly, then began to unsling it instead.

"Quiet!" Conan held up a hand for silence. "Someone comes." The Cimmerian reached behind his shoulder and drew the long blade as easily and smoothly as if it had been sheathed at his hip. Manzur vowed silently that he would master that trick, should he live so long. With his sword properly slung at last, he drew it and stood at guard.

Voices and torches were coming their way. "I heard them over here," said someone. "They were speaking a foreign dialect, and trying not to be heard."

"Probably more Sogarian spies," said another. "We'll corner the fools against the rampart and then cook them over a slow fire. It's an amusing sight, and conducive to great looseness of tongue."

As the torches drew near, three separate groups of hunters could be seen. They had spread wide and were closing in, thinking to herd their quarry toward the rampart and away from the Sogarian camp. Manzur expected Conan to dart away into the gloom, but the Cimmerian did nothing of the sort.

"Should we not be away?" said the younger man.

"You are of a mind to be a hero, are you not?" Conan asked. "Think you that you could do better against these noose-cheaters than you did against me?"

The barbarian continued to amaze him. "I have no doubt of it," Manzur answered.

"Good. Then let us do away with a few of them before we take our leave. It is not polite to make a call upon someone without leaving a souvenir of one's visit."

Manzur had no idea of why his companion was so keen to fight after counseling so much caution, but it was just what he needed. His feelings of frustration and rage were coming to a head, and he gripped his sword hilt with fierce exultation. Enemies to fight at last! The two he had slain during his escape from Sogaria were not sufficient, and the experience had been over too swiftly to be properly savored. This promised to be far more gratifying.

Each torch party had three or four men. They were quite close before they realized that the two they sought were standing before them.

"Mitra!" said a one-eyed man in a green vest. "What are these, black Kushites?"

A torch holder leaned forward and squinted with mock studiousness. "I do believe it's a northern savage and a boy. Perhaps the black paint is some new fashion from the east. Soon we'll all be wearing it."

The men held weapons at the ready, and in their confidence, they showed no fear of the intruders. They revealed gap-toothed grins, anticipating a bit of rare sport.

"Soon you will have no need of paint or anything else," Conan said, speaking Turanian as it was spoken by army officers. "But if you would know who I am, ask the deserters among you if they know the name of Conan of Cimmeria."

The men looked at each other and shrugged. "There are no deserters here," said another torch bearer. "We are all honest bandits, and followers of the great Lord Khondemir."

"We waste time," said the one-eyed man. "Take them in hand and let us conduct them to a suitable fire. There is too much spying going on in this camp."

A man who held a spiky mace raised it and advanced

upon Conan. The Cimmerian's blade made a wide arc, too swift to see. He cut the man from shoulder to waist, nearly halving him. The backstroke was horizontal and took a second man across the belly. All of a sudden, the quiet corner of the camp was a nightmare scene of blood and entrails.

Manzur attacked at once. His opponent raised a talwar and managed to parry two blows before the poet's blade swept across his throat and he went down with a ghastly liquid gasp. Two more assailants pressed Manzur and the young man was forced to defend himself desperately, unable to make an attacking move without laying himself open to a death blow.

Conan slapped aside a gutting lunge from a shortsword and split the swordsman's skull. For an instant he was clear, and with a backhanded blow he removed one of Manzur's assailants before returning his attention to the two men before him. One had a mace and the other held a dagger and a torch. They looked at Conan, then at each other. As if at a signal, the torch dropped to the ground and the two took to their heels. The others had no more heart and beat a hasty retreat while calling for reinforcements.

Conan turned to Manzur in time to see the youth pass his sword through his last assailant's body. Manzur surveyed the scene of carnage with delight, no doubt composing a poem on the spot.

"Come, let us away!" Conan said. As if in a daze, Manzur looked at him vacantly. Then his eyes cleared as he heard the clamor of the aroused camp.

The two ran for the rampart. Behind them the pursuit was confused as men blundered about in the dark, blinded by their own torches. Conan and Manzur ran up the grassy slope and paused at its top. Manzur caught a glint of teeth in the Cimmerian's blackened face.

"Let this be a lesson to you," Conan said. "When you chase a man who hides in the dark, stay in the dark yourself, else you'll never see him. Men do not bear torches in the dark because it helps them search, but because it makes them feel better."

"I shall remember," Manzur said.

They ran down the opposite slope and across the rolling ground toward their horses.

There was no pursuit beyond the rampart, although they saw a line of men atop the earthwork, holding torches aloft.

"What was that all about?" Manzur asked as they paused for breath. "Why did you wish to fight them? We did not reduce their numbers by much."

"There is much conspiring and double-dealing going on in that camp," Conan said. "Khondemir thinks that he is in control of it all. I thought it would not hurt to toss a new and puzzling factor into events. Thus his confidence will be undermined and distrust has been planted."

"And to do this, you were willing to take on such odds?" Manzur said admiringly.

Conan shrugged his massive shoulders as he cleaned the blood from his sword. "What odds?"

Commander Jeku sat before his tent in the first light of morning. An attendant handed him a steaming cup of herb tea, and the officer raised it to his lips just as a delegation of men came from the Turanian camp. Khondemir was at their head, and close behind him were the men he recognized as Bulamb and Rumal. The rest were subchiefs of the Turanian host. Their bearing and attitude were not friendly. If anything, they were hostile.

"Greeting, Lord Khondemir," said Jeku. "Have some

tea. I trust you have come to tell me that you are done with your spells and that we may ride from this dreary place."

"I have come for no such thing, as you know well," said the wizard icily. "Six of my men were killed last night, murdered by spies from your camp."

"So that's it, eh?" said Jeku, smiling beneath his mustache. "I send no spies. It isn't gentlemanly. Your men brawled among themselves, as they do every night, and some were killed. They concocted this story of a fight with my men in order to escape disciplinary action." He looked down his long nose. "Not that your rabble have any discipline to escape. Take my advice and hang a few as an example to the rest. Do not trouble me with the bloody doings of your pack of deserters and runaway serfs."

"They were spies," Khondemir insisted, "and they came from here. Where else could they have come from? The trackless steppe? One called himself Conan of Cimmeria. The other said nothing."

Jeku barked a short laugh. "Just two? And they did for six of your men and walked from the midst of the rest unharmed? I can see why you think they were *real* soldiers." His face lost its humor and he glared at the Turanians. "Cimmeria! It is a land from travelers' tales! No foreigner has ever served in the Red Eagles, but only Sogarian men of good family. Now begone with your accusations, back to your riffraff. And be quick about your charlatan's magic, for I have lost patience. Tomorrow at first light the Red Eagles ride, with or without you and your Turanian scum!"

The one called Bulamb stepped forward. "No pompous ass of a foreigner speaks thus to our sovereign." His hand was upon the hilt of his dagger.

"Sovereign, is it?" Jeku raised a hand to his shoulder. "Look about you, dogs."

The Turanians looked, and saw at least forty Sogarian guards with bows in their left hands, arrows nocked and drawn to the ear. Bulamb's hand fell away from his hilt.

"If I lower my hand," Jeku said, "you will all be riddled with shafts. My men could use the practice. You may try your spells, wizard, but I never heard of magic that was swifter than an arrow's flight."

"You'll not slay us," Khondemir said, "with your assassins or with your arrows. And you'll not be riding from this place at morning light."

"My arm grows weary, wizard, and my tea grows cold. Do not vex me further."

Snarling, Khondemir whirled on his booted heel and stalked off. His followers fell in behind. When the delegation was far enough from the captain, Jeku's guardsmen lowered their bows and returned their arrows to their belt quivers, disappointed.

The captain smiled again as he sipped the pungent herbal brew. The wizard, he was sure now, was a fake. Jeku could return to Sogaria and report that the prince had been gulled and that the supposedly great mage was nothing but a Turanian conspirator, one of the many pretenders to the throne of the late King Yildiz.

He began to compose his report. It would have to be couched in diplomatic language of course, so that the prince would not come out of it looking like an idiot. There would have to be some lowly advisor or chamberlain to take the blame. It was going to be difficult.

"He lies, master!" hissed Bulamb as the Turanian party returned to its tents. "Those men had to come from the Sogarian camp! Let us get our men together and force the foreigners to turn the murderers over to us!"

"Aye," said Rumal. "They were naught more than worthless scum, but the insult to you is intolerable! We cannot let these Sogarians, inhabitants of a small and unimportant city, think they can insult the greatest king in the world with impunity!"

"No, my friends," Khondemir said. "We shall come to a settlement with that insolent dog soon enough. Now is not the time for a split between the forces. We shall face the Hyrkanians before the day is out. We can only chew on our gall and plan our revenge." He turned to Bulamb. "That name, Conan of Cimmeria. Did you inquire among the former soldiers about it?"

"I did, majesty. A few said that they have heard the name, although none has met the man. It seems that a few years ago there was an officer of that name in your beloved father's army. There was some sort of scandal, and in some way he fell afoul of the usurper, Yezdigerd." They all spat ceremoniously.

"One told me," said red-bearded Rumal, "that it is one of the names that is always to be seen on the annual kill-or-capture list. He said he remembered it because of the size of the reward offered: a thousand in gold plus immediate promotion of one grade."

"What would this notable malefactor be doing in this place?" Khondemir mused. "Perhaps he enlisted in the Sogarian service to escape the wrath of the usurper. It is no matter. We shall find him and his companion when we winnow the Red Eagles, after we need them no longer. We have more important things to concern us now."

"The men are upset," said an officer. "They do not like it that aliens come into their midst to slay."

"What of it?" said Khondemir in disgust. "Most nights more than six are killed in their nightly brawling."

"But these are foreigners!" said another.

"Enough," Khondemir barked, making a chopping gesture with one beringed hand. "We have preparations to see to. Let us get back to our command tent."

"What now?" Manzur asked. "All seems quiet. What can we do?"

The two men sat upon a rise of ground overlooking the City of Mounds. With the sun at their back, they ran little risk of being spotted. Should their enemies come after them, their horses were tethered nearby and they could easily outdistance any pursuit.

"We do nothing," Conan said. "We rest. Soon the Hyrkanian horde will be here, and then we shall have plenty to do."

"The Hyrkanians," Manzur said. There was a chill in his blood at the name. "What shall we do when they arrive?"

"That we shall have to play like gamblers, using every advantage that fortune tosses our way. We are between two hosts that would kill us out of hand, but if I can gain an interview with Bartatua, I may win us some time."

The Cimmerian got up and brushed off stray bits of grass. "You may yet win your princess, and I may yet gain the head of Khondemir, with which to buy off Yezdigerd. It all depends upon whether I can speak to Bartatua before that accursed whore of his does."

"That is a large gamble to take with our lives," Manzur noted.

"That is what being a hero is all about," said Conan.

Fifteen

The Hyrkanian host swept across the steppe like the shadow of a cloud, darkening all in its path for a moment, then vanishing as if it had never been. The horses'-tail standards fluttered in the wind of their passing, and there was little sound except for the steady drumming of hooves and the occasional shouts of officers dressing the order of their tens, their fifties, their hundreds, their five hundreds and their thousands.

They had paused only to water the mounts. Men slept in the saddle, giving their reins to companions. All had been left behind except men, horses, the clothing and armor they wore and the weapons they bore. All else—tents, camp gear, loot and other goods—would follow behind, borne on pack beasts led by servants. Thus it was that a mere two days after breaking off the siege of Sogaria, the hordes of Bartatua encircled the City of Mounds.

Shamans came out before the host, shaking their rattles and beating their drums, calling upon gods, ancestors and the Everlasting Sky to witness the infamy of their enemies and the justice of the Hyrkanian cause. There were loud chantings, and many of the shamans went into their whirling dances, strings of bones and amulets standing out from their bodies as they twirled. New arrivals had swollen the ranks of the tribal magicians, depleted since the night of Conan's escape.

The tribesmen sat silently as the shamans went through their rituals. This was serious business and had none of the merriment that attended a common battle. Here there would be no loot and little glory, only the cleansing of a defiled holy place and the working of a terrible vengeance.

A single horse stepped out a few paces before the lines of warriors and the swirling group of shamans. Bartatua sat upon a swift, dappled mare, and the wrath upon his face was awesome to behold.

He wore a spired helmet of Khitan make, its rim rich with the luxuriant fur of the black sable. As he sat staring at the City of Mounds, men swarmed atop its earthen rampart, waving weapons and shouting defiance.

A small group of *kagans* rode up even with Bartatua. Their glares of fell hatred were as fierce as his own.

"There are two groups, *Ushi-Kagan*," said a thousand-commander of the Ashkuz. "See, they stand a little apart from one another. The ones who are all dressed alike must be the Sogarian Red Eagles. The rest will be the other band that joined them some little way back. Turanians, if we read the signs correctly."

"That is what they are," Bartatua said. "Khondemir is from that land, although he shall never see it again. I would know," he swept his gaze over his followers, "what they are doing here?"

"What does it matter?" said the scar-faced eastern *kagan* who had given him advice on dealing with pestilence in a besieged city. "We are going to slay them all anyway. Their business here will die with them."

"There is some reason," Bartatua said, "and on another day some other man may have the same reason. I do not wish to do this twice. Save some alive so that we may question them."

"Not Khondemir!" said the *kagan* of the Budini, fingering an amulet at his neck. "The curse of a dying wizard is more potent than that of ordinary spells. Slay him swiftly."

"An officer, then," said Bartatua, "though it grieves me sorely to give Khondemir a quick, clean death."

"Sometimes revenge must be deferred," said the easterner. "When the day comes that we take Turan, we shall not allow the Turanians to forget that their countrymen performed this sacrilege and caused us so much inconvenience."

"Aye, and Sogaria as well," said the Gerul *kagan*, the green tattoos of his face writhing like a basket of snakes. "The feet of Sogaria's soldiers befoul a Hyrkanian burial place. I rejoice that the Gerul burial place is on the far northern steppe, where sacrilegious city-dwellers will never find it."

"Sogaria shall pay, too," Bartatua said. "Of that be assured. I was minded to deal gently with the city-dwellers, but no more. Where the city now stands, there shall be a pasture for sheep. The stones shall be carried back to their quarries and covered with earth. No man, woman, child or beast shall live. The orchards will be cut down, the tilled fields sown with grass. In future years when travelers shall ask, 'Where is the great city of Sogaria of which the poets sang?' none shall be able to tell them."

The others nodded solemnly. This was vengeance as Hyrkanians understood the word.

"When do we attack, *Ushi-Kagan*?" asked the easterner. His narrow eyes squinted at the angle of the sun. "There is yet time for an assault."

"Nay," said Bartatua. "That leaves no time to instruct the men. This will be a style of fighting with which they are not familiar. How many of us have ever fought on foot, with naught but swords and lances in our hands?"

"A night assault, then," said the *kagan* of the Geruls. "That will give us several hours in which to order our troops. In the dark, the Sogarians and Turanians will not be able to use their greater experience with sword and shield to advantage."

"Nay!" said the *kagan* of the Budini. His brown braids swung back and forth as he waved his hand violently in a negative gesture. "Not at night! We Budini will not follow you thus! If a man is slain at night and is not mounted, he cannot ride to the pastures beyond the moon. Without the spirit-eyes of his mount to guide him through the darkness, his soul is lost forever! Fight in the day if you want the help of the Budini."

Bartatua gritted his teeth to keep his silence for a while. Here it was again, the urge of his people to whirl apart because of their differing customs and ancient antipathies.

"We shall attack in the day," he said at last. "A night's rest will do the men and the horses some good, as well as allow us time to formulate our plans."

"But we will not be using the horses in battle," said the Gerul.

This, Bartatua thought, was the most onerous part of being the *Ushi-Kagan*. Even in small matters, he had to do everyone's thinking. It was not enough to plan campaigns and empires; he had to point out the simplest and most obvious things to men who were supposed to be seasoned warriors.

"Those men down there," he said, "are studying us just as we are studying them. They judge the greatness of our numbers and the smallness of their own. Even now they are considering flight. Our horses have just run for two days and nights with little rest, while theirs have been taking their ease, cropping the grass from the graves of our ancestors."

Bartatua glared fiercely at his chiefs. "Should they try to escape, now or tonight, some might make it through our lines. On tired mounts, we might not be able to catch such as make it away from our arrow storm. Those men have learned the route to our City of Mounds, and not one, *not one!* may be allowed to escape to reveal that secret!"

"Aye," said they all.

In a space behind the Hyrkanian line, warriors were setting up a small tent, the only such shelter to be brought on the hurried forced march. Nearby stood the black-shrouded owner of the tent.

Lakhme walked stiffly, easing the soreness from her body. Never in her life had she ridden as she had in these last forty-eight hours. Her body was a mass of pain, as if she had been beaten with rods and stretched on a rack. She knew that the tender skin of her thighs and buttocks was now red, chafed and galled from constant moving contact with the saddle.

She feared that months of ointments, salves and massage would be needed to restore the beauty of her flesh, but just now she had more than her beauty to worry about. She had planned long and deeply for this moment, and the coming hours must see the climax of all her plotting.

This was the most delicate moment of the entire scheme. Her body craved rest, but she had no time for rest now. Inside the City of Mounds was Khondemir, and she had to make contact with him. The state of his forces, the progress of his sorcerous workings, all had a bearing on the course of her actions over the next few hours.

Her ambition was vaulting but simple. She wanted to rule the world. She could do it through Khondemir and Bartatua. The *Ushi-Kagan* was everything she had hoped to find in a man: a ruthless conqueror with the ambition to subdue the world, and the gifts of leadership and will with which to accomplish it. Plus that, he had the weapon to sweep all resistance before him: the matchless horse-archers of the Hyrkanian steppe. Best of all, he was controllable through his besotted love for her.

Life had taught her, though, that her power over such a man would dwindle as her beauty faded. She needed an ally with whom to cement her mastery over the *Ushi-Kagan*, and that ally would be Khondemir. The wizard, through his magic, would have full control of Bartatua, and she would control the wizard, who was as helpless with love for her as was the *Ushi-Kagan* himself. She would stay close to the wizard until she had ferreted out his secrets; then she would seize control for herself. With both wizard and *Ushi-Kagan* reduced to slavery, she would rule the world through them. She would no longer need to depend upon her beauty, which had never been more than a tool for her. Beauty was a fleeting thing, of importance only to foolish, weak men. Power was everything, and she meant to wield all the power that was to be had.

When the tent was erected and the pallets laid, she went inside to eat and to prepare herself for the night's activities. One supreme effort would see the culmina-

tion of her ambitions. She was a gambler too experienced to risk everything on a single cast of the dice.
Should the wizard fail, she would still have her position
as Bartatua's concubine. There would be another wizard
someday, one to reveal to her the secret of ensorceling a
king's soul. In the meantime, she would be the woman
of the greatest conqueror of the age, and woe betide any
younger, more beautiful woman who should appear.

The heat of summer was stifling in the tent, and she
quickly shed the padded trousers she had worn beneath
her all-swathing black robes. The padding had afforded
her delicate skin some slight protection, but the heat
had been suffocating. She envied the men, many of
whom had stripped to loincloth and boots for the ride.

She called for water, and the warriors returned from
the spring with several skin bags and a collapsing leather
tub. The water was no more than tepid, but it felt
luxurious upon her abraded flesh. As she soaked, she
laid out her plans for the night: first, some questioning
to learn Bartatua's strategy for attacking the City of
Mounds; then, after full dark, a foray into the enclosure
to meet with Khondemir. It was difficult to plan beyond
that because everything would depend upon what the
wizard had to say.

Her perfunctory bath finished, she dried herself and
resumed her silken loincloth. She did not bother with
jewelry for fear of making noise when she made her
nocturnal visit to the City of Mounds. Into the loincloth
she tucked a small dagger in a sheath of thin bronze. It
had no sharp edge, but the triangular blade was needle-
tipped and strong enough to pierce mail, and it had been
steeped in the distilled venom of the Khitan sea snake.
Once, to test it, she had pricked a camel with the tip of
the dagger. The beast had died within minutes. She had

invested in a number of such weapons, to compensate for her relative physical weakness.

After he had made his rounds of the hordes and explained the morrow's battle plan, Bartatua came to the tent of his beloved concubine. She had laid out bowls of the scanty food she had brought: hard cakes of bread, cheese and dried fruits.

"It grieves me, my lord," she said, "that this is all I am able to prepare for you. This is not fare fit for the *Ushi-Kagan*, soon to be ruler of all the world."

He sat before her, admiring as always her unearthly beauty, unmarked by the ravages of the hard ride. "It is no matter. I have already shared gruel with my men. Now, more than ever, they must see that I am one of them, and that I enjoy few privileges when there is true fighting to be done. It is no hardship to me. When I was welding this nation of tribes into a fighting force to be reckoned with, I went many days with no food at all. The steppe is a cruel and unforgiving master, and those who cannot adapt do not last long. Only after conquest do we enjoy the fruits of others' labors. That is good practice, and it has kept us strong."

"Surely it shall not be so difficult a fight, though," she said. "What can that small band do against this great host of the mightiest warriors in the world?"

"Ordinarily, nothing," said the *Ushi-Kagan*. "In a common battle, we would simply fill them with arrows and laugh while we did so. But the ancient laws will not allow it. We must leave our horses and bows and fight on foot. Many of my men do not even have shields, and to them a sword is a tool for cutting down footmen as they flee, thus saving arrows. We have always favored light armor, and many tribes scorn any armor at all. The Sogarian heavy cavalry are well protected with mail, scale and plate, and the Turanians look to be well armored also.''

The *Ushi-Kagan* shook his head. ''No, we shall prevail. With our greater numbers and the honor of our ancestors to avenge, it cannot be otherwise. But the cost! We have never been a numerous people as other nations reckon such things. Our power lies in our mobility and our archery. In this fight—I can scarcely call it a battle—many, many fine bowmen will be lost, more than I would be prepared to sacrifice in a major campaign. And not a foot of ground taken in conquest! This is wasteful and foolish, and all because of that foul necromancer!''

''Well,'' Laklıne said, ''you must remain firm if you are to keep your rightful standing among your people. And never fear, your warriors will take many wives and concubines from among the defeated peoples. They will raise multitudes of strong sons to replace those slain here. My lord is destined to be ruler of all beneath the Everlasting Sky, and no mere wizard can alter that. This is a test that the gods have put before you, to demonstrate your mastery for all to see.'' She poured wine into his favorite skull cup and handed him the vessel. ''How will you go about waging your campaign?''

''The rampart slopes,'' Bartatua said. ''It is not like a city wall. We could attack along any point, or we could attack at every point at once. If we spread our attack too wide, though, we will only make our losses greater. There is much open ground to cover after we are within bowshot.''

''Why not a night attack? They will not see you until you are close.''

'That would be best,'' he agreed, ''but too many tribes will not attack at night for religious reasons.''

That would be a valuable piece of information to take

to Khondemir, she thought. "So it will be an attack at dawn, against a single point?"

"Against two points," said Bartatua. "The City is oriented to the four cardinal directions, with its back to the north, whence come evil spirits. The entrance faces south. At dawn we shall make a feint toward the north wall, riding as close to it as is permitted, then dismounting to attack. The main force shall be hiding in a draw to the southeast. When most of the defenders are drawn away to the north, the main force shall assault the south side of the rampart. If this plan goes well, the foot attack shall sweep all before it, though with many losses."

"With my lord as their leader," she said, refilling his cup, "they cannot fail."

After resting in the tent for a brief time, Bartatua left, telling Lakhme that he would spend the night among his men. It was important that men see much of their leader just prior to a battle, he explained. She feigned reluctance to see him leave, and as soon as he was away, she prepared for her own foray.

Swathed to the eyes in her black robes, Lakhme slipped from the tent. No man watched or stood near, for all attention was directed toward the City of Mounds. The *Ushi-Kagan* had ordered that no one who bore the secret of the location of the sacred site was to pass through Hyrkanian lines. She began to walk toward the lines.

Out of the gloom came the figure of a man in dark clothing. "I am here, mistress."

"Did you follow my instructions, Bajazet?" she asked.

"I did, my lady. There is a draw, not far from here, leading toward the necropolis. I saw to it that my fifty-commander placed me in watch upon it. If you keep low, you may go near the rampart without being seen.''

"You did well," she said as they set out. "Tell me, Bajazet, are you not as incensed as the rest that foreigners are defiling sacred ground?'' If the man was having second thoughts, it would be best to know it now. There was nothing so dangerous as a reluctant accomplice. Better to kill him at once than to leave a possible betrayer behind her back.

"I am no Ashkuz!" he said, spitting. "The burial grounds of Bartatua's tribe mean nothing to me. I only wish to avenge my master, Kuchlug, treacherously slain by the *Ushi-Kagan*!" He gave the title a sarcastic twist.

"Very good," she said. "See that you keep that in mind.''

As they approached the draw, they were so intent upon their errand that they failed to see the two shadowy forms that passed them in the dark.

The sleepy sentries jumped to their feet yammering, startled by the black apparition that had appeared like a vision before them. They presented the points of their lances and the figure lowered a black veil, revealing the face of a beautiful woman, vague in the light from the fires far behind them.

"Tell your master that Lakhme is here," she said.

An officer arrived, drawn by the guards' exclamations.

"Lord Khondemir told us to expect you, my lady," said the man. His silver-chased helmet winked in the firelight. "I will take you to him.''

They walked through the camp, which was quiet for once. Even the licentious rogues who had flocked to Khondemir knew better than to spend the night in drunken revelry when battle was imminent. The officer led her to the base of a titanic mound. Looking around the City, she saw that this was the largest of all the tumuli.

"Up there," the officer said, pointing to the top of the great grassy heap of earth. "My lord Khondemir is at the top. Men have toiled up there all day, helping him with his preparations. Since sundown he has forbidden any to ascend this mound, save only you when you should arrive."

She climbed the mound, which proved to be even steeper than it appeared from the bottom. Her legs, already tired from the ride, grew wobbly as she approached the crest. A wave of dizziness swept over her, but she refused to let Khondemir see her in a moment of weakness. She paused briefly and summoned all her willpower. With her stamina restored, she strode up the last few yards at an easy stride, betraying no trace of the weakness that she felt from scalp to toes.

"I am here, Khondemir," she said, her voice steady and calm.

"I expected you," the wizard said. He was in his full ceremonial robes. Strange and disturbing figures were embroidered with threads of silver and gold upon a robe dyed with the blood of Khitan dragons, and he wore a short cope made from the skin of a virgin princess of Zamora, captured and sacrificed by a Turanian mage three hundred years before.

"Did you bring the things I need?" he asked.

"Here, this should be sufficient." From a pocket sewn into the lining of her robe she withdrew a silken bag and a small vial of glass. Khondemir took them from her and turned back to the curious structure that had been erected upon the mound, next to a tall, stark standard of iron. From the top of the standard, white horses' tails waved in the moonlight and the skull of some fantastic beast grinned down at them.

The wizard set her offerings upon the structure, which was a low altar made of wood and leather. It had buckled straps at its corners, and the wizard had covered it with strange, writhing figures much like those embroidered upon his robe. Lakhme stared at them in fascination, for here was a source of power she had not yet mastered. The figures seemed to crawl before her gaze and she looked away.

Around the base of the mound she could see the fires of the Turanian-Sogarian camp. Beyond the fires there was a broad belt of darkness behind which were the smaller fires of the Hyrkanian horde. It was a circle of fire so immense that she felt a sinking in her belly.

"I see why you do not allow any of your men up here after dark," she said. "Such a sight would turn to ice the stoutest of hearts."

"There are other reasons," said Khondemir. "This place is now consecrated. No others may tread upon this spot save myself, you, and the Princess Ishkala. The stars are in their proper places. The phase of the moon is correct, and the focus of events has moved to this ground. Tomorrow night I shall summon a great Power. When I plunge the sacred dagger into Ishkala's breast and rip forth her still-beating heart, all of our plans will come to fruition. I shall be in complete control of the *kagan*, Bartatua. When the confusion of battle is sorted out, I shall be the true commander of a mighty conquering army, and soon thereafter shall be the king of Turan."

He smiled benevolently. "And you, my dear, shall ascend the throne with me. Not as my queen, of course. The Turanians would never accept a Vendhyan pleasure-slave as their queen. But you shall be my chief concubine."

"Of course," she said, her smile as perfect and

seductive as ever, "I would never aspire to a position so high and public as that of queen. However"—she swept her gaze over the huge encircling ring of fire—"I had hoped that you would be able to work your magic tonight. You may not be alive to work sorcery tomorrow night. The Hyrkanian host is vast, and its members are incensed that foreigners profane one of their burial grounds. Even without their bows and their horses, there are enough of them to sweep over you by weight alone."

His superior smile reappeared. "Have no fear. My men are very expert in war and will make the best use of their arms and of this position. Besides, not all of the Hyrkanians are so eager to avenge the profanation of this place. Only the *kagan*'s own people, the Ashkuz, hold the City sacred. The others may be making fierce noises, but that is only to display their loyalty to Bartatua. Tomorrow, when they advance across open ground on foot, about to fight in a manner they have always despised, they shall not be so eager. Mounted and armed with their fine bows, they are all but undefeatable. Afoot with hand weapons, they are little more than rabble."

She remembered the scornful words of Bajazet. "You may be correct."

"I am. And I shall be king of Turan. It is destiny." At that moment, seeing him standing atop the mound in his magnificent robes, she could readily believe it.

"I have obtained Bartatua's order of battle for the morrow," she said. "Will you hear it now?"

"Come down to my tent. You may relate it to my officers as well."

They descended the mound. She had no fear of being seen by Khondemir's officers, for they could never betray her to Bartatua. Should Khondemir's plans fail on the morrow, should the *Ushi-Kagan* be victorious, none of the enemy would be spared. Even should one or two be taken for questioning, she would see to it that they died before their tongues could give her any anxiety.

They passed by a fire where men were conversing while they oiled and sharpened their weapons. Almost unconsciously her instinct for eavesdropping caused Lakhme to listen to their words.

"There goes the master," said one as he thumbed the edge of a long, curved dagger. "He said that the savages would not attack tonight, and it looks as if he is right. We are safe until daybreak."

"True," said another with a sardonic smile. "We are safe barring another midnight visit from Conan of Cimmeria." The men around the campfire laughed at the witticism.

Lakhme felt icy fingers closing around her heart. She had barely been able to understand the rough Turanian dialect of the hill bandits, but the name caught her as surely as a noose cast by a Hyrkanian tribesman. She stopped in her tracks and turned on Khondemir.

"Conan! The Cimmerian! What do your men know of him?" Her voice was low, but urgent.

Khondemir was as one thunderstruck. "Conan of Cimmeria? Why does that name distress you?"

"Tell me!" she insisted.

"He is merely the men's latest bugaboo. Last night a man calling himself by that name came into the Turanian camp to spy. He had a companion with him, but that one did not speak. They were surrounded by my men, but after announcing himself, this Conan fellow proved to be a lion among hyenas. He slew a great swath of troops and fled without a trace. The men have made a night goblin of him, half in jest."

"What did he look like, and whence came he?" This news could not be true, she thought.

"The survivors described him as a veritable giant, with black hair to his shoulders and eyes that looked gray in the torchlight. He was painted black to escape detection. I suspect that he came from the Sogarian camp to spy upon me, but the pompous oaf of a captain denies having any such man in his following, and treated me insolently. He lies, of course. Where else could the man have come from? Men do not just wander in from the trackless steppe. What does the name mean to you?"

"An enemy," she said. "An upstart who grew too close to the *kagan*. He seemed a needless complication, so I sought his downfall, both to rid myself of a rival for Bartatua's trust and to cement my secret relations with the shamans. I had him bound and naked and ready for sacrifice, but his friends rescued him and they escaped pursuit."

She rubbed her bare arms, although the night was warm. "It is he. Everything fits—the size, the hair, the eyes. And I know that he darkened his skin on a mission into Sogaria. He is a fearsome swordsman, and it is no wonder that your rogues were no stop to him."

Khondemir shrugged. "It is a minor matter. The man must have fallen in with the Sogarian column after his escape. He will have offered his services to Captain Jeku, including his expertise as a spy. Have no fear, he can cause you no harm now. After the fighting is over, should he still live, I shall give him to you as a plaything. Pray do not vex yourself over this trifling matter."

"As you say," she said. "Perhaps it is just a coincidence." Still, she could not rid herself of a feeling of dread. "Enough of this," she said. "Let us go to your tent. I must return to the Hyrkanian lines long before it is light."

"Why?" Khondemir asked. "Stay here with me. You have done all that was necessary, now that I have those items which shall confer upon me power over the mind and soul of Bartatua."

"No, I may still spy upon the Hyrkanians. Who knows when some new factor, some change of plans, may be important?" In truth, she did not want to be in the City of Mounds should Khondemir fail.

He shrugged beneath his robes. "No matter. Perhaps it is best that you sit out the fighting in a safe place and join me afterward." He looked up and studied the full moon, hanging skull-like above them. "At any rate, it will all be over after the sun sets tomorrow."

Sixteen

"The important thing to remember," Conan said, "is to keep your mouth shut, whatever anguish that may cost you. No matter what the Hyrkanians say, no matter what the threats to your city or country, do as I have told you or you are surely a dead man."

"I will remember," Manzur said. He was filled with tremendous fear and elation. They were in the midst of a vast enemy host! How dangerous, yet how heroic! What verses he would write when all this was over.

"Good," Conan said, clapping him on the shoulder. "Think of the loss to the world of poetry should you die before your time."

As they made their way toward the Hyrkanian lines, they passed two figures, one of them muffled in black robes. Manzur took no notice, but Conan smiled grimly as the black-robed one passed from view.

Among the tribesmen, who wore the dress of many steppe peoples and the armor of many nations, the two went unnoticed. They avoided fires, and the moonlight was not sufficient to reveal facial features clearly. Conan was looking for a fire larger than the others, and soon he found it. As they drew nearer, he saw faces he recognized, those of the *kagans* and the high officers of Bartatua's great horde.

"Greeting, *Kagan*," Conan said as he stepped within the circle of firelight. Bartatua looked up and his face went blank.

A man seated at Conan's feet turned and snapped: "That is the *Ushi-Kagan*, you mannerless—" Then the man's jaw dropped. "By the Everlasting—" He struggled to his feet, yanking at his sword hilt.

Conan felt a dozen pairs of hands laid upon him, but he made no move to resist. A struggle would mean certain death.

"Hold! Do not slay him!" said the *Ushi-Kagan*. The grip upon Conan did not loosen. Bartatua rose to his feet and stood face-to-face with Conan, separated by no more than a handbreadth. "I never thought to see you again, Cimmerian." He turned to look at Manzur. "Who is this? His garb is Sogarian."

"A man without power of speech, *Ka—Ushi-Kagan*. He found me lost upon the steppe. He is a caravan drover. His last stop was Sogaria, hence the clothes."

The assembled chieftains goggled at the apparition. They were ready to kill, but their leader seemed more thoughtful than wrathful.

"Come, Conan," Bartatua said. "Let us walk together. Release him."

A dozen voices shouted protest. "Nay, my lord!" cried the Gerul *Kagan*. "This is some trick! This foreigner proposes to slay you."

Bartatua barked a short laugh. "He walked to within three paces of where I sat unaware. Think you this man could not have slain me before you even knew he was in our midst?"

"Take my weapons if you wish," Conan said. "I mean the *Ushi-Kagan* no harm."

"You do not fool us, Conan," said the Budini chief. "Our leader is a mighty man, but we have all seen your strength. You can snap the neck of a powerful man in an instant."

"Bind my wrists, then," Conan said impatiently.

"No," said Bartatua. "I sense this is something important." He turned to his men. "Take his weapons and follow us at a little distance." He turned back to Conan. "I am curious, but I am no fool. Come with me. Your companion will be given food and wine."

The two walked a short way from the lines, where they could observe the fires of the City of Mounds. Behind them trailed the group of chiefs, hands gripped tight around the hilts of their weapons.

"I confess," Bartatua said, "that I was saddened to condemn you to death, and I felt little rage when I was told of your escape. Especially"—he grinned— "when I learned of how many of those scurvy shamans you sent to hell in getting away." He sobered again. "But that was a foolish thing you did, attacking my woman. I should kill you now for that."

"It is about your woman that I wish to speak," Conan said.

"Well?" said Bartatua, his voice dangerously gentle.

"She has betrayed you."

The *Ushi-Kagan* turned to face Conan, and his expression would have stopped a charging bull. "Betrayed me? You mean with you?"

"It is not that kind of betrayal," said Conan. "And it is with Khondemir."

"Speak swiftly, Cimmerian," Bartatua ordered. "Your life hangs by a fine thread."

"My life has hung by many a thread," said Conan,

"and some of them have been finer than I care to remember." Then he told the *Ushi-Kagan* of the events upon the night when Lakhme had brought her false charge of attempted rape against him. He spoke of her orgiastic dance with the shamans. Bartatua's face became twisted with an immense pain in the telling, but Conan could not spare him.

The Cimmerian told of his escape and his wandering in the duststorm, and of how he was found by Manzur. He held back nothing save Manzur's true identity. At the end he told of the words he had heard issuing from Khondemir's tent on the previous night. For some time the *Ushi-Kagan* was unable to speak.

"Conan," he said at last, his voice little more than a husky croak, "if you lie, you shall die a death such as no man has ever known. It shall be a death so terrible that the demise of Conan the Cimmerian must resound through the centuries as the ultimate horror to be endured by mortal man." His tone left no doubt as to his sincerity.

"I do not lie, *Kagan*," Conan said. "Or should I say *Ushi-Kagan*?"

"*Kagan* is a good title," Bartatua said. "There is none nobler beneath the Everlasting Sky. *Ushi-Kagan* is the vaunting boast of a conqueror. I know not why, Conan, but I find it in my heart to believe you. Your words strike me harder than would the arrows of an enemy, but they carry the terrible sound of truth. Yet still I find it difficult to believe. Perhaps I gave her my heart because I always wanted a woman to love. But then, perhaps I trusted you because I always wanted a friend I could trust."

Conan found that his own heart was stricken by his next words. "If you would be convinced that I speak the truth, Bartatua," he said, "go now and call for your woman. As I came hither, I saw her skulking toward the City of Mounds. She had a tribesman with her. She has gone to deliver to Khondemir whatever it is that he must have."

For a while Bartatua was again speechless. "After this," he said upon recovery, "even when I mount the throne of the world, the taste of triumph will be as the taste of soured wine. My destiny was to be pure, as ordained by the gods beneath the Everlasting Sky. Now it is corrupted by the perfidy of this woman, by my foolishness as a man, by my very acts. I was like a puppet in a Khitan shadow play, manipulated upon sticks by shadowy slaves behind a screen. Thus I betrayed and persecuted my only friend, while I foolishly was led by a faithless woman, as easily as a drover-boy leads a gelded ox!"

"Bartatua, my friend," Conan said, "you are not the first man to be gulled by a beautiful woman. Certainly you shall not be the last."

"But how many of those men," said the *Ushi-Kagan*, "aspired to the throne of the world? I am such a man. And what is to be expected in an ordinary man is unforgivable in an *Ushi-Kagan*. Come, let us go back and speak to my chiefs. None of this makes any difference as far as our attack on the City of Mounds goes. Whatever plots Lakhme and Khondemir have hatched are out of my hands. The dawn assaults shall be as scheduled. Will you lead one of them? I know that I have forfeited your loyalty through my foolishness, but some things can still be made right."

"I would be willing, *Kagan*," Conan said, "but would your men follow me? You have looked into my eyes. You and I are men of the same sort, save that I am Cimmerian and you are Hyrkanian. But your men will need more than my word ere they will accept me as one of their leaders once again.''

Bartatua took Conan by the arm. ''Come with me, my true friend. We shall make all right. I know of a way not only to confirm your story, but to expose Lakhme's perfidy. Upon the morrow you shall lead my armies against the enemy, and you shall have honor before any other. Beneath the Everlasting Sky, there shall be no man second to the *Ushi-Kagan*, Bartatua, save Conan of Cimmeria!''

The stars had not yet begun to fade in the east when Lakhme returned from the City of Mounds. Around her she could hear the sounds of the camp waking, of men making their final preparations for the battle to come. She took deep satisfaction in the knowledge that soon she would be done with the barbarous camps of the nomads.

She would live in a palace in the center of a great and rich city. Slaves would pander to her every whim, and the greatest men of the world would approach her on their knees to beg for her favor. That was the proper ordering of the world. She who had been sold into slavery by her parents would be the greatest of women. The figurehead upon the throne might be Khondemir, or Bartatua, or some other man of her choosing, but in time there would be little doubt of where the true power lay.

In her mind she began to build her palace. It would be gorgeous beyond belief, with spired towers high enough to pierce the clouds. Her floors would be paved with gold and pearls. There would be no cloth in the palace save the finest silk. Her slaves would be the most beautiful—She was jarred from her dream when iron fingers closed around her upper arm.

"We meet again, my lady," said Conan of Cimmeria.

"You!" she hissed. "When Khondemir said—" She stopped herself abruptly. There might be listeners nearby. "When my lord sees you, his vengeance shall be terrible. How have you come here, traitor? Do you yet plot against the *Ushi-Kagan*?"

"You may as well forget your pose, Lakhme," he said. "I have already spoken with the *Ushi-Kagan*. He knows everything now. Perhaps I should say that he knows the more important points of your betrayal. What mortal mind could comprehend all the schemings of a lovely serpent such as you?"

"What lies have you poured into his ears?" she asked accusingly. She spoke loudly now, for she was sure that listeners stood in the darkness nearby. "The *Ushi-Kagan* is too trusting. He sees courage and battle skill in a man and he thinks that these mean the warrior is honorable. You are a traitor!"

She saw that the man was taking her toward a large fire, and she thought of the dagger tucked into her loincloth. No, she thought, the time is not yet. She might still retrieve her situation by smooth words and the *Ushi-Kagan*'s love for her.

"Words will not help you," Conan said. "The *Ushi-Kagan* is not as trusting as you think. When he heard my tale, he wanted proof. He has found it."

Now she saw that there were many men around the fire. At the center, near the fire, stood Bartatua. At his feet were three shamans, trussed like calves for branding. Other shamans knelt with their hands tied behind them and terror upon their faces. In the *Ushi-Kagan*'s hand was a shortsword, half of its length glowing bloodred. A wisp of thin smoke drifted from its tip, and the stench of scorched flesh was heavy in the air.

When Bartatua looked at Lakhme, she almost fainted. She knew now that she should have used her dagger when she had the chance. Her nimble mind raced. What lies would divert Bartatua's wrath? It never occurred to her to use the dagger upon herself.

"These amulet-rattling frauds," Bartatua said to her, "have been providing us with some rare entertainment. They have spoken freely, with many clever embellishments. They threatened me with the wrath of the gods at first, but a taste of the hot iron loosened their tongues and refreshed their memories. It seems that there have been ceremonies to which I was not invited, but which you attended. Indeed, I understand that you participated with rare zeal."

"I knew they plotted against you, my lord," she said. "I but spied upon them to learn their plans."

"Yes, spying and secret nocturnal missions are a specialty of yours. Where did you find her, Conan?"

"There is a small gully not far that runs near the City of Mounds. A tribesman on guard there let her pass without challenge."

"Go and arrest that man," Bartatua said to a warrior who stood nearby. "He is a traitor. From him we will learn if there are others."

"What fate for the woman, *Ushi-Kagan*?" asked the scar-faced eastern *kagan*.

"It can be no ordinary death," Bartatua said. He glared at Lakhme with an expression of pure stone. "You could have been the woman of the ruler of the world. Why did you betray my trust?"

She said nothing, but stood with eyes downcast.

"She schemed against you," said Conan, "because it is her nature to do so. She could no more act in good faith than could a scorpion turn into a dove. She would betray Khondemir as well, or any other man. Even now she stands here plotting some way out of this trap that she has prepared for herself.''

''Kill the slut and be done with it, my lord,'' advised the Gerul *kagan*. ''The sun will rise soon and we have a battle to fight.''

Bartatua's hand closed around his hilt, and he stared at Lakhme for a moment. Then he released the weapon. ''No. After the fighting, when we reconsecrate our place of burial, then she shall die. Then all shall see what happens to one who betrays the trust of the *Ushi-Kagan*. Take her to her tent and put her under guard. She has no place whence to run, but watch her well lest she slay herself and cheat me of my vengeance.''

Two trusted warriors led Lakhme away. She did not speak and she kept her face lowered. Those who watched thought that she averted her eyes in shame or fear, but they were wrong. She did it to hide her smile. She would be placed under guard, and the guards would be mere men. Men were tools, instruments for her use. She knew that she would not die on this day, and her thoughts turned on the empire that still lay before her.

''To more important things,'' said Bartatua when she was gone. ''The Budini and the Gerul will make the first assault at sunrise. That is the feint to the north wall. We shall give the defenders time to align most of their forces against the feint; then the mass of the horde shall make the true assault against the great entrance in the south wall. Conan will be in charge of that assault. Conan, have you anything to say before we go to prepare our forces for the coming battle?''

Conan stood before the assembled chiefs. The shamans still lay moaning upon the ground, but he ignored them. ''I wish that I had time to train the men properly for this sort of combat, but that is a futile thought. The thing to remember is that the defenders have horses and bows and that they will have no compunction about using them. The Turanians are not bowmen as mighty as your own, but they are adequate. In any case, the range will not be great, and your men wear only light armor. In a massed charge, nearly every shaft will find a man.

"The important thing is to cover the intervening ground as swiftly as possible. The sooner you can come to hand strokes, the better. The enemy has swords, lances and shields, and knows well how to use them. Do not try to fence or to match swordplay. You must mob their forces, three or four men piling atop every defender. Leap over their shields and go for the throat. You will take many casualties in this way, but the alternative is to be massacred without inflicting any casualties yourselves."

This was a sobering prospect, and it was a grim group of men who began to seek out their followers. "What shall we do with these, *Ushi-Kagan*?" asked a warrior who stood guard over the bound shamans.

Bartatua turned back for a moment. "Those fraudulent traitors? Kill them all. From this day forth, any shaman who sets foot within my camps shall die on the spot." He turned away and left for his position as the warrior began methodically cutting throats.

Conan signaled Manzur, and the two walked off alone. When they were well out of earshot, Conan said, "You may speak now, but keep it low."

"Conan, those are my countrymen in that camp! I care nothing for the Turanians, but the Red Eagles are Sogarians. I cannot stand by and see them slaughtered."

"Manzur," Conan said grimly, "those are dead men.

This great mob of nomads will not let one survive. The Sogarians have trodden upon sacred soil, and even if a few break away and run, the tribesmen will track them down relentlessly and slay them. They will die cleanly in battle. That is the way soldiers should die. The day they took up arms they knew that this time might come.''

"But they guard Ishkala!" Manzur protested.

"You must abide here," Conan said. "I shall be first into the City of Mounds. If it is at all possible, I will find your little princess and bring her out. Perhaps in the confusion the two of you may make your escape."

"No!" said Manzur obstinately. "I will go down there and die with my countrymen!"

Conan sighed. "I feared this. Well, there is only one thing I can do."

Without warning, his great knotted fist flashed out. The heel of his hand cracked into the side of Manzur's head below the edge of his helmet. The youth crumpled to the ground like a sack of oats. The Cimmerian checked his breathing and was satisfied that the lad was merely unconscious. He slung the boy over his shoulder and went in search of a gully where Manzur might wait out the day of battle, securely bound and gagged.

It was growing light as the two guards conducted Lakhme to her tent. She knew how she would manage her escape and decided that the sooner the better was the best policy. She had studied her guards closely. They were ordinary Ashkuz tribesmen, not extraordinary men such as Bartatua and Conan. This would be easy.

As she ducked into the tent, she turned to the two guards. "Surely you must come inside with me. How else may you be certain that I will not kill myself?" The two followed her in.

The interior of the tent was small and cramped so that the guards had to stand close to her. "Is this not more pleasant than going to fight a battle on foot?" she said teasingly. "And am I not more pleasing company than the blades of your enemies?"

"Silence, woman," said one. "We are here to guard you, not to converse with you."

"But you have not searched me," she said. "After all, I might bear some hidden weapon." She let her black robe fall to the ground, and the eyes of the men betrayed her effect. Never had they seen the *kagan*'s woman save in her all-enveloping robes, and now she stood before them attired only in a brief loincloth and low boots.

"Am I not fair?" she asked, stroking her silken flesh. "I am a Vendhyan pleasure-slave, schooled in the arts of pleasing men. I know all the hundreds of ways to give a man the ultimate pleasure, ways that common soldiers could never hope to experience." One hand lifted a perfect breast as if offering and pleasuring herself at the same time. The men stood as though hypnotized.

"But you have not finished your search." She stepped from her boots; then her hands went to one hip as she began to unfasten her loincloth. As the silk fell away, she deftly kept her dagger masked by the cloth. "There," she said. "Now I can conceal nothing. But if you would be sure, you may search me more closely." She stepped toward them.

Slowly one of the guards put forth a hand to touch her unearthly white flesh. Her dagger flashed out and scratched a red line across his palm. In an instant it streaked across the face of the other guard, scoring his cheek. She sprang back as the two sought to gather their wits, so swiftly had seduction turned to violence.

"Slut!" said one. He dragged at his sword; then a look of surprise enveloped his face as he found that drawing the weapon required a terrible effort. He tried to say something to his companion, but his tongue would not move.

Lakhme laughed with delight as the men toppled to the ground and lay there gasping. Their backs arched, their eyes started from their sockets, and their stiffened fingers clawed at the empty air.

"Did you really think that you could have me?" she taunted as she stepped across their bodies, flaunting her nakedness at them. "Common warriors were never born to enjoy the wisest and most beautiful woman in the world, soon to be the most powerful as well. Men like you live only to be sacrificed to my purposes." She continued to laugh as, with a final drumming of heels on the ground, the two guards died.

Quickly Lakhme resumed her clothing. A glance out the door of the tent told her that no man stood within sight. All were at their stations, preparing for battle. She began to hurry toward the tethered horses.

Conan stood at the fore of the horde that waited in the dry riverbed to the southeast of the necropolis. He did not like the position at all. The men lay on their bellies, packed together like stockfish in a jar, and they were strung out for hundreds of paces. There was much ground to cover between this place and the rampart, and they would be exposed to arrow fire for most of the distance. There was no other way, though. This was the only place in the entire rolling plain where so many men could escape being seen from the highest of the mounds.

Besides mail shirt and helmet, Conan carried the largest shield he had been able to find. It was less than two feet across, but it was made of fine Vendhyan steel and it might suffice to protect him from arrows until he was past missile range and could use his sword.

There came a sound of shouting from the necropolis. Then there were trumpets braying and drums beating, followed by a pounding of hooves.

"They begin!" cried Bartatua, who stood next to Conan.

"Give them a few more minutes," said the Cimmerian. He saw his men stir restlessly, inflamed by the sounds of battle.

"No man stands until I give the word!" said Conan. "Each of you shall soon have plenty of opportunity to die. Be not so eager!"

Carefully the Cimmerian gauged the din from the necropolis. When the greater part of the noise had faded away toward the north, he stood and waved his shield overhead.

"Forward!" he bellowed.

With a howl of bloodlust, the men sprang to their feet and swarmed over the rim of the draw. With his shield ready for the storm of arrows, Conan began to run. But as the sounds of the horde behind him faded away, he turned and was dismayed to see that he was far in front of the Hyrkanians.

"Run, you sons of whores!" he shouted. "You are nothing but archery targets if you walk!"

Some of the men broke into an awkward shuffle, and Conan realized that most of these men had never run in their lives. Few of them had even walked more than a few-score paces at a time. Their bandy-legged waddle would have been laughable except that he knew they were now within arrow range.

As they continued their maddeningly slow progress toward the rampart, it seemed that the wall was all but undefended. A lone warrior stood atop the crest, and Conan did not at all like the look of the situation. When the horde was still two hundred long paces from the rampart, the lone soldier raised a silver trumpet and blew a long, snarling blast. Within moments warriors stood shoulder-to-shoulder atop the rampart. Each held a bow raised at a high angle. A dark cloud arced lazily toward the Hyrkanians.

Conan raised his shield and crouched as much of his body behind it as he could. He heard shafts glance from its surface and he heard the shrieks of stricken men. All around him bodies toppled, transfixed by long shafts.

"Faster, curse you!" he shouted. They continued their slow, sullen advance, and Conan sensed the heart going out of them. This was not their kind of warfare. Already he could see men in the garb of many tribes lagging behind. Almost all of the men in front were Ashkuz tribesmen, for it was their ancestral tombs that lay under defilement.

As the attackers drew nearer to the rampart, the archers began training their bows downward. Suddenly behind the line of bowmen there appeared mounted men. From the saddle, these fired over the heads of the standing men, increasing the firepower of the defenders by at least one third.

Conan groaned to see so many of the tribesmen dropping. And they had yet to inflict a single casualty upon the enemy! "Up on the rampart now!" he shouted. "Another few paces and they can't use their bows."

At that moment a thunder of hooves cut across his shouting. From around the east and west corners of the necropolis came two wings of the Red Eagles. This was the kind of fighting for which heavy cavalry was made, and they sliced through the lightly armored footmen like a spear piercing smoke. Axes and swords fell, and rose bloodied to fall again. Spears thrust, and no thrust failed to bury a sharp steel point in the entrails of a Hyrkanian raider. Each time the spiked head of a mace descended, the flanks of horses were spattered with blood and brains. Here and there a horse was hamstrung and its rider mobbed and slain, but for the most part, the charge was little more than a slaughter of stymied men.

The two lines of horsemen smashed into the great mob of nomads who were trying to force their way into the gateway. Here the butchery was truly terrible, as the horsemen cut back and forth through the footmen like the blade of a scythe harvesting wheat.

Conan cut a man from the saddle and turned to Bartatua, who was wrestling with a warrior he had hauled from his speared horse.

"This is no good!" Conan said as the *Ushi-Kagan* pulled his bloody dagger from the horseman's body. "We must fall back and regroup. At this rate, they'll kill us all!"

"Aye," said Bartatua. An arrow narrowly missed his face and buried itself in the throat of a nearby tribesman. The man went down with a torrent of blood spraying from his lips.

"Fall back!" Bartatua shouted. He signaled to the nearest men, as did Conan. Gradually, all along the line, men began to break away and flee. Many who did so fell upon their faces, arrows in their backs.

Conan backed away, always keeping his shield between himself and the enemy. Once a shaft brushed his thigh, making a shallow cut. Another nicked his ankle. His skill and his armor saved him from serious injury.

When they were out of arrow range, the men regathered. The *Ushi-Kagan* surveyed the scene of carnage with dismay and rage. "How many have we lost?" he demanded.

"Thousands. And I doubt that wc slew a hundred of them. Probably not half that many." Conan surveyed the shattered warriors who sat upon the ground. "And at least one man in three is wounded, many seriously."

They were rejoined by the northern party. These tribesmen had not suffered as badly, for the feint had not been pressed far within arrow range and the northern wall had been thinly defended. Nor had this horde met with a heavy cavalry charge. After receiving his chief's report, Bartatua led Conan a distance away from the others and spoke with him.

"They knew," he said. "They knew that the attack from the north was to be a feint. They were fully prepared to savage my horde, with archers and horsemen waiting below the southern rampart until we were within range. They had their heavy cavalry massed at the eastern and western walls, ready to ride over the rampart and take us in both flanks." He brooded for a few minutes. "It was Lakhme. When that witch went into the City of Mounds last night, she told them of my strategy. How long before my *kagans* figure that out, Conan? Who will respect a leader who reveals his most important secrets to a foreign slave woman?"

Conan said nothing. When Bartatua wanted advice for the next attack, he would say so.

"And too many of those who died were Ashkuz, my own tribe. They are the strong pillar that upholds my sway. Must I start all over again, building my power among the tribes, reforging the broken alliances that were built upon their trust in my invincibility?'' Conan saw that the most self-confident man he had ever known was beginning to doubt himself. ''Well, Conan, tell me how I may retrieve this sorry situation.''

''For one thing, we do nothing for the rest of the day,'' said the Cimmerian. ''Let the men rest and regain heart. Let them also brood upon slain comrades and kinsmen. We shall strike at sunset. That will leave enough light for those who fear to die in the dark.'' He looked toward the ramparts, where warriors had descended to finsh off the wounded and retrieve arrows from the bodies.

''Their concentrated defense is too much to face,'' he continued. ''We will divide into four groups and assault all four sides at once. There will be many slain, but nothing like this morning. The enemy will be spread too thin to concentrate its fire. If your men could just run, their losses would be far fewer, but that is asking the impossible.''

''At least we shall be able to avenge our honor,'' said Bartatua, ''whatever happens after that.''

''You brood overly much,'' said Conan. ''Perhaps you will have to defer your campaign for another year. Once you give your men victories and much booty, they will love you as before. Warriors are easily replaced. A new crop of youths comes of age with every passing year. This is a valuable experience. Now you know how the people you attack feel when you slaughter them and they have no way of striking back.''

The *Ushi-Kagan* managed a grim smile. ''It is a good thing that I do not require much sympathy, for you give very little.''

Conan shrugged. ''I never felt the need of it, why should you? Leaders of men have more important things to do than to feel sorry for one another.''

"So they have," said Bartatua. "Come, let us brief the men." He was about to turn away when something caught his attention. A horse was galloping across the rolling ground toward the gate in the grassy rampart. Its rider wore flowing black robes.

"The witch has done it again!" Bartatua shouted. "May all the gods curse the flesh from her bones!"

"I suppose," said Conan, "that it is too much to hope that some archer will put a shaft through her delightful body."

Such hope indeed proved futile, and Lakhme rode through the gate unmolested. "No matter," Bartatua said. "I vowed to kill her in the City of Mounds, and so I shall. We must be careful not to slay her in the fighting. That would be too quick. Come, let us make our dispositions."

Seventeen

The sun was touching the horizon as Khondemir prepared his great spell-casting. This was a summoning more ambitious than any he had ever before attempted. He had no doubt of its outcome, though, for his faith in his destiny was absolute. Bound before him on the altar was the Princess Ishkala, her tender limbs pinioned. It had been a simple matter to send men to her tent while the Red Eagles were occupied with the morning's battle. Since then, the Sogarians had been busy with preparations to repel another assault. It had not occurred to them to check on Ishkala's welfare.

In the red light of sunset he could see the enemy arrayed in four hordes. As the sun began to slide below the horizon, the hordes surged forward.

"They come!" cried Lakhme. Attired only in her silken loincloth, she stood next to the altar. She had assisted Khondemir in his final preparations. It had been she who had stripped the clothing from the Sogarian princess, strapping the girl down upon the altar with a kind of unholy pleasure on her face. Even now she stroked Ishkala's white flesh as she would a favorite pet.

"No matter," Khondemir said. "In a few minutes they shall see that which will stop them in their tracks. Let us begin."

With his sorcerous apparatus assembled before him, the wizard began to chant, casting upon a fiery brazier the items Lakhme had brought him. Gradually the sky above the altar changed in color. Ishkala's eyes filled with terror, but her screams were confined within her throat by a tight gag across her mouth. Lakhme stroked the princess's brow and crooned soothing words as the girl eyed the sharp dagger in Khondemir's hand.

"When they know they are defeated," Bartatua shouted to his men, "some will try to break away. I want no man to seize a horse and give chase. It is sacrilege to go mounted in a burial ground. I have already detailed a thousand men on the swiftest horses to chase down any who flee. They are stationed beyond the limits of the City, in territory where it is lawful for men to ride. You have heard Conan's words, and you remember what happened this morning. Cover the ground as swiftly as possible. The arrow fire will not be as intense this time, and their cavalry cannot attack all four hordes at once. Now go to your places. When the sun touches the horizon, we attack!"

The host split into four divisions and each began making its way to its attack point. Even with their depleted numbers, few had been able to hear the *Ushi-Kagan*'s words, but their officers had delivered the gist of them. Morale had been restored, and they were determined to avenge their honor.

Side by side, Conan and Bartatua prepared to charge with their men. Once again the assault would be from

the south, wence they would head for the great entrance
gate. Bartatua had determined to keep up with the
Cimmerian and to stay well before his men. If all could
see him, they would be less likely to falter. It would be
unendurable disgrace for Hyrkanians to allow their *Ushi-
Kagan* to plunge alone among the enemy.

They gripped their weapons tightly as they watched
the sun. The bloody orb was at the horizon. As the fiery
edge touched the steppe, Bartatua raised his arms.

"Forward!" shouted the *Ushi-Kagan*. The shout was
echoed by his tribesmen and was soon taken up by the
men surrounding the other walls.

Conan started out at a steady lope. Beside him, Bartatua
tried to match stride. As they covered ground, the
Cimmerian looked back to see if the men were keeping
the formation he had ordered. They were in four ragged
lines, with plenty of space separating them. This was
because the great enclosing square would contract as
they neared the rampart. If they charged as a single
mob, they would be crammed together shoulder-to-
shoulder by the time they reached the rampart. They
would become an easy target for arrows and would be unable to use their weapons when they had the opportunity

The sleeting arrows began to fall among them. As
Conan had predicted, the fire was not as heavy and
concentrated as that of the morning. The men were no
longer quite so helpless either, as the lighter arrow fall
and their recent experience allowed them to make better
use of their small shields. Many had equipped themselves with extra armor, taken from the wounded and
slain.

As they drew within a hundred paces of the gate, a
thunder of hooves betokened another cavalry charge.
The Red Eagles came storming through the gate, splitting into two wings as they emerged. They smashed

into the Hyrkanian line at two points. On this occasion their progress was not as easy as it had been that morning. As the first cavalry entered the horde, nooses snaked out to encircle mount and rider. Horse and man crashed to the ground, to be mobbed and overwhelmed by footmen.

Following riders toppled over the fallen. As others swerved to avoid the bloody, kicking heaps, they made easy marks for more cast ropes. The cavalry charge began to falter, then completely halted in a wild melee of slashing horsemen and screaming, blood lusting footmen.

Conan roared a wild Cimmerian war cry as he charged into the defenders blocking the gateway. As soon as the last of the cavalry had cleared the opening in the rampart, the defenders had blocked it in a shield wall three lines deep. He was out of the range of arrow fire now, and no longer needed to preoccupy himself with defense.

A Turanian raised a lance to cast at Conan, only to lose lance and arm in a single, terrible blow of the Cimmerian's sword. Conan blocked a sword with his shield, then smashed the swordsman's face with the shield's edge as he cut down a man to his right, the blade shearing through light mail, snapping collarbone and ribs and biting deep into the entrails. Blood sprayed over the Cimmerian and those standing nearest him.

A thousand Hyrkanians, howling the shrill war cry of the steppes, were piling onto the Turanians. Conan saw a man claw at a shield with his bare hands, climbing over its rim to attack the man behind it. The defender thrust his sword into his enemy's bowels, toppling backward as the dying Hyrkanian's teeth sank into his throat.

The gateway became a scene of demented slaughter as men fought with no hope or thought of quarter. The footing grew treacherous as blood and spilled entrails carpeted the grass and the pile of bodies grew deeper. Fallen weapons threatened the feet of unwary combatants.

Not wishing to linger in an environment so unfavorable, Conan sprang over the heap of corpses, landed catlike with his feet firmly planted, and with two blows of his sword felled two men who bore down upon him from right and left. He looked about, to see that he was standing within the City of Mounds. Bartatua stood beside him, and screaming Hyrkanians were pouring into the breach. The defenders were falling back in disorder, and the true slaughter had begun.

As the blood-maddened horde smote and slew, Conan sprinted after a fleeing Turanian who had mounted the horse of a fallen defender. The Cimmerian discarded his shield to run the faster, and without breaking stride, he resheathed his sword. The Turanian was headed toward the center of the City of Mounds. Conan wanted a live man to question, and soon there would be none.

The rider circled a low mound, giving Conan the opportunity he needed. He ran to the top of the mound and from there he leaped to the shoulders of the Turanian, toppling him to the grass. The man's eyes started from their sockets with terror as Conan presented a dagger to his throat.

"If you would live, speak quickly," the Cimmerian growled. "Where are Khondemir and the Sogarian princess?"

"There!" gasped the man, pointing upward. "Atop the highest mound! The Vendhyan woman is with them. He makes mighty magic!"

Conan's gaze followed the pointing finger. "Crom!" he half-whispered. He released the man to escape or die, and paid no attention as the Turanian scrambled away. Conan was entranced by the spectacle above him, and his battle lust turned to horror.

The sun was down and the stars were appearing, but above the great mound was a single, boiling black cloud. In its center was a glare so red that blood was colorless by comparison. All around the necropolis the sounds of battle were tapering off as the terrible sight overhead filled men with a fear greater than that of mere death.

Within the red glare writhed something, a vast, hulking form of unutterable blackness.

"What is it?" said a voice beside Conan.

He turned to see Bartatua standing at his side. The *Ushi-Kagan* was bloodied to the shoulders but he seemed to be unwounded. He stared upward with the same mixture of awe and fear that Conan felt.

"The wizard is up there," Conan said. "He works some terrible spell. He must be summoning a nightmare creature from another world with which to slay us all. Lakhme is up there with him."

The *Ushi-Kagan*'s face knotted with rage. "He works his unclean arts upon the tomb of our first ancestor! Come, Conan, we still have killing to do!"

Bartatua strode for the great mound and Conan went beside him, leaping up the steep grassy side of the mound. As they ascended, the cloud above grew blacker and the red glare clarified, revealing a portion of the creature that lurked behind its veil. A pair of slit-pupiled eyes, larger than shields, stared out above a nest of huge tentacles. It was some unthinkably vast cephalopod, and its body hulked gigantic in the red distance. It bore the vague likeness of a spiral shell.

A smell as of an incomprehensibly ancient sea bed washed down the sides of the mound, and the huge tentacles pushed against the veil, seeking a way into the world of men. As Conan and the *Ushi-Kagan* gained the crest of the mound, they saw two human forms silhouetted against the redness. A third form lay supine before them. The taller of the two standing forms raised a hand aloft, revealing the glitter of a dagger.

As the hand paused in its ascent, Conan ripped his sword from its sheath and cast it sideways, the blade flashing in a horizontal spin.

In the fading light, Lakhme stared aghast at the slaughter below. "Hurry, wizard!" she urged, "or soon there will be no army left to carry you in triumph to Agrapur!"

"All shall be over soon," he assured her. He had been chanting for several minutes in words for which human vocal equipment was never intended. "There is but one formality to attend to, and I shall have full control of our visitor."

Lakhme shuddered as the hideous thing took form above them. She knew not whether it was god or demon, but it represented power in a form that frightened even her. The girl who lay upon the altar had stared in horror as the thing took form, but at last her eyes had rolled back to expose only crescents of white and she lay unconscious as her terrible fate approached consummation.

"In a moment," Khondemir said, exultation writ upon his face, "I shall rip forth her heart, and this Lord of the Deep shall be my servant. Bartatua and all the hordes of Hyrkania shall be my slaves!" He raised the knife with unholy glee as the demon pushed against the last resistance of the veil.

The wizard stared at the naked girl stretched upon the altar. It would be a single stroke below the left breast, plunging in, then ripping across to open a great rent. Within an instant he would reach into the wound and tear forth the still-beating heart, to proffer it in unholy propitiation to the dark god above him.

"To thee, oh lord of all power!" he cried, as something whirred past his head.

With a triumphant howl, he brought his hand streaking down toward the prone girl. He stared in total incomprehension as, slowly, he realized that he no longer held the dagger. It took another moment's thought to understand that he no longer had a right hand. His eyes gazed in horror as blood spouted from the stump of his wrist and flowed over Ishkala's white flesh. Then the first tentacle wrapped around his body.

Lakhme watched her ambitions crumble as the wizard was raised high in the air until he was held above the horses'-tail standard of the Ashkuz. He screamed and disgorged hideous noises as the creature plucked an arm from his struggling body and fed it into a fanged mouth in the midst of its nest of tentacles.

Then Bartatua stood before her. "My love," she said desperately, "it was the wizard! He cast his spell over me! Now that he is finished, I am returned to my senses! Let us be away from this place."

The Kagan's hands closed around her slender neck. The thumbs bore into her windpipe and her head swam as the blood flow to her brain was constricted. His face was grim and vengeful, but there was a trace of doubt in his eyes. His powerful bowman's hands could have snapped her neck instantly, but he was unable to bring himself to this final, irrevocable step.

As she struggled for breath, Lakhme panicked. Her hand went to her loincloth and brought out the little thin-bladed dagger and plunged its full length into Bartatua's side. His eyes widened; then their stare became fixed as he fell, bearing her down with him, his hands still locked around her throat. She grasped his fingers and tried to break them away, and then she saw someone standing above her. It was the Cimmerian. He was her only hope now, and she stretched forth a hand, pleading for help.

Conan looked down at his dead friend and at the faithless woman. He knew that he could yet save her. Such was his strength that he could break even Bartatua's death grip. The pleading in her eyes was a terrible thing to see.

He stepped over her writhing body and began to cut the straps that held Ishkala. Above them, the monster was finishing off the last of what had been the wizard, Khondemir, would-be king of Turan. Conan tossed the girl's bloodied body over his shoulder and began to run down the face of the mound. He did not look back at the Vendhyan woman.

At the base of the mound, all was confusion as men knew not whether to fight or flee. The thing above seemed to be satisfied with the sorcerer and was retreating back into its cloud. Conan snatched a cloak from a dead man and wrapped it around Ishkala's pale body. At a steady trot, he headed for the rampart.

In the little gully where he had left Manzur, he found the young poet still securely trussed. "Keep quiet," he ordered as he loosened the young man's bonds. "We must be away from here, and swiftly. Bartatua is dead. So is the Vendhyan woman."

"Ishkala?" Manzur gasped as the gag was untied.

"She is this bundle. She is unharmed, at least in body. We must get to the horses. Now there is enough confusion that we may make our escape, if we move swiftly."

They emerged from the gully and began walking toward the horses. Although there were men all around, they attracted no notice. Many Hyrkanians were coming back from the City of Mounds, aiding or carrying wounded compatriots. The most seriously injured were desperate to mount their horses lest they die afoot in the dark. The unique horrors of their recent battle had left them half drugged.

Conan found his own horse where he had tethered it, a little apart from the others, saddled and bearing his bow and arrows. A packhorse with supplies stood next to it, along with a string of remounts. As the two men mounted, with Ishkala held in the saddle before Conan, they heard an unearthly ululation behind them. It was the mourning cry of the steppes.

"Someone has summoned the courage to ascend the great mound," Conan said. "They have found the body of Bartatua. That should keep them occupied for a good while. Let us be away." Into the gloom rode the three survivors.

On the fifth day of their southward wandering, they saw two riders approaching in the distance. "Who may they be?" asked Ishkala. She rode in a spare tunic of Conan's, her bare legs glossy and dark from exposure to the sun. She had fashioned an impromptu hood from the cloak Conan had earlier wrapped her in.

"We cannot tell until they come closer," the Cimmerian said. "Two men are not much threat." They rode on, and soon Conan grinned as he saw who came to meet them.

"You see, Fawd," said Rustuf to the man who rode beside him. "I told you that this Cimmerian knave would not be done for by a mere duststorm. How goes it, Conan?"

"Very well. Which is to say that I am still alive and moderately healthy."

"Fawd and I plan to ride to the west," Rustuf said. "I long to visit with my brothers of the *Kozaki*, and Fawd wishes to gaze upon the towers of Agrapur once more."

"I'll go with you," Conan said. "I was going west when my journey was interrupted by the Hyrkanians."

"Surely, Conan," protested Manzur, "you are coming to Sogaria with us! The prince will heap you with honors. You will be given riches and land, and a high command in the army."

The Cimmerian shook his head. "Just now I wish no further dealings with monarchs, especially one that might remember me as the man who cost him a fort. Nay, I ride west. That is where my destiny lies."

Before they made their final farewells, Manzur took Conan aside. "I am grateful to you, Conan," he said, "but it grieves me that I missed the final battle, and that it was not I who rescued Ishkala."

"I'll warrant you've not told her that," said Conan with a grin, "and I know perfectly well that that is not how your poem will come out when you've finished it. You see, you are not the first poet I have encountered."

As the two young people rode off, the three warriors turned the heads of their mounts westward.

"Bartatua was slain," Conan told them.

"No man is immortal," Rustuf said philosophically. "So perishes another would-be Emperor of the World."

"He could have been," Conan said. "He was a great man, perhaps the greatest I have known. All that defeated him was his love for a worthless woman."

"It's just as well," Rustuf said. "I do not think I would like living in a world with only one king. The first thing you know, he would be enforcing peace so that the flow of taxes would not be interrupted. No, I like a world with many little kings and many little wars. That's the world for a warrior."

"Aye," Conan said. "In a world like that, even men such as we can earn crowns of our own."

Together the three men rode toward the setting sun, across the endless grassy steppe.

CONAN

☐ 54238-X CONAN THE DESTROYER $2.95
  54239-8   Canada $3.50

☐ 54228-2 CONAN THE DEFENDER $2.95
  54229-0   Canada $3.50

☐ 54225-8 CONAN THE INVINCIBLE $2.95
  54226-6   Canada $3.50

☐ 54236-3 CONAN THE MAGNIFICENT $2.95
  54237-1   Canada $3.50

☐ 54231-2 CONAN THE UNCONQUERED $2.95
  54232-0   Canada $3.50

☐ 54246-0 CONAN THE VICTORIOUS $2.95
  54247-9   Canada $3.50

☐ 54248-7 CONAN THE FEARLESS (trade) $6.95
  54249-5   Canada $7.95

☐ 54242-8 CONAN THE TRIUMPHANT $2.95
  54243-6   Canada $3.50

☐ 54244-4 CONAN THE VALOROUS (trade) $6.95
  54245-2   Canada $7.95